VOYAGE OF THE WANDERLUST

A TRI-GALACTIC TREK NOVEL

MARY E. LOWD

CONTENTS

CHAPTER 1
PREMATURE METAMORPHOSIS

Kynnis put four of her pudgy green hands against her face and wrapped another two around her nauseated middle. She could feel the soft skin of her face wrinkling and cracking, preparing to split open. It was too early. Much too early. She wasn't supposed to go through her chrysalis phase for years yet, but she could feel it happening. "I'm scared," she said.

"Should I take you home?" Korvax asked, his pointy muzzle twitching to one side in the funny way he had. The quills on his back rattled, fluffing out with worry for his young friend. She was only a child. He shouldn't have agreed to bring her up in his spaceship to see her world from a distance. But she'd pleaded so prettily, and he was a sucker for enthusiasm. A fool, as all of his own people had always said. That's how he'd ended up traveling so far away, making himself part of an entirely different world, surrounding himself with an entirely different people—aliens who looked like butterflies when they were fully grown. He loved living among them.

"I think... it's too late," Kynnis said, and those were the last words she ever spoke with her caterpillar lips. They shriveled away, leaving a smooth, crystalline surface underneath. A faceless face.

Korvax crouched beside his young friend, pleading and coaxing, "Don't die, don't die."

Kynnis wanted to reassure him, but her old mouth was gone, and the new one wasn't finished forming. She wasn't dying. But she was changing. Korvax had never seen one of the Ollallans he lived among transform from child to adult. Mostly, he lived among the children, knowing they transformed but not knowing what it looked like. So, he didn't know this was normal. Technically, normal. Physically, normal. Just... early. So very, very early.

Kynnis wasn't ready.

But she had to be ready.

It was happening.

Like her mouth, now her eyes began to crack and crumble. Her vision fractured, then grew milky around the cracks. The milkiness spread, placing a film between herself and the outside world. She could still see Korvax, but the vision was blurry. Only a dark shape, kneeling over her. Then even his voice began to grow muffled, as if he were speaking to her through a pane of glass.

And Kynnis found herself separated from the outside world. All the parts of her that had interfaced with the outside world—eyes, aural canals, mouth, and even her pudgy green hands and feet—were withering away as replacements grew inside. But right now, she was a soupy, gooey mush of organs, rearranging and restructuring. Maturing. It was terrifying. And exciting.

Why was this happening? Had she done something wrong? Something that triggered her chrysalis phase so many years earlier than it should have come?

Kynnis spent all her time with Korvax, the funny quill-backed Xantrosian. She ate the strange foods he cooked, played with the high-tech devices he'd brought from his world, and had even let him take her up in his spaceship to see her world from above the sky.

But questions of why faded from Kynnis's mind as the world outside faded farther and farther away. Questions of *why* were related to memories, and the deeper her mind fell inside itself—with nothing external to draw her thoughts away—the more she found herself pondering different futures.

"The past is already chosen. The future is full of possibilities."

The words echoed in Kynnis's mind, larger than any thought she'd ever had before. As if someone was speaking to her. Someone so large, so large she could hardly conceive of them. As large as an entire world. Her mind felt almost too small to hold such words. And yet, the meaning of them became crystal clear to her: she could see the threads, the pathways, the different options for the future, as if she were looking at a tangle of yarn. A spider's web of futures opened up in front of her, and she saw the threads glisten, sparkling like dew drops on strands of nearly invisible silk.

Her mind was at the center. All she had to do was: choose.

Choose a thread.

Choose a path.

Choose the reality that would become real, the one she would emerge into as a full grown Ollallan, wings still wet and waiting to unfurl.

She would have wings! In every future, she would have wings.

Kynnis had always known that one day she would have wings, but that day had always seemed so far off. That was why she had begged Korvax to take her beyond the sky on his funny metal spaceship that didn't look like it should be able to fly. She hadn't been able to wait.

"Which path will you take, little one?"

The voice was filled with warmth and love.

Kynnis considered the possibilities. She saw paths that led to long lives surrounded by children—caterpillars of her own, who she would hatch and raise with Korvax's help. In every path, he stayed her steadfast friend. Kynnis's mind slid from one path to another, each bright and shining. There were so many choices, but many of them were marred by a great darkness, looming and overshadowing the happiness.

Then—away from the great tangle of threads, all twisted together, all similar in many ways—Kynnis saw one path, unlike the others.

A short life. A single egg laid which she wouldn't live to see hatch, but Korvax would tend to it and raise the caterpillar who hatched.

And oh, the life of that child!

Kynnis saw faces around her potential, hypothetical, possible child—funny, fuzzy, furry faces. More mammalian creatures— like Korvax, but also different—would come to her world, and her child would meet them.

Could meet them.

If Kynnis chose that path.

But better yet?

The looming darkness, the overshadowing cloud didn't mar that path. The thread glistened brightly as far as Kynnis could see into the future. Somehow, the funny, fuzzy, furry faces kept the darkness away.

If Kynnis understood what she was seeing with her newly multi-faceted eyes, still growing inside her chrysalis-ensconced self, she had the chance to save her entire world by choosing the right path.

Her choice became no choice. How could she choose a long life for herself at the expense of her entire people?

Kynnis's mind snapped into place, and the visions of alternate realities, a whole multiverse of possible futures, began to fade. All that was left was a singular, certain vision that would haunt and tantalize her for the rest of her days, the entirety of her life to come, her life with wings.

The image was of a feline face, gray and fluffy, with piercing green eyes that stared mysteriously at Kynnis from a future she wouldn't live to see.

But her daughter would.

CHAPTER 2
BELATED PROMOTIONS

Commander Janessa Carroway's green eyes reflected the stars as she watched through the shuttle's windows. She knew the shuttle was approaching Nexus Nine Base, but she didn't look at that looming metal structure. She'd heard about the space station's unusual architecture—all interconnected hexagons and triangles; pointy and angular instead of smooth and sweeping like most Tri-Galactic Union star bases, since it had originally been a Reptassan station. Carroway didn't want to be here. It was a bad sign for what her next assignment would be.

"Jan, do you think that will be our new ship?" the Morphican piloting the shuttle asked, pointing at a small ship docked at Nexus Nine Base. His long rabbit ears were flat back behind his head, and his nose twitched furiously. In spite of the cyborg components that explicitly regulated his emotions, Lt. Vossie looked concerned.

Mild concern was the strongest emotion Jan Carroway had ever seen reflected in her rabbit-like compatriot's demeanor.

Carroway was a Norwegian Forest cat with wild, untamable fur. She stood a head taller than most other cats, fluffy gray fur straining to escape the collar and cuffs of her Tri-Galactic Navy uniform. For an uplifted Earth feline, she was huge, which still left her substantially smaller than a lot of dogs. And the Tri-Galactic Navy was filled with dogs.

Lt. Vossie, on the other paw, was a tawny brown rabbit-like alien, approximately the size of a small cat. With his long ears standing tall, he came to Carroway's shoulder. But in addition to his small size, he had the blunt claws and buck teeth of a vegetarian prey animal. His people were so naturally fearful that they'd developed highly advanced cyborg tech to elevate themselves above their fear.

Tubes in Lt. Vossie's tawny neck fed artificial hormones into his body, constantly tweaking the chemical mix that bathed his brain, keeping it emotionally steadied, and a computer implant on his brow allowed his brain to interface directly with an AI that could whisper soothing probabilities straight into his mind, reminding him that fear was only fear and he didn't need to let it rule him.

Cmdr. Carroway had come to depend heavily on Lt. Vossie and his preternatural calmness in dangerous situations. The fact that the hot-headed Norwegian Forest cat and cool-minded Morphican worked so well together was part of why they were here, approaching a space station she didn't want to go to.

Carroway deigned to follow the angle of Lt. Vossie's gesture and gazed, briefly, at the small ship. It looked brand new. But it also looked small. And well-armed. Very well-armed. The whole tiny ship was bristling with electron torpedoes and blazor canons.

"I don't want to captain a ship like that one," Cmdr. Carroway grumbled. Her voice was deep for a cat. She supposed she looked warlike with her sharp teeth, pointed ears, and bushy fur that flared around her face like an unruly mane. But she wanted to pursue science, diplomacy... The peaceful side of the Tri-Galactic Union.

"We still don't know that you're being promoted," Lt. Vossie pointed out pedantically as he finished docking their shuttle with a satisfying ka-thunk. The sound felt very final, like a prison door sliding shut.

Carroway gave Vossie a withering look. Her feline eyes could smolder like green fire when she wanted them to.

Lt. Vossie folded, admitting, "Okay, yes, the probabilities suggest very strongly that we're being re-stationed because you're about to be promoted. It is exceedingly rare for a TGN officer with the rank of commander to receive a Silver Paw award for exceptional service during military action and not receive promotion to captain within the year."

It had already been more than a year since the skirmish with the Archidopteran fleet where Cmdr. Carroway and Lt. Vossie had distinguished themselves by disregarding their captain's orders and executing an extremely difficult maneuver that resulted in saving their ship and three other vessels as well. Lives had been saved. Hundreds. And yet, Carroway had barely escaped being court-martialed for disobedience. Even though she'd been right. She'd been right to trust Lt. Vossie's probabilities, and their captain had never forgiven either of them for it.

The last year had been a long one full of demeaning orders and duties beneath both of their statures in rank. Subtle slights and obviously held, but unspoken, grudges. And now, instead of being promoted at a proper ceremony aboard the ship they'd been serving upon for years, Carroway and Vossie had been shipped off here to this backwater, converted-Reptassan station with no explanation of what to expect.

Janessa Carroway had dreamed about being promoted to captain since she was a mere kitten, still only daydreaming about someday joining the great and grand Tri-Galactic Navy, let alone ever becoming a celebrated officer.

Her daydreams had never gone like this.

This didn't feel like a celebration. It felt like a punishment.

"Let's get this over with," Carroway rumbled, rising from her seat in the shuttle. She led the way to the shuttle's airlock in the back, and Lt. Vossie followed her.

As soon as the pair stepped through the second pair of airlock doors, placing paw upon the metal floor of Nexus Nine Base, they were greeted by a widely grinning German shepherd dog wearing a TGN captain's uniform. Carroway was tall for a cat, but this dog dwarfed her. "Welcome, welcome!" the dog barked. "I'm Captain Shep Bataille, and it's an honor to meet you—" He held out a paw toward the bristling Norwegian Forest cat. "—Captain Janessa Carroway."

Carroway heard the change in her rank like a slap to the face. Her pointed ears wanted to flatten tight against her skull, but with the force of effort, she kept them tall. She even put out a paw and politely shook the gregarious dog's hand. She was a well-trained cat. Never hiss or growl around dogs. Don't let them see what you're really feeling. *Even when their slights burn you up inside.*

"And you must be Lieutenant Commander Vossie," Captain Bataille barked, offering his paw to the Morphican.

Lt. Vossie kept a cool head, but he looked genuinely confused as he stared up at the much taller dog. "There must be some mistake," the rabbit-like alien demurred. "I'm a lieutenant, and my commanding officer here is Commander Carroway." Instead of taking the dog's proffered paw, Vossie gestured at Carroway. "At least, *last we heard.*"

And there lay the crux of it.

All three officers—dog, cat, and rabbit—stood awkwardly in the hall outside the airlock as they figured out what had happened, tension rising between them.

"I'm so sorry," Captain Bataille barked, his own triangular ears having dipped to half mast. "There's no ambiguity in the reports I've received. Both of you should have received your promotions before arriving here." A stricken look flickered over his long muzzle. "Your promotion ceremonies should have been performed before leaving your previous post."

Carroway's scowl made it clear that there had been no promotion ceremonies. Some feelings are so well earned that they're not worth hiding, even from touchy dogs who don't believe a cat is surrounded by hidden slights all of the time.

"I could get my officers to try to throw something together..." Captain Bataille offered, his eyes going hazy as he tried to figure out logistics. "It'd have to be quick..."

"Don't worry about it," Captain Carroway said, trying out her new title for herself in her own mind. It didn't feel right. It felt fake. Probably because she was supposed to have had a ceremony, and it never happened. Her promotion felt like an afterthought.

Lt. Cmdr. Vossie cast a quick glance at his newly minted captain. She spotted a muted note of disappointment in his eye, and for a moment, she wondered if she should have taken this dog up on his offer to throw together a last-minute, ramshackle, hackneyed promotion ceremony for the two of them. Perhaps Vossie would have enjoyed the ceremony, even if she didn't think that she could. Ah well, it was too late now. Captain Bataille was already telling them about their new post.

"I assume you'll want to see your new ship! The Wanderlust is a beauty." Captain Bataille's brush of a tail wagged as he led them down the metal hallway, past other airlock berths, most of them empty, but a few hosting various docked vessels.

"The Wanderlust?" Carroway asked, in spite of herself. The name was pretty, and it conjured ideas of meandering through the universe, simply discovering for the sheer joy of discovery. That's what she'd joined the Tri-Galactic Union to do. So, maybe, even if she'd missed out on a silly ceremony to celebrate her promotion, she'd still get a post that made it all worthwhile. And hey, once she was the captain, no one would be ordering her around on her own ship.

"Yes," Captain Bataille woofed. "The Wanderlust is a long-range, small crew vessel."

"How small?" Lt. Cmdr. Vossie asked, always one to pin down exact numbers.

"She can be run by a crew of six in a pinch, but she's

designed for a crew of twelve to eighteen." Captain Bataille stopped walking and gestured at an open airlock with one of his large paws.

Through the airlock doors, Carroway could see the central hall of a standard-design TGN ship. No clues about the ship's capabilities could be seen here, just closets for spacesuits, maintenance tools, and other supplies kept near an airlock.

A head popped out of a door farther down the hall—the head of a short, very pretty dog, approximately the same size as Lt. Cmdr. Vossie. The orange fur on the pretty dog's ears was so long and draping, it made his face almost look like a butterfly with the white sploosh down his pointed nose serving as the butterfly's body. Carroway recognized his breed immediately as Papillon.

"Captain Bataille!" the Papillon squeaked, clearly surprised by the group's arrival. "I wasn't expecting you for another hour."

"I'm sure the ship's fine, Ensign Lee," Captain Bataille woofed. Turning back to Carroway and Vossie, the German shepherd added, "This is Ensign Barry Lee, one of Nexus Nine Base's finest. We'll be sorry to see him go."

"You're part of my new crew, Ensign Lee?" Carroway asked, trying to strike the right note between coldly commanding and warmly welcoming. She didn't want to let any members of her new crew get the wrong idea about her being too soft. She didn't need them arguing with her about whether they needed to follow the orders of a cat. On the other paw, this pipsqueak of a dog didn't look too intimidating, and she did want to be on good terms with her crew. A ship works better when the whole crew gets along.

"Yes, captain!" Ensign Lee yipped while executing a smart salute with his paw. "I've been working with the engineering team on Nexus Nine Base for the last few months, retrofitting The Wanderlust for her upcoming mission. I know this ship inside and out, and while she's an older model, we've spiffed her up good as new. Better than new!"

With a sinking feeling, Carroway realized that The Wanderlust must indeed be the heavily armed ship Vossie had pointed out to her during their approach. The ship's name might carry connotations of peaceful, meandering missions of first contact, science, and diplomacy... but it was an old name. The blazor canons and electron torpedoes? Those would be the retrofits. She was sure of it. She'd distinguished herself during war; she was being given command of a war vessel. She feared learning what their first mission would be.

The Tri-Galactic Union wasn't at war with anyone right now. Except for the Archidopteran skirmishes over a year ago, the TGU hadn't been at war for a long time. But there are always dangerous patches of space—places where you can't trust your allies not to turn on you or aggressive newcomers to arrive. Like the Archidopterans. Carroway shuddered at the memory of fighting those insectile aliens, whose queen had been intent on conquest. Similarly, until quite recently, the Reptassans had been at war with Avia, the planet orbited by Nexus Nine Base. Even if the Tri-Galactic Union hadn't officially been involved in that conflict, there had been plenty of room for dangerous missions and the loss of life.

Captain Carroway had no interest in taking lives, but sometimes, it was necessary when another military attacked a peaceful target. She had never meant to become a war captain during a time of peace, but it looked like that was what the Tri-Galactic Union was going to want from her.

Ensign Barry Lee led Captain Carroway and Lt. Cmdr. Vossie through The Wanderlust, from stem to stern, an extremely thorough tour. The ship had two barracks rooms, each capable of housing a half dozen officers comfortably. There were individual quarters for both the captain and the first officer—meaning Carroway and Vossie—which were equipped to be shared with an additional two officers, in the case where the ship took on a fuller complement. According to Ensign Lee, the ship had only been assigned six officers so far, including himself, Vossie, and Carroway. An extremely minimal crew. A fact that should have seemed reasonable—why not leave room for the new captain to pick a few officers of her own?—but somehow set off alarm bells between Carroway's fluffy ears.

In addition to the barracks and quarters, there was a small multi-purpose room with a synthesizer where officers could eat and do minimal exercise, and of course, there was the engine room.

The tour of The Wanderlust ended on the small ship's bridge where Captain Carroway reverently walked a circle around her new captain's chair, right in the middle where she could keep an eye on all the other officers who would serve in this room. Serve under her. Serve her.

It wasn't a ceremony where her previous captain and crewmates celebrated her excellence, saying nice things about her and her accomplishments, and ending with the ritual addition of a captain's rank pin to her collar. She'd have to synthesize one and add it to her collar herself, later...

But sitting down in her own captain's chair for the first time... It did feel like an accomplishment. Even if everything had been done wrong, in ways specifically designed to hurt her, and it was the wrong kind of ship... It was still *her* ship.

As soon as Captain Carroway's fluffy tail curled around her seated self, fluffy tip landing on her lap, all twitchy, Lt. Cmdr. Vossie whispered, "Congratulations, Captain. You deserve it."

Captain Carroway smiled fiercely, pointy fangs peeking out and whiskers rising. It felt good to be a captain.

Carroway's previous captain may have given her criminally negligent orders, tried to court martial her for disobeying them, and then spent more than a year punishing her for being better at his job than he'd been. But that buffoon of a dog still hadn't stopped her from earning her own captain's chair.

"How's it feel?" Captain Bataille barked from behind her. "I know my first captain's chair felt like..." He paused, stepping around to where he could make eye contact with the newly minted Norwegian Forest cat captain. "...like I was finally home, and I'd been searching for home for a long time."

Captain Carroway's smile softened, becoming no less real, but less savage, and her green eyes glazed, like she was looking at herself from a distance in her mind's eye.

"Yes," Carroway agreed. "That's exactly what it feels like." Though, she thought, it would feel even more that way if another captain—a dog, no less—weren't standing on her bridge, waiting to brief her on the orders for her ship's first mission. No worries. Captain Bataille wouldn't be on her ship much longer, and whatever horrible mission the Tri-Galactic Union had planned for this overclocked warship, she'd find a way to make the best of it. She'd have Vossie at her side, and they'd pick a few more officers they could really rely on. It would work out. She'd prove herself, and she'd get better missions after this one. Maybe even—one day—a better ship. But this would do, for a start.

CHAPTER 3

THE UNSAVORY NATURE OF THE MISSION

Captain Shep Bataille whirled around the pilot's seat at the front of the bridge and sat down, his brush of a tail still wagging behind him. His positive demeanor made Captain Carroway almost hopeful about the nature of the mission he was about to assign her. But deep inside, a quiet nagging part of herself knew better: he was a dog. He'd have looked at the bright, optimistic side of even the worst situations.

"I bet you're ready to hear about your mission," Captain Bataille barked.

"Yes, I am," Carroway answered, tail tip twitching uncontrollably in her lap. She swished her tail around behind herself where the twitching would be less obvious.

Lt. Cmdr. Vossie took a seat at one of the scanning posts to the side of the bridge where he could listen. His long ears were standing tall, but his bunny nose was twitching about as furiously as Captain Carroway's tail tip.

Ensign Lee was still standing, looking a little awkward, paws shuffling like he wasn't sure what to do. Captain Carroway was about to invite the Papillon to take a seat next to Vossie at one of the scanning stations, but Captain Bataille beat her to the punch.

"Alright, then," Bataille barked. "First thing's first. Ensign Lee, you're dismissed."

Carroway's nose wrinkled, and she felt twitches crawling all over her back, rankling her with the impudence of this dog who thought he could order around her officers on her own ship. Sure, it had only been her ship for about twenty minutes, and she'd only just met Barry Lee... But was she captain, or wasn't she? Maybe things would never change, even if she did have a senior rank.

Ensign Lee saluted smartly, his delicate paw briefly touching the tip of one of his butterfly-wing ears. Then he scurried off the bridge.

"I thought Ensign Lee was one of my officers," Carroway hissed sharply between her fierce fangs.

"He will be," Bataille answered smoothly, unbothered by the angry Norwegian Forest cat glaring at him with green eyes as sharp as broken glass. "Technically, though, while this ship was yours from the moment you stepped paw aboard it, Ensign Lee and the other crew members you'll be taking from here don't transfer from their posts on Nexus Nine Base to The Wanderlust until the beginning of first shift tomorrow."

This news soothed Captain Carroway's raging heart some. The German Shepherd wasn't slighting her or impugning her rank. He was simply following protocol to a strict degree. Honestly, if her previous canine captain had been so precise, she would have liked him better. It also would have stopped him from messing with her nearly as much.

"Tell me about the mission," Captain Carroway meowed, trying to make her voice as pretty and palatable as possible. As if that had any chance of changing what mission this dog had already been told to assign her. It didn't. But she couldn't repress the urge to act placating to him in that moment anyway.

"You're familiar with the Reptassan situation in this arm of the galaxy, yes?" Captain Bataille asked.

Both Norwegian Forest cat and Morphican cyborg nodded.

"It's a bad situation," Bataille woofed, a grimace crossing his long muzzle.

The Reptassans, a spacefaring species of cold-blooded reptilian aliens, had occupied several less technologically developed worlds in their region of space for years, oppressing those planets' native peoples, including the deeply religious, bird-like Aviorans whose world Nexus Nine Base orbited. Both Carroway and Vossie had known about that. But neither of them had heard about the wolf-like Lupinians whose world orbited a neighboring star until Captain Bataille filled them in now. The Lupinians' world had fallen into a region of contested space until recently when the Tri-Galactic Union had signed that space over to the Reptassans as part of a highly politically charged peace treaty.

The Tri-Galactic Union had offered to help any individuals living on Lupinia—which included the native wolf-like Lupinians, a colony of Arborealist squirrel settlers, and even a splinter colony of Aviorans—to a new world safely within the limits of union space, if they wished.

Very few of the people living on Lupinia had wished to leave the world they were living on. The world they knew as their home. A world that now legally belonged to the Reptassans who also had a colony there.

According to the Tri-Galactic Union and the Reptassan government, Lupinia was a world whose situation was peacefully, legally, and bindingly settled. According to the mishmash of colonies living there, it was a world at war. By and large, the colonists themselves weren't fighting. They were living their lives, but under the constant threat of attack from Reptassan retaliation against an illegal group of freedom-fighters who called themselves Anti-Ra, short for anti-Reptassan.

"So, we're dealing with illegal freedom fighters," Captain Carroway mused.

"Freedom fighters who deeply believe in their cause," Lt. Cmdr. Vossie added, pensively.

"Yes," Captain Bataille agreed. "They believe they're defending their homes. Except..."

"It's not their home anymore." Captain Carroway's tail lashed behind her.

"I mean, it is," Captain Bataille corrected. "If they want it to be. They just have to live under Reptassan rule."

"Not the easiest stricture," Lt. Cmdr. Vossie said drily. "From what I've heard."

"No," Captain Bataille agreed. "My first officer is an Avioran. She grew up under Reptassan occupation of her world, and she has a lot of sympathy for the Anti-Ra. Regardless, we can't let them threaten the peace between us and the Reptassans."

Captain Carroway drew a deep breath between her fangs. "So, what is The Wanderlust supposed to do about all this?"

"There's a small, dense nebula near Lupinia. It's called the Dirt Cloud, because it's such a mess to fly through. The Anti-Ra forces have been hiding out there. We need you to fly The Wanderlust all the way to the white dwarf star in its center—you can barely even see that there *is* a star in its center from outside —and use a vacuum bomb to ignite the white dwarf."

Lt. Cmdr. Vossie blinked. On him, that was an expression of absolute shock. "A vacuum bomb?" he asked.

"Yes," Captain Bataille agreed, grimly. "It's already loaded into The Wanderlust's canons."

"Those are extremely rare," Captain Carroway said, slowly, measuring out the words. "Highly regulated."

"Into a white dwarf?" Vossie continued.

"Yes," Captain Bataille agreed again.

"Inside a super dense nebula?" Vossie pressed.

"Yes. Is there a problem?" Bataille asked, his muzzle twisted into an expression of confusion.

"No," Vossie said, firmly. His nose had stopped twitching, and somehow, that was much more disturbing to Carroway than when it had been keeping pace with her nervous, restless tail tip. "I'm just making sure I understand the mission properly."

"Well, it sounds like you do." Captain Bataille grinned wolfishly. It wasn't that he looked predatory, just that his face had a wolfish shape to it. He looked happy. He'd done a good job of briefing the new captain and her first officer on their upcoming mission.

He didn't seem to have seen beneath the surface of that mission. He was a dog, and he tended to take things at face value, like most dogs did. But Captain Carroway could see the gears turning in her Morphican compatriot's head. Not literally. Though, sometimes, the little lights on the computer implant in his brow flickered in a way that suggested to her that it was processing data. Those lights had been flickering a lot during this conversation.

"Captain," Lt. Cmdr. Vossie said, speaking directly to Carroway, bypassing the German Shepherd entirely. "I'd like to suggest that you request Timothy Melbourne be added to The Wanderlust's crew as our main pilot."

"Done," Captain Carroway said without hesitation. She could ask the Morphican about what he was up to later. She trusted his judgment implicitly; a request from him was enough for her to take immediate action, even if the name Timothy Melbourne only rang the weakest of bells in her brain. "Captain Bataille, you heard my first officer."

"Yes... I did..." Captain Bataille equivocated, looking oddly nervous for such a big dog in such a safe position. "Isn't Timothy Melbourne the cat who was stripped of his rank and arrested for—"

"Yes," Vossie agreed, pleasantly, not waiting for the end of Bataille's sentence. "We need him. He's the best pilot in the union."

"Well..." Captain Bataille frowned. "I can put in a request to my higher ups, but it's really not my decision. He's still in jail, serving his sentence on that penal asteroid."

"Yes, please, do put in a request," Captain Carroway said. "That's all I'm asking."

"Very well," Captain Bataille agreed, looking placated. The question would be out of his paws, so he didn't need to worry any more about it. "Then I guess we're done here. Unless there's anything else you need?"

Captain Carroway gazed levelly at her Morphican first officer, watching the flickering lights on his computer implant settle down to steady green before answering the dog. "No, I think we're good, Captain Bataille."

"Excellent!" Captain Bataille stood up, straightened his uniform and said, "You're both welcome to enjoy the amenities on my station until The Wanderlust is prepared to embark. The rest of your crew will report to you, here, first thing tomorrow. You're welcome to review their manifests, and if you'd like to request any changes or any additional officers be added to your crew, I'll review those requests immediately. As I understand it, this mission is of the utmost importance, so I expect you'll want to get underway as soon as possible."

"I suppose we will," Lt. Cmdr. Vossie said with such an acerbic tone that it brought both captains to a stop.

After an awkward moment, Captain Bataille barked a laugh. "You're a funny one, Lt. Cmdr. Vossie."

The very tip of Vossie's left ear twitched, giving him a skewed, skeptical look. "Morphicans are not usually known for their humor," he said. The acid hadn't left his voice, but it had curdled, turning flat and toneless.

"Thank you, Captain," Carroway said to the hesitating German Shepherd, hoping it would hurry him on his way, so she could talk to her first officer in private. She wanted to know what was bothering him so badly. The mission hadn't sounded too bad to her, but she was clearly missing something. "I think we have all that we need for now."

Placated, Captain Bataille took his leave, and as soon as he was gone, Carroway turned to Vossie, green eyes asking him to spell out what he'd seen without any need for her to say the actual words.

Vossie watched the hall leading to the bridge for several beats longer than Carroway felt was strictly necessary. However, his long ears could hear Captain Bataille's canine tread walking down the hall, and he waited until the German Shepherd was all the way off their ship before speaking.

When Lt. Cmdr. Vossie finally spoke, his captain felt like her feline patience had been stretched well beyond its natural limit. The Morphican said, "It's a suicide mission."

CHAPTER 4
THE FATE OF BARRY LEE

"Are you sure?" Captain Carroway asked, already feeling hollow inside. The Norwegian Forest cat wanted her Morphican first officer to say he wasn't sure, that he might be wrong. But he wouldn't say that. And she didn't doubt him. So, Carroway asked another question, instead of waiting for a confirmation she didn't need and wouldn't like hearing. "How? And why didn't that bastard just say so?"

The Norwegian Forest cat scowled down the empty central corridor of her new ship—a giant space coffin, apparently—at where she'd last seen the scoundrel of a German Shepherd who had so cheerfully informed her of the facts necessary to send her and her ship's crew to their deaths. A crew she mostly hadn't even met yet, but she already felt responsible for them.

"I don't believe the captain knew," Lt. Cmdr. Vossie said. His voice sounded as hollow as Captain Carroway felt. "I only know because I happen to have an obscure interest in the physics of super dense nebulae."

Even with the specter of her death thrown over her, Captain Carroway couldn't help smiling at Lt. Cmdr. Vossie's confession. He had a lot of obscure interests. It was one of the things she liked about him. She never knew what kind of obscure trivia he might share with her. Obscure trivia proved very useful—sometimes life-saving—more often than most people seemed to expect.

"So, what can we do?" Carroway asked.

"We can hope that Tim Melbourne is as good of a pilot as he was when he got thrown into jail."

"Anything else?"

Lt. Cmdr. Vossie shrugged his narrow rabbity shoulders. "I can hole up in my new quarters and do some research, but basically, we're supposed to set off a bomb deep in the middle of a nebula that will lead to a collapsing chain reaction which we're very unlikely to escape alive. Our vacuum bomb will turn the Dirt Cloud into a brand new black hole, and it'll neatly take out the entire Anti-Ra resistance with it. But unless Tim Melbourne can slingshot this little ship off the growing gravity well as it expands..." Vossie shrugged again. "I don't have any other tricks up my sleeves."

"You'll find something," Carroway said, fervently believing it.

The tip of Vossie's long left ear twitched, and his prim mouth quirked into half of a smile around his buck teeth. "I will do my best," he said. "What will you do?"

"Get to know our new crew," Carroway said. If she was going to lead them to death, she should get to know them as much as she could first. "We'll meet back here in the evening."

"I will synthesize a bottle of cream wine and appropriate, new rank pins for our collars," Lt. Cmdr. Vossie said, anticipating his captain's request.

"Exactly," Carroway agreed. "We'll have our own little promotion ceremony, just the two of us on our new ship. Then we'll discuss what we've learned and figure out a plan to make the best of this mission."

With that, Vossie retired to his new quarters, and Carroway grabbed a tablet computer with the manifest for her new crew on it and headed out to explore Nexus Nine Base. It didn't take her long to find the esplanade in the middle of the station, lined with shops and stalls where merchants sold local goods. The real hub of activity, though, seemed to be Scharm's Bar, so Carroway got herself a table, ordered the local specialty which seemed to be a fruit juice called Jumaria nectar, and settled down to study her crew manifest.

When the bartender—a Sliggurm who was basically a giant slug-like alien with rows of tiny hands all along each edge of his translucent body and four bulbous eyestalks on the top of his head—brought Carroway her order, she put out the word with him that if anyone on her manifest showed up, he should send them her way. A gray squirrel at a nearby table overheard and invited himself to join her. He turned out to be the station's doctor—a bright-eyed, bushy-tailed, and fast-talking fellow who seemed to know everyone on the station. Which made sense... as the doctor, he'd do regular check-ups on everyone, and given his extremely friendly demeanor, it wasn't surprising that he seemed to think of practically everyone he'd ever met as a close friend.

Captain Carroway learned more than she'd wanted to know about the two cats and a dog who'd be reporting to her tomorrow morning alongside Ensign Kim. They were all junior officers; the highest ranking was the canine lieutenant. All four of them were young, green, untested. And most ominously, it sounded like none of them had much in the way of close family members nor any obvious romantic partners. Both cats had been orphans raised in catteries; both dogs had come from rare one-puppy litters and had already each lost at least one of their elderly parents.

Maybe Captain Bataille didn't know he was sending her and her crew on a suicide mission, but she would have bet her fluffy tail that whichever admiral dreamed up this plan knew exactly what they were doing. Which raised all sorts of questions. For instance, if the Anti-Ra were hiding all of their forces in the Dirt Cloud—including low level officers who weren't necessarily responsible for the policy choices of their commanders—then wasn't it a war crime to simply destroy the whole nebula too fast for anyone to escape?

Or it would be a war crime. If they were at war. And if the admiral who ordered the firing of the vacuum bomb would admit to understanding what it was going to do.

Captain Carroway didn't want to be the Tri-Galactic Union's fumbling, "accidental" assassin. She was a throwaway officer who'd caused trouble with Lt. Cmdr. Vossie's help, and now the higher ups were going to get rid of her, along with her accomplice and a handful of young officers who'd been deemed disposable. All of Carroway's thoughts were dark, dismal, and horrible, in spite of the effervescent Jumaria juice buzzing through her veins like strong coffee, making her mind feel bright and far too awake.

If it weren't for the looming specter of her suicide mission, Carroway would have had a lovely time chatting with the pretty little squirrel doctor. He was very handsome and flirty, and Carroway had always had a soft spot for pretty little squirrel men. But as it was, after a few rounds of Jumaria juice, she excused herself and went back to The Wanderlust.

Carroway and Vossie had a quiet little ceremony where they took turns pinning their new rank insignias on the other's collar, followed by a solemn toast with stemmed glasses of synthesized cream wine. Then they spent the rest of the day reading everything they could about super dense nebulae, vacuum bombs, the growth patterns of artificially induced black holes, and the situation between Reptiss and Lupinia. It was a bleak way to spend one of their final days, but neither of them would give up hope that this suicide mission could be survived.

Lt. Cmdr. Vossie wouldn't give up, because he truly believed that knowledge was salvation and had a chance to save them. Captain Carroway wasn't so sure of that. But she couldn't give up, because Vossie, Lee, another dog, and two cats were all going to be following her orders. She owed them her best attempt to save their lives, even if she felt ready to despair about her own.

Come night—or what served for it aboard a ship docked at a space station—Carroway was about ready to give up and hope that for the first time ever, Vossie was wrong, and this wasn't a suicide mission. The two of them had read the situation entirely wrong. Clearly, the Tri-Galactic Union wouldn't send them on a death march to murder an entire fleet of freedom fighters. She was on the verge of insisting that she and Vossie get some rest before facing their fresh-faced junior crew officers the next morning. When suddenly, Carroway received a brief communication from Captain Bataille on her tablet computer: her request to requisition Timothy Melbourne had been approved. The felonious feline had been released on a temporary, conditional parole and was already in transit to Nexus Nine Base. He would arrive, ready to join their crew, only hours after the other new officers would report to her in the morning.

Captain Bataille relayed the information with obvious surprise, and as soon as their conversation was over, Captain Carroway felt her heart breaking.

After reviewing the dossiers on her new crew members from Nexus Nine Base, Captain Carroway had looked up the records on Timothy Melbourne. He'd never even graduated from the Tri-Galactic Union Naval Academy. Not technically. He'd been a really promising student, part of an elite squadron on track to get plum positions as soon as they graduated and received their first postings. But he'd coerced several of his friends in that elite squadron to join him in performing an overly complicated and dangerous flight maneuver during a performance they gave to set off their year's commencement ceremonies.

Tim Melbourne had pulled his part off flawlessly, but one of the students he'd coerced hadn't been up to such a challenge. Two of the five shuttles involved in the maneuver crashed into each other, sending them into a spiral that took down two more. All in all, three students died. Of the remaining survivors, one student was dismissed dishonorably from the Tri-Galactic Navy with no further retribution, and Tim Melbourne had been serving hard for the last three years.

If the admiral who'd ordered this mission was willing to send Tim Melbourne to Carroway without even asking questions... There was no question here. Vossie was right. This was a suicide mission, and it was condoned by top brass. There was no way out. Any attempt from her to dodge this fate would just leave it to fall on another officer's shoulders, while the dogs who didn't like Carroway found another way to get rid of her and Vossie. She didn't have a weighty enough voice to actually stop this mission from happening, and if she was honest with herself, based on what she'd been reading about the Anti-Ra's terrorist tactics, she wasn't sure it would be the right thing to do anyway. The Anti-Ra needed to be stopped.

All Carroway could do was figure out how to handle her singular tenure as captain gracefully. Maybe Vossie could pull a trick out of his sleeve, or maybe Tim Melbourne was a good enough pilot to beat the odds. But in case they weren't... Well, Carroway had to do her best by her crew, and that meant dismissing as many of them as possible before the mission even began. She needed Melbourne, and Vossie was in this with her from the start. But did The Wanderlust really *need* six officers to crew her?

Carroway wanted to ask Vossie for his advice, but she also didn't want to place this choice on his shoulders. She was the one responsible for her crew's lives, not him. So, she studied The Wanderlust's schematics, made a few judgment calls, and decided she would dismiss all but one of the additional officers assigned to her crew. It would be tight, but The Wanderlust could achieve this mission with only four officers at her helm: Carroway, Vossie, Melbourne... and one other.

Carroway's first instinct was to dismiss Ensign Lee, but she knew that was only because she'd already met him. He was real to her, and the idea of bringing that cheerful, optimistic, young

Papillon with her to die... It was heartbreaking. But as soon as she met the other officers, the idea of bringing them along instead would be heartbreaking too. Everything about this was heartbreaking. But Carroway didn't have time to let her heart crack open and bleed right now.

So, she studied the dossiers on the four Nexus Nine Base officers who'd be reporting to her in the morning, looking for who she could most afford to spare while giving this mission every possible chance of succeeding, in spite of being designed to fail. At least, in the sense of being survivable.

No matter how many times she read through the dossiers though, Carroway couldn't get around it: Ensign Barry Lee was the most qualified of the four officers who'd be reporting to her in the morning. He'd been working with The Wanderlust, installing her upgrades and working with her unusual systems for the last several months. And The Wanderlust did have some unusual systems. Many of the ship's components were tied together with an organic, mycelial network of fungal tissue grafted onto the usual mechanical parts, meaning the ship could repair itself, and the AI algorithms in the computer could adapt much more quickly than with traditional inorganic hardware. And Ensign Lee was the only one of the officers assigned to The Wanderlust who'd had significant time training on those unusual systems.

It was either bring Barry Lee aboard as a crew member of The Wanderlust... or replace him with two other officers to do the same amount of work. And if this suicide mission ended as the higher ups intended... then one death was better than two.

Barry Lee was going to be coming with them.

CHAPTER 5
A MINIMAL CREW

aptain Carroway slept fitfully that night. It was her first night as a captain, her first night sleeping in captain's quarters, but her dreams were haunted by the faces of the officers she hadn't met and intended to dismiss as soon as she did meet them. All night, her sleeping mind struggled with the tasks that lay ahead of her, as if by focusing hard enough, she could work her way through them in her dreams and complete the suicide mission inside her own mind, where no one could really die, because nothing was real.

By the time morning rolled around, Captain Carroway was a rumpled, grumpy, irritable mess. At least, that's how she felt on the inside. On the outside, she brushed her fluffy, tufted fur until it looked smooth and flowing. Downright glossy. She stared at her own green eyes in the mirror until she could make them sparkle appropriately and her pointed ears stood tall.

When she greeted Vossie, who was already on the bridge waiting for her—punctual as always—the Morphican looked glum but well-rested. Carroway had asked him in the past about how he managed to always look well-rested, even in situations where sleep evaded her like a tricksy little song-bird teasing a pre-uplift cat, singing so appealingly but always fluttering just out of reach of her claws. Apparently, his computer implant helped regulate his sleep, so he'd never known a night of sleep that was less than utterly easy and restful in his entire life.

Sometimes, Captain Carroway thought that having a computer implanted directly into her brain, whispering numbers at her all the time, would be worth it just for that side-effect. This was one of those mornings. A morning when she looked at Lt. Cmdr. Vossie's computer implant, flickering peacefully on his brow, beneath his long ears, and just wanted to yank it right out and jam it into her own head, hoping for just a little touch of the restful sleep it could grant.

Of course, it didn't work like that. Lt. Cmdr. Vossie's implant wouldn't pull out of his head easily—it would leave a gaping, bleeding wound filled with ripped wires—and even if it did, the device wouldn't do anyone else any good without brain surgery.

So, instead of sleep or computer implants, Captain Carroway settled for synthesizing herself a mug of steaming hot coffee, thick with cream. Most uplifted animals from Earth didn't drink coffee, even though it was a characteristically earthen beverage, but it was one of Carroway's most treasured pleasures.

Back before uplift, the caffeine in coffee had been toxic for cats and dogs, and a lingering distaste made it uncommon as a choice these days. However, coffee was known to have been popular among humans before they disappeared, so some religious dogs drank the bitter elixir as a way of paying tribute to the species who'd uplifted them.

Carroway wasn't religious; although sometimes, coffee made her feel that way. She just drank coffee because the caffeine made life more tolerable for her. She was hooked on it. Completely hooked. Though, the Jumaria juice she'd had at Scharm's bar the previous afternoon had been pretty good too. She might consider it a reasonable substitute in a pinch, but she did prefer the milky, acrid taste of creamy coffee. The way it burned and tortured her tongue was a profound pleasure, and as she sipped the scalding drink, she found herself wondering: how many cups of coffee were left in her life?

Captain Carroway shuddered as she settled into her captain's seat, hot mug in paw.

Precisely on the dot, four junior crew members padded their way onto the bridge in an orderly row. Ears perked, tails wagged, and at the sight of such youthful optimism, Captain Carroway's heart felt like it had been hit with a vacuum bomb and was imploding on itself like an unlucky white dwarf star.

She tried to remind herself that she was about to save the lives of the two tabby cats and scruffy mutt who stood in front of her. Sure, some admiral who'd never looked these kids in the face had consigned them to death under her command, but she was going to commute their sentence.

She was a savior.

Sure.

The coffee in the mug between Carroway's paws wasn't the only bitter thing on the bridge of The Wanderlust this morning.

The four young officers announced themselves to Captain Carroway, and she stared at their faces longer than she probably should have. Trying to memorize them. Trying to soak up everything about them that she could, so she could hold it close and tell herself that she'd accomplished something meaningful when this mission went to hell.

All of them except Ensign Lee. Of course. She couldn't bring herself to look the poor Papillon in his eyes. She would need to. She couldn't bring him on a suicide mission without looking him in the eyes. But she would give herself time. She would work up to it.

"All of you except for Ensign Lee are dismissed," Captain Carroway hissed through her pointed fangs.

The cats looked miffed; the mutt just looked confused. But all three of them filed away without giving her any trouble. They had no idea what a favor she'd just done them. That was okay. Captain Carroway wasn't interested in being a hero. She never had been, no matter what her previous captain had thought about her stunt during the Archidopteran skirmish. She'd been trying to save lives then, and she was trying to save lives now.

"Captain, may I ask you a question?" Ensign Lee woofed, his voice high and quavering. He was clearly troubled by the dismissal of his colleagues. They were probably his friends. They'd probably been looking forward to sharing this assignment together.

Captain Carroway still couldn't bring her green eyes to look at his face, only his hind paws standing on the floor of the bridge. Her bridge. Her ship.

Her junior officer.

Captain Carroway raised her gaze until her eyes met Ensign Lee's. His brown eyes were filled with feelings: confusion, certainly, but also hope. He shouldn't hope. The fact that Carroway could see hope in Lee's eyes killed her.

But not as much as the vacuum bomb would when they succeeded at their mission.

Before Carroway could give her junior officer permission to ask his question, Lt. Cmdr. Vossie piped up from his station at the side of the bridge: "I also have questions," he said.

Captain Carroway sighed, and instead of letting her crew question her, she said, "You're wondering why I dismissed half of our crew."

"Yes," Lt. Cmdr. Vossie agreed, sardonically. His left ear tip had flopped forward in the way that made him look skeptical and questioning.

Ensign Lee refrained from speaking, but Captain Carroway could see in his eyes that she'd pinpointed his question exactly.

"Do you have replacement officers in mind?" Lt. Cmdr. Vossie pressed.

"No," Captain Carroway answered. "We're going to carry out this mission with a crew of four. The three of us, and a pilot I've already requisitioned."

"Regulations state that this ship requires a crew of at least six," Ensign Lee barked, looking like he felt his paws were on steadier ground now that there was a regulation he could quote.

"This isn't going to be a regulation mission," Captain Carroway snapped. "Can it be done with four officers? The four officers I've listed?"

Ensign Lee got very quiet for a moment, but Captain Carroway stared at the pretty little butterfly-eared dog until he admitted, "Yes." Then he hedged the statement adding, "I believe so."

Captain Carroway felt like she was beating up a puppy. But no matter how she felt, it wasn't true: Ensign Lee was a full grown dog and an officer in the Tri-Galactic Navy. He had signed up for this job. And sometimes...

Sometimes this job was horrible. Just immeasurably horrible.

Captain Carroway sighed. She forced herself to keep looking Ensign Lee in the eye as she said, "I'm sure this wasn't what you were expecting from this posting. And I'm sorry that we've gotten off on the wrong paw here. But you should know: I selected you to stay aboard The Wanderlust as part of this abso-lutely minimal crew because the records showed you were far and away the most qualified."

Ensign Lee's butterfly ears perked up a little at his captain's praise.

"For reasons that I'm not going to get into right now—" Captain Carroway couldn't help shooting a glance at Lt. Cmdr Vossie, but the Morphican showed no reaction to her words. He was steady as ever. "—it's absolutely essential that this mission be run with as small of a crew as can be managed, and from what I've seen in all of the dossiers I read last night, it would take two officers to replace you."

Captain Carroway wanted to tell Ensign Lee that his compe-tence was saving the lives of his friends. But it would have been cruel and unnecessary to burden him with the weight that she and Vossie were carrying. He didn't need to know. At least, not yet. So, she stayed vague, saying only what she felt she could safely say: "You should know that your exemplary record is proving *invaluable*."

Ensign Lee still looked a little troubled, but his long-furred tail wagged behind him. And after a moment, his delicate muzzle broke into a smile. When that little Papillon smiled, he absolutely beamed. The radiance of it burned inside Captain Carroway's heart, and she had to look away. She couldn't let herself care too much about this officer. She was responsible for him, but they weren't going to have a long and satisfying working relationship together.

They were going to do something far more intimate: they were going to die together. And soon.

How many more cups of coffee?

Captain Carroway wanted to take a savoring sip of the coffee gripped in her paws—she was gripping it like the mug was the anchor holding her steady in a universe she might just flicker out of if she let go—but suddenly, the idea of eating or drinking anything made her feel sick. She couldn't even enjoy one of her very last cups of coffee.

"We need to prepare to embark," Captain Carroway said. "Make sure everything is ready, so we can leave as soon as our pilot arrives."

If she had to die, she wanted to get it over with as soon as possible. That wasn't logical. Everything would be over for her. There was nothing to look forward to after this mission, nothing worth racing toward. Shouldn't she savor every moment left? But also, how could she enjoy anything with this mission looming over her tufted, fluffy ears?

If the crew of The Wanderlust dragged out their preparations, there could be several days between now and the end. But this was hard enough, Carroway couldn't afford to drag it out. It was better to face her fate today.

For the next few hours, Ensign Lee trained Captain Carroway and Lt. Cmdr. Vossie on The Wanderlust's unusual systems. The Norwegian Forest cat and Morphican learned more about how to handle the mycelial components of The Wanderlust's computer systems than they'd possibly have time to use during the remaining hours of their lives, but learning something new was a better way to stay occupied and distracted from their impending doom than anything else Captain Carroway could think up. Besides, there was a minuscule possibility that something learned could save their lives.

Captain Carroway couldn't let go of that hope, even if she didn't believe it. They did learn one neat trick though—Lt. Cmdr. Vossie's computer implant could be plugged into his station using a mycelial cord, allowing him to interface directly with The Wanderlust's shipboard AI. It wouldn't save their lives, so far as Captain Carroway could tell, but it might shave seconds off of his reaction times here or there, and maybe, just maybe, that would make a minor difference.

When Timothy Melbourne finally arrived, he was escorted by an ursine security guard. The snow white cat had bright blue eyes, hearing aids in both ears, and an immediately obvious sense of humor. He exuded a self-mocking jocularity, joking with the bear—who towered over him, dressed in a chainmail sash draped over her normal Tri-Galactic Navy uniform—about how she didn't need to show off her strength by carrying around such a heavy accessory. Or maybe it was secretly a weapon that she'd wrap around him if he tried to run away?

The ursine officer did not seem amused and was clearly pleased to be dismissed as soon as Captain Carroway officially took over custody of the paroled cat.

"So, what're the breaks?" Timothy Melbourne practically purred as he draped himself over the seat at the pilot's station on the bridge. He was wearing a Tri-Galactic Navy uniform, which surprised Captain Carroway, but there was no rank pin on his collar, which surprised her less. "I've been smashing rocks with a pickaxe for months on a mining asteroid, and suddenly, I'm here. What can I do for you, oh Fluffy Savior?"

"You can start by referring to me as 'Captain,' Mr. Melbourne," Carroway sniffed at the insubordinate young cat, subtly stressing the fact that he had no rank of his own.

"Can do, Captain," Melbourne meowed, sitting up straighter in his seat, like he really did intend to do his best to impress this cat who had rescued him from hard labor, in spite of whatever his jocularity might have implied. Of course, he didn't know what he'd been rescued for.

Captain Carroway could have simply melted into the floor and become a pile of loose, shed fur with nothing holding it together at that moment, realizing she couldn't harden her heart against this cat—criminal or not—any more than she'd been able to harden it against Ensign Lee. Neither of them deserved what was coming. No one did. No one could. Being swallowed up by a burgeoning black hole wasn't the kind of punishment one could earn, only be unlucky enough to stumble into.

For a second—no, not a whole second, only the barest fraction of a second—Captain Carroway pictured confessing the nature of their mission to her two junior officers and begging her tiny crew to mutiny with her, take this ship and run, see what kind of lives they could carve out for themselves as outlaws with a heavily armed top-of-the-line little ship.

But Vossie would never go for it. And Carroway didn't know this impudent white cat or the driven little Papillon nearly well enough to want to spend her life tied to them like that.

And beneath it all, she didn't want to betray her uniform. She believed in the Tri-Galactic Union, and this was what the union needed from her. She would do her duty. She would shoulder this weight.

At least, she wouldn't have to shoulder it much longer.

With more bitterness than could be crammed into a year's worth of coffee, Captain Carroway realized that this was the moment when she should give an inspiring speech to her crew before they disembarked. She wasn't sure she could muster it. She took a sip of her now cold coffee, letting the taste—which was ashy in her mouth—bolster her as much as possible. Then with mug still in paw, she walked to the front of the bridge and stood in front of the viewscreen, which showed a lovely view of Nexus Nine Base in all its architectural complexity—triangles, hexagons, all tangled together in a beautiful pattern.

"Welcome to The Wanderlust," Captain Carroway said. "We're a small crew, and we have a simple mission today." She cringed at her own choice of words, but they weren't inaccurate. If the mission were more complex, perhaps there'd have been more hope for her and Vossie to find a way to survive it. "We're going to defend the peace between the Tri-Galactic Union and Reptiss by delivering a crippling blow to the Anti-Ra, an illegal terrorist organization that's been assaulting Reptassan colonies on the planet Lupinia. They've been hiding in the Dirt Cloud, a nebula in the neutral area between Tri-Galactic Union space and Reptassan space."

"And you needed a crack pilot," Mr. Melbourne meowed, looking troublingly ponderous, like he might see right through the veneer of this mission to its heart. He knew he wouldn't be here if there weren't something strange going on.

"Yes," Captain Carroway agreed, hoping to sweep past the point quickly. "We needed the best pilot we could get our paws on, and my first officer, Lt. Cmdr. Vossie—" She gestured at the rabbit-like officer, seated at his post, still plugged into the mycelial computer. "—suggested you."

Timothy Melbourne frowned. The somber expression on his ghostly white face provided a solemn contrast to his earlier joking demeanor. He was a very handsome young cat. That shouldn't make any difference, but somehow, the handsomeness of his features highlighted his youth. He glowed the way that only the young can glow. In spite of working on a mining asteroid, incarcerated, for the last three years, he was still so young and untouched by the world. It was a crime that the potential for his life was being thrown away like this.

Captain Carroway turned away from Melbourne and faced Ensign Lee, which only made the feelings she was struggling with worse. The Papillon was a blameless young officer with a perfect, exemplary record. Her voice caught in her throat, coming out as a low rumble, when she said, "Ensign Lee, would you please contact the station and request permission to undock. It's time we got underway."

Ensign Lee nodded, his expression similarly solemn. He might not know the depth of what was wrong aboard this ship, but he could read the room. And no one aboard The Wanderlust was having an especially good day. At least, that was what Captain Carroway thought.

Once The Wanderlust was truly underway, it became clear that—regardless of his earlier thoughtful expression and clear perceptiveness—Timothy Melbourne was having a very good day. He was flying a ship again—the thing he'd been born to do, and something he hadn't been allowed to do in three years. His paws were meant to steer the helm of a spaceship, racing between stars. He was a natural born pilot.

Captain Carroway was glad that someone was enjoying this death march. Even if she couldn't enjoy the taste of her coffee—she'd gotten herself a second mug, fresh and hot, extra creamy—she couldn't help smiling at Timothy Melbourne's evident joy. The ghost white cat might have intuited that he was heading toward the gallows—trading incarceration for extinction—but he was the kind of feline who intended to relish every last bite of his final meal, metaphorically speaking.

To Lt. Cmdr. Vossie and Ensign Lee's dismay, Timothy Melbourne kept up a constant patter as they flew toward their doom, asking questions about what had been happening in the universe outside his asteroid prison, sharing anecdotes about particularly amusing fellow prisoners, and just generally insisting on keeping some form of conversation alive. Captain

Carroway found it kind of charming, and she didn't mind the distraction. She didn't want to be left alone with her thoughts. None of her thoughts were any good right now anyway. Everything between her fluffy ears was as dark and murky as the Dirt Cloud they were approaching.

CHAPTER 6
PROTEIN BARS AND CUPS OF COFFEE

The closer The Wanderlust got to the Dirt Cloud, the more of the starry sky it blotted out on the viewscreen wrapped around the front half of the bridge. By midday, crenellated clouds in shades of dark purple and muddy orange filled their entire view. No stars at all. Even the white dwarf that was their target, deep in the middle of the nebula, was completely hidden by the clouds of thick, dark dust.

"At our current rate of travel, we'll enter the Dirt Cloud in twenty minutes, Captain," Mr. Melbourne meowed. "This might be a good time to share some details about what exactly we should expect, and how you want me to deal with it."

The charming white cat continued to be impertinent. Captain Carroway should have minded, but under these unusual circumstances, she actually appreciated the prodding. She couldn't keep Melbourne in the dark if she expected him to fly well.

Carroway exchanged a look with her first officer. The Morphican nodded, understanding her request without her having to say anything. Still hooked into The Wanderlust's computer, he swiveled in his seat until he could see both of the junior officers stationed at their posts—Melbourne in the pilot's seat at the front of the bridge, and Lee at a monitoring post on the other side of the bridge. There was still a comfortable amount of slack in the mycelial cord between his implant and the computer it plugged into.

"Intel shows that these clouds are crawling with Anti-Ra ships," Lt. Cmdr. Vossie said, his tone unfathomably even for someone who knew he only had a matter of hours left to live. And it's not like they were going to be especially wonderful hours. "Their ships are older and more worn down than The Wanderlust. On a one-by-one basis, we should have no trouble facing them. However, they have an entire fleet. We are one ship. Logically, we must operate through stealth. Ideally, we will make it to the star system at the center of the Dirt Cloud without a single one of the Anti-Ra ships discovering us."

"Stealth," Mr. Melbourne repeated. "Got it. I can do that." The white cat's blue eyes twinkled as he smiled.

Captain Carroway felt cold. She never felt cold, not with all her thick fluffy fur, but watching Timothy Melbourne smile at the idea of facing a challenge made her feel cold.

"When we reach the white dwarf in the center of the nebula," Lt. Cmdr. Vossie continued tonelessly, "we'll fire on our target, and then we will need to escape the Dirt Cloud as quickly as possible."

The two junior officers—who'd had no chance to interact privately so far and knew each other hardly at all—exchanged a meaningful glance. A pretty little butterfly-eared dog, best and brightest of Nexus Nine Base, and a handsome, smooth-talking criminal of a cat. They were both bright young officers. Too bright not to notice that Vossie had neatly side-stepped telling them the nature of their 'target' or what to expect after they fired on it. But it wasn't their place to ask. Not when their commanding officer was making such a clear point of refusing to say.

Timothy Melbourne didn't seem like a cat who usually stayed in his place, but this time, something stopped him from asking a question that he could tell his superior officers didn't want him to ask. Maybe he could tell that he wouldn't like the answer. Maybe he sensed that it wouldn't help him accomplish his goals: it wouldn't help him fly better, and right now, flying was all he had to live for.

Ensign Lee opened his muzzle and closed it again several times, seemingly getting up the courage to press Lt. Cmdr. Vossie or the captain for more information. But Mr. Melbourne, with his quick, easy way with words, had set the tone.

Now was a time to obey, not a time to ask.

"Well, then," Timothy Melbourne meowed, "shall we get underway?" He said it so casually, like they weren't headed toward their dooms, and yet, somehow, it didn't sound like Melbourne didn't know. It just sounded like he refused to care; he refused to let it drag him down.

Captain Carroway was growing very fond of these young officers very quickly. She might have a small crew, but damn her tail if it wasn't a good one. "Thank you, Mr. Melbourne," she growled. "Please take us into the Dirt Cloud."

With a larger crew, it would have been possible for all of them to take a break, leave replacement officers to babysit the bridge and keep an eye on the ship, while they took a final meal in the small multi-purpose room. A real final meal. Of course, that would have meant there was an entire extra shift of officers who'd need to eat a final meal. Twice as many deaths.

As it was, there were barely enough officers on The Wanderlust to fully man the bridge with all four of them working all the time. They couldn't take shifts for full meals; instead, they took turns ducking off one at a time to synthesize quick snacks that could be eaten at their stations, making sure there were always three officers on the bridge.

Protein bars and cups of coffee, that would be Captain Carroway's final meal. And none of them would be sleeping again. Four officers was not enough to set up stable shifts, so they'd all serve on the bridge until this was over. Which should be soon.

The Wanderlust shot like an arrow into the Dirt Cloud's dusty gloom. Mr. Melbourne steered her with a deft paw, and as soon as the gloom closed around them, he began wefting and weaving the ship between especially dense clusters of dust, large space rocks, and electro-magnetic field phenomena. He was every bit as skilled as Lt. Cmdr. Vossie had said he would be. His skills couldn't have deteriorated hardly at all during his incarceration, in spite of the fact that he wouldn't have had his paws on a starship's controls for three years.

The dust ahead of them began to glow as their sensors showed they were approaching the white dwarf. The glowing intensified, lightening the gloomy dark purple and muddy orange clouds to twilight violet and the warm orange of a campfire.

"It's almost pretty," Mr. Melbourne observed.

"It's crawling with Anti-Ra ships," Lt. Cmdr. Vossie countered, admonishing the young feline. "Remain vigilant, Mr. Melbourne."

"Will do," Melbourne meowed, unconcerned by Vossie's light rebuke. Compared to years in jail, the displeasure of one Morphican was nothing. But then, the white cat swore, "Dammit," at exactly the same time as Ensign Lee announced grimly from the back of the bridge, "We're being hailed."

"I'm sorry, Captain. I've been dodging ships all morning without a problem," Mr. Melbourne meowed defensively. "I swear that ship was entirely powered down and didn't show up on our sensors until we were practically on top of it."

"I believe you, Mr. Melbourne," Captain Carroway said, leaning back in her seat and placing one paw against her brow as if the advent of an Anti-Ra ship spotting and hailing them was a literal headache for her. "Regardless, we now have to deal with this complication."

"Their ship is small," Lt. Cmdr. Vossie said. "We should be able to take it down with relative ease."

"Show the Anti-Ra ship on the viewscreen, please," Captain

Carroway ordered, and instantly, the view shifted. Instead of the empty expanse of clouds in front of them, the viewscreen showed a darker segment of the nebula's clouds to their side. Silhouetted against the gentle purple-orange glow of the clouds was a small vessel. Smaller than The Wanderlust. Less well armed. It looked old and like it had seen heavy fire in its time.

Captain Carroway knew the Anti-Ra ship would be swallowed up by a black hole soon enough, even if The Wanderlust did find a way to take mercy on it. Unless, of course, the Anti-Ra ship summoned a bunch of other Anti-Ra ships, and they managed to take The Wanderlust down together.

There was an idea. She could fail. If she failed, she might live.

As a traitor...

As a prisoner...

Even having these thoughts was treasonous.

"Should I answer the hail?" Ensign Lee asked.

"Orders, Captain?" Lt. Cmdr. Vossie asked pointedly.

And yet, even knowing that their mission was to destroy the entire nebula—which would destroy all the ships inside it—Captain Carroway couldn't bring herself to order Lt. Cmdr. Vossie to fire on a vessel whose greatest act of aggression so far was to hail them. She had been ordered to fire a vacuum bomb on a white dwarf, not to fire upon less-armed vessels.

"Answer the hail," Captain Carroway rumbled through gritted fangs. "Put them on the main viewscreen."

Within moments, the view of the glowing nebula clouds, silhouetting the Anti-Ra ship, was replaced by the face of a golden-mantled squirrel with bright eyes and round ears decorated with tiny gold and silver hoop earrings along their edges. This squirrel's features were a little broader and plainer than the flirty gray squirrel doctor at Nexus Nine Base, but in his own way, he was just as pretty. Captain Carroway had bigger concerns right now than how pretty a squirrel man was... but he was, nonetheless, nice to look at, and this would likely be the last time she got to enjoy looking at a pretty squirrel man.

The squirrel was seated on a bridge that looked as rundown and battle-torn as the outside of the Anti-Ra vessel he was hailing them from looked. Around him, manning the other stations, were another squirrel, a Morphican who didn't seem to have the usual computer implants, and an individual who looked to be half-Avioran, half-Reptassan with feathered plumes framing her otherwise scaly, beaked face.

"Greetings, Tri-Galactic Union vessel," the squirrel said. "I'm Captain Chestnut of The Last Chance. My vessel has been patrolling this nebula, and we wondered if you would be so kind as to inform us of what you're up to here."

"Do you usually patrol with all your systems powered down?" Captain Carroway countered in a purring tone.

The squirrel smiled warmly; his eyes sparkled with kindness. Captain Carroway would think of his face sadly if she survived this mission. It would be a shame, knowing he'd perished due to her actions. But, hey, maybe if The Wanderlust could dodge its way out of the nebula ahead of the crashing wave of gravity sucking everything into an unnatural singularity, maybe this Anti-Ra vessel would manage to ride out the danger by chasing after their tail. It was a long shot. Such a long shot.

"Touché," the squirrel eventually conceded. "Regardless of what my vessel was up to, we're both here now, and I have to ask you to turn around and head back out of the nebula for your own good."

"Our own good?" Captain Carroway meowed archly. "I don't think your vessel is a match for mine." She didn't need to out-argue this squirrel, just keep him talking long enough to complete her mission and high-tail it out of here.

"Perhaps not," the squirrel admitted. "But the Tri-Galactic Union has ceded control of this area of space, and I don't think you really want to be here."

"You're right," Captain Carroway agreed. "We don't, and we'll be out of your fur shortly, if you leave us be."

As the two captains—large cat and small squirrel—traded

quips, both of their ships continued barreling toward the brightest part of the nebula, the center where the white dwarf lay waiting for them. Waiting for its destiny.

A destiny none of the animals on either ship could possibly anticipate.

"This really isn't a safe region of space for a Tri-Galactic Union ship," the squirrel said, his thin brush of a tail flicking behind him like a marsh reed whipping in the wind. "If you'd like, my ship would be happy to escort you back out of the Dirt Cloud."

"How generous," Captain Carroway meowed, gesturing with a paw for Ensign Lee to cut the sound on their transmission.

"Sound is off," Ensign Lee announced.

Captain Carroway immediately turned to her first officer and asked the Morphican: "Are you ready to fire on our target as soon as we're in range?"

The rabbit-like alien nodded solemnly, lights twinkling on his computer implant that was still plugged into the ship's computer.

"Excellent," Carroway said. "Consider the order already given." Then addressing her pilot, she said, "Mr. Melbourne, I want you to alter our trajectory to take us within firing range of the white dwarf star; then as soon as Lt. Cmdr. Vossie has fired on our target, you will sling-shot The Wanderlust off of the star's gravity well in whichever direction will get us out of this nebula fastest. I'm talking faster than you've ever flown or even imagined flying before. Understood?"

"Exciting," the white tomcat said sardonically; except underneath the cynicism, he really did sound excited. "And yes, Captain, understood," he added more formally.

"Correction," Lt. Cmdr. Vossie interjected, "please sling shot us in whichever direction the nebula's dust clouds are least dense. I've patched a course through to your console."

"Perfect," Mr. Melbourne said. This time, he sounded too

focused on his flying to play at sardonic tones. "The new course is laid in, and adjustments are being made..."

On the other side of her bridge, Captain Carroway heard paws shuffling and glanced over to see Ensign Lee looking uncertain. "Is there an Anti-Ra base in close orbit of the star?" the Papillon woofed, sounding like he was getting a little too close to figuring out there was something wrong with this mission, something more than he'd already seen.

On the viewscreen, the golden-mantled squirrel was still chittering away, looking extremely irritable, but the sound was off and none of his words were coming through. Instead of answering her junior officer's question, Captain Carroway said, "Please turn the sound back on, and I'll see if I can keep this Anti-Ra captain arguing with me until it's too late for him to interfere with our mission.

Out of the corner of her eye, Captain Carroway saw Ensign Lee stiffen at receiving an order instead of an answer. The Papillon looked like he felt slighted and a little angry about being actively excluded from understanding what to expect when The Wanderlust reached the white dwarf. But it wouldn't help for him to know. He followed his order and said crisply, "Sound will be on again in three, two, one..." And Ensign Lee went silent.

"I'm sorry, Captain Chestnut," Carroway purred smoothly. "Our systems lost sound for a minute there, but I believe we have it fixed now."

The golden-mantled squirrel sputtered, but then he regained his composure, tail stilling behind him. "If you don't leave this nebula at once, I'll be forced to call for reinforcements." The other officers around him—the rabbit, other squirrel, and reptilian-bird—were looking increasingly tense and nervous.

"Oh, I don't think that will be necessary," Carroway purred. She was almost enjoying toying with this squirrel man who thought he had any sort of upper hand.

"If you don't allow us to escort you out of this nebula at once," the squirrel said, "then I think it will be."

"Is that a threat?" Carroway asked, her own tail was lashing beside her in the captain's seat now, almost taking on a life of its own with the rush of feelings that could barely stay contained in her body. Adrenaline, excitement, fear, and perversely, a strong attraction to the squirrel captain, which was probably just a weird side-effect of all the other emotions. Too many emotions for a cat—even a big, scary, intimidating Norwegian Forest cat— to handle at one time. But this would all be over soon. *Too soon.* Carroway just had to hold on a little longer. She lifted her mug of coffee, hoping to steady herself, and tried to take a sip, only to be startled by finding it empty.

No more cups of coffee...

Too late for cups of coffee...

That was it. Her last cup of coffee. Ever.

The murky purple-orange clouds on the viewscreen suddenly melted to nothing in the middle, and the bright white light of a dwarf star shone like an angel of doom and destruction.

"Look," Carroway said, trying to buy her crew the last few minutes they needed, "we're just here on a scientific mission. We're going to fire a research probe into the heart of that dwarf star. We'll leave immediately afterward. We don't even need to stick around for the results. The data will be transmitted directly to us when it's ready." The lies came easily. It hardly mattered what she said anymore, not with the end this close.

And yet, to her side, Captain Carroway heard her ensign gasp. The Papillon couldn't help himself from saying aloud, "We're firing on the star *itself*?"

Captain Carroway had made a miscalculation. Ensign Lee knew they weren't going to be firing a research probe. This ship didn't even have any probes suitable for such a mission. And despite his exemplary record, he was young and untested. With this first test... He'd just failed and revealed information Captain Carroway didn't want revealed.

"Why are you firing on a white dwarf star?" the squirrel captain asked, bright eyes narrowing.

"Anything less than a vacuum bomb would have minimal effect on a full-fledged *star*," the reptile-bird on the Anti-Ra bridge hissed at her squirrel captain. "Are they firing a *vacuum bomb?*"

"Are you?" the squirrel captain asked pleasantly, passing along his underling's question. "That would be a war crime."

"*We're firing a scientific probe,*" Captain Carroway growled, repeating her lie. Then turning to her own underling, she snapped at the stunned-looking Papillon, "Turn off that viewscreen. I'm done with this conversation."

Ensign Lee disengaged the comms, and a peaceful view of the orange-purple nebula clouds glowing around a shining white dwarf returned to the viewscreen.

Captain Carroway didn't like the way that reptile-bird had asked about the vacuum bomb. Something in her hissed tone had implied to the Norwegian Forest cat that she knew exactly how deadly a vacuum bomb would be in this situation, and the idea of their enemy knowing their secret plans—plans that half of her own crew didn't know about—made every nerve in Captain Carroway's body sizzle.

But it didn't matter, she told herself, looking at the size of the white dwarf star on the viewscreen. It was too late for the Anti-Ra ship to stop them.

"The Anti-Ra ship is keeping pace with us, continuing to follow us toward the white dwarf star," Ensign Lee woofed. Then he added, softly, "I'm sorry if I spoke out of turn earlier."

When Captain Carroway turned to look at him, she saw the Papillon's butterfly-like ears were splayed, hanging low. Her heart melted. He shouldn't die feeling ashamed and guilty. He deserved better than that. She said to him, "Ensign Lee, you have performed beautifully on this mission." Raising her voice to speak to the rest of her crew—all three of them—she added, "You all have. You should all be proud."

Only moments later, Lt. Cmdr. Vossie announced, "We have fired on the target."

On the viewscreen, a streak of light zoomed toward the white dwarf. It looked like a shooting star. Instinctively, Captain Carroway muttered under her breath, wishing on the star like she would have as a kitten: "*Live, please, let us live.*" Then speaking up to be heard, she said, "Ensign Lee, please keep the viewscreen centered on the white dwarf, and Mr. Melbourne, I hope you're flying faster than a cheetah on caffeine can run."

The white tomcat didn't answer. He was too focused on flying.

CHAPTER 7
THE CHOSEN THREAD SNAPS INTO PLACE

Every muscle in Captain Carroway's body clenched as she watched the white dwarf on the viewscreen—the vacuum bomb was still careening toward it, and if she hoped fervently enough, she could imagine the white dwarf was already shrinking. They were already flying away from it. They were going to escape. Maybe, just maybe, they were going to escape.

"Captain?" Ensign Lee woofed tentatively.

Captain Carroway tore her eyes away from the view of the shrinking white dwarf star to look at her ensign. His butterfly ears were standing tall again, but there was concern in his eyes and a shakiness in his stature. Carroway meowed impatiently, "Yes? What is it?"

"The Anti-Ra ship, The Last Chance, is on a collision course to intercept our... uh... scientific probe," Ensign Lee barked with a quaver in his voice.

"Will that work?" Captain Carroway snapped at her Morphican first officer.

"No," Lt. Cmdr. Vossie stated plainly. "Even this close to the star, there's enough space dust per cubic kilometer for the explosion to spread from the Anti-Ra vessel to the star."

There was something so deeply tragic about the Anti-Ra crew sacrificing themselves on a gambit that wouldn't even work. And yet, was it truly more tragic than simply dying because they were caught in a rapidly growing black hole? Either way they would die. Though, Captain Carroway supposed this way was more noble. And that made it more tragic. She'd only spoken with that squirrel captain—Captain Chestnut, it was worth remembering his name, he deserved that—briefly, but the Norwegian Forest cat felt a profound respect for him.

"They're brave souls," Captain Carroway meowed.

"Are we about to die?" Ensign Lee woofed. There were more than enough puzzle pieces available for him to have put the whole picture together by now.

"Not if I have anything to do about it," Mr. Melbourne meowed through gritted teeth.

"There is a small chance," Lt. Cmdr. Vossie observed, "that the Anti-Ra vessel intercepting our vacuum bomb will give us the extra time we need to escape unscathed. The black hole will grow much more slowly at first, beginning with the Anti-Ra vessel as its seed."

"Those are people," Ensign Lee woofed, staring at the Anti-Ra vessel growing ever closer to the arc of the vacuum bomb on their viewscreen. His statement was less a rebuke of Lt. Cmdr. Vossie's matter-of-fact tone and more just a statement of horrified wonder at the train wreck he was watching.

None of them had been prepared for this, even the two of them who'd known the truth about this mission.

On the viewscreen, the small Anti-Ra vessel collided with the streak of light that was the vacuum bomb, and for a moment, everything flashed white. Bright and piercing. When Captain Carroway's eyes cleared from the flash of light, she saw the Anti-Ra vessel burning, smoldering; then it impossibly shrank in on itself like a trick was being played on her eyes.

Captain Carroway blinked, and next she saw, the Anti-Ra ship was gone. White light from the dwarf star began snaking across the empty space toward where the ship had been. Then the star itself began elongating, stretching from a shining sphere to a glowing oval. Then one end of the oval—the end closer to where The Last Chance had disappeared—snaked out, twirling across invisible gravity lines, circling the minuscule but rapidly growing black hole that the Anti-Ra ship had become.

"Will we make it?" Captain Carroway breathed, barely voicing the words at all.

"It's hard to say," Lt. Cmdr. Vossie answered.

"Those people..." Ensign Lee woofed, overcome by grief. "We were just talking to them..."

"At least, they didn't have time to suffer." Commander Carroway tried to say the words softly; she was trying to be comforting, but all she could think was: they didn't have to wait and wonder whether they'd survive, like I'm having to do right now. It was wrong to envy people who were already dead, but in a way, Carroway did.

As a kitten, one of Captain Carroway's littermate's had tried to interest her in watching sports games together, but she'd never understood the appeal. If you waited until a game was over—doing something else while it was happening—you could just look up the score and skip past all that unnecessary drama. It saved so much time.

Captain Carroway wanted to look up the score after this was over, but the only way out was through...

The white dwarf star's light continued to stretch out and swirl around the dark patch where the black hole must be. It was eerie and beautiful, and it didn't feel like it was getting any smaller on the viewscreen. Of course, it was growing... so maybe that was an optical illusion? But Captain Carroway didn't think The Wanderlust was pulling away from the black hole.

"We are stuck in the black hole's gravity well," Lt. Cmdr. Vossie announced. His long ears had both drooped forward hopelessly. He'd never looked more defeated. "We cannot escape by flying forward."

"Could we..." Captain Carroway felt like an idiot saying it, but this wasn't a time to let dignity get in the way of brainstorming. "...I don't know, turn around and fly through it?"

"It's a *black hole*," Lt. Cmdr. Vossie said bleakly. "It's not a worm hole. It doesn't *go anywhere*."

"*Are you sure?*" Captain Carroway hissed.

"One hundred percent," Lt. Cmdr. Vossie replied primly. Even this close to death, he could still find room for annoyance.

"Not a thousand percent?" Mr. Melbourne quipped. The white tom cat's narrow tail was lashing frantically behind him. "I dunno. Only one hundred percent seems low to me right now for basing decisions on."

"No, Mr. Melbourne, that would be hyperbole," Lt. Cmdr. Vossie said, tall ears perking back up a bit now that he had a chance to defend clear communication and the pursuit of reason. "Neither hyperbole nor flights of fancy will help us here."

"I'd take a flight of fancy over nothing right now," Ensign Lee woofed.

Captain Carroway looked at the young, pretty dog. He was staring at the viewscreen like it would swallow him up, and he wasn't wrong. Ensign Lee might have spoken out of despair, but he had a valid point. Whether a plan would work right now might be less relevant than whether it would give The Wanderlust's crew something to do with their final minutes...

There wasn't time to do anything meaningful like share a last meal that had more substance than protein bars and coffee or record final messages to send to the loved ones they would be leaving behind—something that Captain Carroway should have thought to do the night before. But her brain had been in a fog, ever since Lt. Cmdr. Vossie had said the word "suicide" to her. And at this point, nothing The Wanderlust sent would escape the growing black hole's rapidly expanding gravity well anyway. They were lost. They might as well embrace it.

"To hell with probabilities," Captain Carroway announced

with as much bravado as she could muster. "Turn this ship around and take us straight into the black hole."

"To hell with logic, science, and reason too, then, I suppose," Lt. Cmdr. Vossie muttered, but he didn't argue more than that. He understood what his captain was doing. He didn't have to like it or agree with it, but he did understand. And even though his body was perfectly regulated to keep himself from panicking at the imminent prospect of his death, the rabbit-like alien understood that the other three crew members of The Wanderlust didn't have that advantage. Terror would be coursing through their veins in the form of all kinds of stress hormones. They couldn't help letting fear of mortality unbalance them.

"Aye, Captain!" Mr. Melbourne meowed in delight. If he was going to die, at least, he was going to die doing what he loved, what he was best at, and doing it in the most extreme way possible.

What other cat could say they'd flown a top-of-the-line starship straight into a rapidly expanding baby black hole? None that he knew of! Of course, he might not get much of a chance to brag about it after the fact either, but that was a problem for later. Right now, his paws were doing the driving, and it was time to let them dance over The Wanderlust's controls.

Toward the back of the bridge at his station, Ensign Lee was facing his own mortality for the first time in his young life. He was a young enough dog who'd lived a blessed, privileged enough life that—while he'd faced his father's death as a young puppy—he'd never really considered the idea that he would someday die. Not really. He knew it academically, of course, in a sort of abstract way, but it had never been a real, serious concern, staring him right in the face, unblinking, unflinching, coming for him.

Ensign Lee found himself wondering about what he might have missed out on by spending his whole life so dedicated to the pursuit of his Tri-Galactic Union career. And yet, even with the seconds ticking down, he couldn't think of anything wild or reckless he'd ever done, and he couldn't think of anything glorious but foolish he wished he could do, if only there were time left. He couldn't think of anything at all. Fear had frozen him. He'd never been brave and bold like the tomcat steering their vessel with dancing white paws.

Ensign Lee watched Mr. Melbourne, and maybe it was just the crazy, heady mix of hormones flooding his body, but he felt a little bit in love with that cat. Only half an hour ago, he'd wished Mr. Melbourne would shut his muzzle and stop telling silly stories about his exploits among the prisoners on the penal asteroid for the last three years, and yet, suddenly, those stories felt so vibrant, so full of life. Even life on a penal asteroid sounded wonderful and delightful when described by that charming tomcat.

If Mr. Melbourne could pull The Wanderlust out of this black hole, Ensign Lee swore to himself, he would try to become more like that tomcat. He would try to live life such that Mr. Melbourne could tell stories about him to pass the time. Nothing Ensign Lee had done in the last few months—or years, even— would make a good story. All he'd done was work, focus, study, and follow the rules. If he got a chance, Ensign Lee wanted to be more than just a Good Dog. He wanted to be a vibrant one.

On the viewscreen, the white dwarf's stretched out strings of light blurred and blended together. The air aboard The Wander- lust's bridge grew thick and heavy, like the officers on her bridge were breathing—or rather, choking on—molasses. Then the ceiling contorted, metal screaming as it bent inward, and the viewscreen cracked right down the middle. Liquid crystal fluid leaked down the cobweb cracks on the display like blood.

Flame licked its way onto the bridge from The Wanderlust's central corridor, followed by billowing bursts of thick gray smoke, dotted with glowing red sparks that filled the air. All of the officers on the bridge began to cough and gag. Thick air was hard to breathe, but ember-filled smoke actually burned.

Captain Carroway tried to cry out—she wasn't sure if the cry was the start of an order to Mr. Melbourne to turn the ship back around or simply a primal war cry meant instinctively, irrationally to scare the big, looming black hole away—but the roar returned to her throat before it could escape from between her fangs.

The smoke cleared, flowing backward to the corridor where it had come from.

The viewscreen repaired itself, cracks smoothing back together and liquid crystal fluid flowing back into place behind the smooth screen.

The ceiling screamed its way back to its original convexity, and the air began to thin, becoming easier to breathe again.

Everything was undoing itself.

Except the view on the viewscreen?

Blank darkness. An endless void. Nothing, nothing, nothing.

"Is the viewscreen broken?" Captain Carroway choked out from her lacerated throat, still burning from the smoke she'd breathed in.

Mr. Melbourne, with his fur fluffed out like an asterisk, turned back to look at his captain; the expression on his ghost-white face showed that he thought she was crazy. Clearly, the viewscreen had repaired itself. The cracks that had been there only moments before were entirely gone.

"Yes," Captain Carroway snapped impatiently, her voice still rough and rumbly, "I know it's not still *broken*... but... is it *working*? Where's the star? Are we... inside a black hole?"

The Norwegian Forest cat captain looked over her shoulder at Ensign Lee, but the Papillon was staring at the controls on his console, paws hovering uselessly above it like he'd been about to do something but then forgotten what it was. He was far too absorbed and bewildered by whatever readings his console were showing him to notice anything as inconsequential as a question from his captain. The young dog was clearly stunned.

The white tomcat, on the other paw, looked like he'd been

startled into action, ready to fight anything and everything that came his way. "What the hell was that?!?" he caterwauled.

"I believe," Lt. Cmdr. Vossie said, voice shaking and ears flopped completely downward, "that we just experienced a blip in time."

The rabbit-like alien's brow was bleeding, fur matted and red above his left eye. His computer implant was gone. At least, with horror, that's what Captain Carroway thought at first. Then she saw the implant had been yanked out somehow and was lying on the console beside her stunned first officer, still plugged in by way of a mycelial cord to the ship's computer system, but no longer serving any purpose now that it's connection to Vossie's brain had been severed.

"Oh, Vossie!" Captain Carroway yowled. *How would her friend get by without his implant?* She needed to get him to a doctor immediately so the implant could be reinstalled in his brow and the connections restored to his brain.

"Actually..." Ensign Lee's voice was halting and hesitative. He was still staring at his paws, hovering just above his console. "We've moved in space as well... A long way in space..."

"Well, where are we?" Captain Carroway asked distractedly. She had gotten up and was trying to help Vossie, but there wasn't much she knew how to do for him. She was afraid to touch the displaced implant. She didn't know how delicate it was or if she might break it further by trying to unplug it from The Wanderlust's computers. So, she let the implant be and settled for checking Lt. Cmdr. Vossie's brow directly. The wound was mostly shallow, but like head wounds do, it was bleeding profusely.

"I believe, based on these readings, that we're in the empty expanse between galaxies." The Papillon's butterfly ears had splayed and were hanging low. His bright eyes had a frantic shine to them. "Unless I'm mistaken, we're on the far outer reaches of the fringe of... the Tetra Galaxy."

Captain Carroway whirled around, exclaiming, "The Tetra

Galaxy!" Mr. Melbourne reacted much the same way, and the two cats' exclamations coincided.

"A blip in space-time..." Lt. Cmdr. Vossie muttered. "Intriguing." They were the words he would normally say, but his voice was weak and his whole body shook like his heart was racing with fear and probably a plethora of other emotions that his implant would usually be keeping in check.

"Mr. Melbourne, could you see if you can scare up a med kit, please?" Captain Carroway meowed, trying to gather her wits together. Then she added, "And Ensign Lee, could you please calculate the quickest route home?"

The Tri-Galactic Union was centered in three galaxies—The Milky Way, Twilight Spiral, and Ursa Dentatus. Those galaxies were thoroughly explored and interconnected by various hyperspace jump points that made it possible to navigate through them and between them fairly quickly.

The Tetra Galaxy, however, was much farther away. And while a nexus did exist that bridged between the far outer reaches of Ursa Dentatus—the galaxy where the bear-like Ursine aliens had come from—and the Tetra Galaxy, the Tetra Galaxy itself was still almost entirely unexplored. There were no maps of hyperspace jump points that would make it quick or safe to navigate. And at a rough estimate, a direct course from the outer edge of the Tetra Galaxy back home to the Milky Way, without any hyperspace jump points, would take many months at top speed. At best. At worst? It could be years.

Four Tri-Galactic Union officers, all alone, trying to crew a ship of this size for months on end without any help or support would be untenable. Even if it were a crew who had been carefully picked to get along with each other. That wasn't the case here. Sure, Captain Carroway and Lt. Cmdr. Vossie had been best friends for years, and Mr. Melbourne might prefer a long voyage to his incarceration... but Ensign Lee had been betrayed by the Tri-Galactic Union he believed in when he was sent on this mission. The bright, young Papillon had every right to be angry.

None of them were prepared for what they might be facing.

"Uh... Captain..." Ensign Lee was now looking at his computer console like it had turned into a snake and might bite him. "We're being hailed?"

"Out here?" Captain Carroway meowed in bewilderment. "In the middle of nowhere?" The Norwegian Forest cat sighed and shrugged. Maybe this mission would involve scientific discovery and diplomatic first contact after all. "Put whoever it is on the viewscreen, I guess."

Mr. Melbourne returned with a med kit and began cleaning up Lt. Cmdr. Vossie's head wound. Meanwhile, Captain Carroway returned to her captain's seat and composed herself for whatever might appear on the viewscreen, whatever strange, new, alien race might live out here in the dark between galaxies.

CHAPTER 8
TWO CREWS ON ONE SHIP

Captain Carroway could not have been more surprised when the face that appeared on The Wanderlust's viewscreen was the very familiar golden-furred face of Captain Chestnut. "What the hell?" she spat. "We watched your ship explode!"

"And I felt it explode," Captain Chestnut said, shuddering. The reptile-bird behind him had a haunted look in her eyes, and Captain Carroway noticed that the other Anti-Ra officers—the Morphican and other squirrel—were no longer on the ship's bridge. "But more importantly, my engineer tells me that our ship has sustained enough damages from that first explosion that unless we power down immediately, it might very well explode again. And believe me, I do not want to experience that twice. None of my crew do..." His voice went hollow in a way that suggested to Carroway that maybe not all of his crew had survived the return from that first explosion. "Especially when I expect the second time might be... well... more final. It's not often that you get a reprieve from your ship exploding around you." He smiled weakly.

"What can we do to help?" Captain Carroway asked. Minutes ago, she'd been responsible for the Anti-Ra ship's total and complete destruction. Now she was asking how she could help the survivors...

Of course, minutes ago, she was facing the prospect of her own death. And now... Now she didn't know what she was facing at all.

This day was dizzying.

"If your ship has room and is in a more stable condition," Captain Chestnut said, "could my crew evacuate to it?"

"Yes," Captain Carroway agreed without hesitation. "We can bring you all onboard. Power your ship down, and we can tow it... well... wherever we end up going."

"We'll figure it out when we get there," Captain Chestnut said. The lights on his bridge flickered. He looked over his shoulder and shouted, "All paws prepare for immediate evacuation. And Diaz? Power it all down. Everything." Looking back at the screen, he said, "Thank you, Captain—?"

"Carroway," the Norwegian Forest cat provided. Then she said to Ensign Lee, "Please teleport all life signs on The Last Chance into The Wanderlust's second barracks room." Then turning so her face couldn't be seen by Captain Chestnut through the viewscreen, she quietly hissed, *"Make sure our teleporter disables any weaponry they might have on them, and set up a force shield across the barracks' door."* She wanted to help the Anti-Ra crew, but she didn't want to give them the opportunity to take over her ship.

Ensign Lee nodded in acknowledgement and then woofed, "I'm reading four life signs." Then lowering his voice, the Papillon added, "That's two fewer than showed on the ship before..." He waved a paw loosely, indicating the bewildering space-time blip they'd all just experienced. "...before all this happened."

Captain Carroway drew a deep breath between her fangs to steady herself.

The Anti-Ra officers would be mourning their lost crewmates. Individuals who had died because of an order she'd given and a vacuum bomb her ship had fired. She hadn't expected to have to look survivors in the face after committing the atrocity she'd been ordered to commit.

She hadn't expected to look at anything at all.

No matter how hard and confusing all of this was... it was better than being squeezed to death inside a baby black hole, which was what she and Vossie had expected would happen.

There was a certain freeing quality to having expected her own death so completely and to have come out the other side alive. Freeing and a little unreal. Surreal, even. Like she was floating through an impossible dream.

Captain Carroway had faced the certainty of her own death and survived; anything else could be figured out.

First off, Captain Carroway needed to deal with her new guests. If she had a proper crew for her ship, she'd be able to send an underling to deal with the Anti-Ra refugees while she stayed on the bridge, figuring out what was going on. As it stood, there were now as many Anti-Ra on her vessel as Tri-Galactic Union officers. That was not a good balance.

Captain Carroway made her way to the back of the bridge and opened a supply cupboard filled with hand weapons—half a dozen blazors and two blazor rifles. She hoped she wouldn't need one. But in case she did... It was better to be armed and not need it than the alternative. Captain Carroway hooked a blazor onto her uniform's belt, took down another two blazors which she handed to Ensign Lee and Mr. Melbourne, and then locked the cupboard. She didn't offer a blazor to Lt. Cmdr. Vossie.

The injured Morphican was in no shape to wield a weapon. He was still shaking uncontrollably. Though, Mr. Melbourne had bandaged the wound on his brow.

"How did your implant get pulled out?" Captain Carroway meowed gently. "Why didn't it... I dunno... get repaired like the viewscreen and the ceiling when the, uh, *blip* reversed time?"

Buck teeth chattering, Lt. Cmdr. Vossie stuttered, "Don't... know... time effects... patchy..."

"A similar question," Ensign Lee woofed, "is why didn't the Anti-Ra ship repair itself? Why did two of their officers die?"

"Their ship was damaged earlier than ours," Captain Carroway meowed. "Presumably the blip simply didn't reverse time far enough to repair their ship."

"Except if the time blip didn't go all the way back to before their ship collided with our... *scientific probe*—" Ensign Lee positively glared at Captain Carroway as he repeated the words of her lie. "—shouldn't the cascading explosion of their ship that led to the birth of a baby black hole simply have started over again?"

"And then led to another reversal," Mr. Melbourne offered. "Rocking back and forth forever and ever, trapping us in a tiny, horrible time loop?" The white cat shuddered. Even a lifetime of servitude on a penal asteroid sounded better than living through the last few minutes, backward and forward, over and over again for eternity.

Maybe he shouldn't have been so excited to receive parole. Maybe this mission wasn't worth it...

Too late now.

"Time loops..." Lt. Cmdr. Vossie spoke bitterly and haltingly. "...are... nonsense."

"But time *blips* aren't?" Mr. Melbourne meowed.

Captain Carroway looked at her Morphican friend. He was doing poorly. He needed a doctor. Someone who could perform brain surgery and put his implant back in place. "Is there anything we should do with your implant?" the Norwegian Forest cat asked. "To protect it? Should we unplug it from The Wanderlust's computer system?"

Lt. Cmdr. Vossie shook his head emphatically, and Mr. Melbourne said, "The implant and the mycelial... uh... tendrils from The Wanderlust's computer system seem to have fused together. I don't think we can remove it without doing damage to it."

Captain Carroway scowled. That was a problem she would have to deal with later.

"In fact," the white tomcat added, "the fungal tissue attached to the implant... seems to be growing. Ugh." He poked at the lumpy pinkish-gray fungal flesh attached to Lt. Cmdr. Vossie's implant with a carefully extended claw. The flesh shuddered, reacting to his poke.

"Don't do that," Captain Carroway snapped. "Lt. Cmdr. Vossie needs that implant. So, I'm going to go deal with our... visitors. While I do that, I want Ensign Lee to continue scanning the nearby area. We could use a planet to land on—"

"Not likely out here," Ensign Lee woofed pessimistically. "We're at least a week's travel from the nearest star..."

"—or any other potential source of resources, as it doesn't sound like we'll be able to get home... well..." Captain Carroway still didn't have a good estimate of how long to expect their voyage home to be. Maybe they could find a way to reverse whatever phenomenon had sent them here? And possibly end up back inside the gravity well of a growing black hole... No, she'd rather be on the far side of the Tetra Galaxy than crushed to death. The Norwegian Forest cat decided to pivot to a different topic. "Mr. Melbourne, please start researching what we can do to help Lt. Cmdr. Vossie handle the removal of his implant and what might be necessary for us to get it placed back where it belongs in his head, given the resources we have aboard The Wanderlust."

"Aye, Captain!" Mr. Melbourne meowed.

Vossie managed a weak buck-toothed smile at his captain and friend. Ensign Lee just kept frowning at the console in front of him.

Captain Carroway stalked off the bridge and down the central corridor of The Wanderlust with her fluffy tail lashing behind her. When she got to the second barracks room, she found the Anti-Ra officers had already opened its door and discovered the glittering sheen of the force shield holding them in.

"You didn't have to disable our weapons and lock us in," a canine woman growled from within the room as Captain Carroway stepped into sight on the opposite side of the force shield from them. The canine woman was the largest person onboard The Wanderlust right now. She probably stood head and shoulders taller than Captain Carroway. She had short, dark, brown fur, bat-like ears, and wide set eyes. She wore a necklace of braided reeds over her clothes, and the fur on one side of her face had been dyed reddish in an ornate pattern. She was also glaring absolute daggers at the Norwegian Forest cat who had incarcerated her. If she'd been loose aboard the ship, she could have caused a lot of damage.

"Ah, but see, the fact that you have weapons and have already noticed that they're disabled—" Captain Carroway countered, tail still lashing, refusing to show that she was intimidated by the canine's size, "—says to me that I most definitely did."

The towering canine woman growled. Captain Chestnut stepped in front of her. He was barely a third of her height, but the canine responded to his posturing by backing down and shrinking away from the shielded door like a shadow melting from the light. She moved farther back into the barracks and sat down on one of the bunks beside the Morphican man without any implants who seemed to be holding a small bonsai tree in his arms, cradling it like an infant. The tree had pink and white blooms among its lime green leaves and was planted in a small, beautiful glazed pot. The final Anti-Ra officer—the reptile-bird woman—was approximately the size of the Morphican—both of them being about the size of a small cat—and, she was pacing the room restlessly, claws on her talons clicking against the metal floor. Her plumes of red and blue feathers were all puffed out.

"Touché again," Captain Chestnut chittered, clearly trying to block the view of his distraught crew members with his small body which was entirely incapable of such a task, except for the way that his intense aura of energy made eyes draw to him like moths to a light. Captain Carroway wasn't sure if the squirrel captain was trying to stop her from looking at his crew or stop his crew from looking at her. Either way, he tried and failed to smile, before saying, "I think we have a lot to talk about, and it might be best if we were to talk in private, away from either of our crews. Is there somewhere we can do that?" His rounded ears flicked, causing the rows of tiny gold and silver hoops lining their outer edges to jingle.

The other three Anti-Ra officers were clearly listening to Captain Chestnut as he spoke. The tiny squirrel captain looked about as haggard as Captain Carroway felt, and she knew he had even better reason than her. He had lost friends today. He had possibly lost his ship. And he hadn't seen any of it coming. She'd had two days warning that a catastrophe was coming, and it hadn't been nearly enough.

"Yes," Captain Carroway agreed looking down at the much smaller squirrel. "I suppose we do have a lot to talk about. Perhaps, we could discuss things in my quarters."

Captain Chestnut gave her a forced attempt at a grin. "I'd be happy to—" He gestured at the force shield with one of his tiny, delicate paws. "—if you'd just be so good as to let me out."

Feeling a little uncertain, Captain Carroway reached a paw out to the control panel beside the door and dropped the force shield. The squirrel captain had taken one step through the door's threshold when his reptile-bird officer came rushing toward him.

Automatically, Captain Carroway took a step back and brought her paw to the blazor clipped at her waist, but the reptile-bird stopped as soon as she reached her captain. She placed both scaly, talon-like hands on his narrow shoulder and squawked intensely, *"Don't forget. We can't leave Maple's spirit tree behind!"* The red and blue feathers framing her face flattened down in a way that made her look even more distraught than when they'd been puffed out.

Captain Chestnut took the reptile-bird's talons gently in his own small paws and said, "I won't forget. We won't leave her tree behind, and it'll be fine for a while longer, even without life support. It's a tree. It's sturdier than we are, right?" He nodded encouragingly up at the reptile-bird until she nodded back at him.

"You're right. Thank you." The reptile-bird drew her talons away and wrapped her wing-like arms around herself. She went back to pacing the room.

Captain Chestnut stepped all the way through the door, and Captain Carroway was relieved to be able to reengage the force shield and close the door, locking the squirrel's crew away. The squirrel himself was small enough—and unarmed—that Captain Carroway had no worries about releasing him, alone, onto her ship. She was more than twice his size and still had one paw on the butt of a blazor. Not to mention that she had two more armed officers on the bridge.

The Anti-Ra squirrel would behave himself during their conversation. He had no alternative.

"Captain Carroway," Captain Chestnut said. "Before we begin discussing anything in depth, perhaps I could get you to do a favor for me?"

"About the spirit tree?" Captain Carroway asked.

"Yes, I grabbed my own tree before we were teleported off of our ship, but..." The golden-mantled squirrel faltered. He didn't look like the captain of a squad of resistance fighters; he just looked like a man who had lost a friend today. "My crewmate, Maple, was another Arborealist, like me, and none of us had a chance to get to her spirit tree before being teleported away."

Maple must have been the other squirrel who Captain Carroway had seen on the Anti-Ra bridge, before all the chaos had occurred. The chaos she'd caused by following her orders, by carrying out her mission.

"It's small, like the tree my Morphican officer is holding, if you noticed it..."

"I did," Captain Carroway meowed. "It was lovely. And of course, I'll have one of my officers locate the life signs of your friend's tree and beam it aboard immediately. Why don't you wait for me in my quarters while I take care of that?"

The Norwegian Forest cat gestured with a paw at the doors to her quarters. She wasn't too worried about leaving the golden-mantled squirrel alone in them for a few minutes. He couldn't get up to too much trouble in that time. And right now, it looked like he simply didn't have the energy or heart for causing trouble in him. There'd been a gleam in his eye when he'd matched wits with her over the viewscreen, before The Wanderlust has triggered the creation of a black hole. That gleam was gone now. Gone since he'd died, come back to life, and been forced to face the loss of two of his friends.

Captain Chestnut opened the door to Carroway's quarters and stepped inside, his fluffy reed-like tail dragging behind him.

Captain Carroway took a deep breath to steady herself. Then she walked back to the bridge and explained the situation about the spirit tree to Ensign Lee. The Papillon promised to locate it—which he'd failed to do originally because its life signs were so much smaller than for the crew members of The Last Chance—and teleport it directly to the barracks where Captain Chestnut's crew was still incarcerated.

With that taken care of, Captain Carroway checked in on Lt. Cmdr. Vossie who was now draped over his computer console, shaking and crying, trying to hide his face behind his long ears out of shame over his lack of emotional control. He turned away from Carroway—even though she was his oldest and closest friend, he didn't want her to see him like this. He didn't want anyone to see him like this. He didn't want to be this way. He wanted his implant back; he wanted it to whisper directly into his brain that everything would be okay, listing precise probabilities for every likely occurrence that might happen in the coming minutes, while releasing soothing hormones into his blood-stream, bathing his brain in the bright, cool, clarity of a properly balanced body.

Captain Carroway reluctantly left Lt. Cmdr. Vossie to his misery, since there didn't seem to be anything she could do for him right away. And she had other problems to deal with.

"Keep researching the implant," Carroway said to the white cat who was sitting beside Vossie, clearly already deep in research. Articles streamed across the screen in front of him, reflecting in his clear blue eyes. Then a thought struck Carroway and she added, "There's a Morphican Anti-Ra officer locked in the second barracks room right now. Maybe he knows some-thing that can help Vossie. He doesn't have implants, but maybe he knows something useful about them. Or..." She hesitated to say this, because she knew it would only upset Vossie further right now... but it needed to be said. "Maybe he knows some-thing that can help Vossie adjust to... living without his implants. We may be out here for a while... He may need..."

Captain Carroway didn't finish her sentence. Lt. Cmdr. Vossie had tilted his head to where he could see her between his long ears and was glaring at her even more sharply than the canine Anti-Ra woman had been doing only a few minutes ago.

Captain Carroway was getting the distinct impression that she was stuck on a ship, several galaxies away from home, with a whole crew of people who hated her. Two crews of people who hated her.

Well, maybe not Mr. Melbourne. The white tomcat seemed deeply absorbed in researching Morphican implants. He didn't seem unhappy. Why would he be? The asteroid where he'd been imprisoned was galaxies away, and right now, he was an integral member of this small crew. He was the only person aboard the ship who was having, arguably, a good day.

Before leaving the bridge, Captain Carroway glanced one more time at Lt. Cmdr. Vossie's implant, lying on the computer console. The implant was barely even visible now; only a corner of it peeked out of the growing glob of pinky-gray mushroom flesh that kept growing around it. The blog of flesh was the size of a baseball now.

Looking back to Ensign Lee, Captain Carroway said, "You're the closest thing we have to an expert on The Wanderlust's mycelial systems. When you've finished scanning for nearby resources, I want you to figure out if we can get Vossie's implant unplugged from this fungal matter without hurting it... or... hurting the ship's computer."

With that, Captain Carroway stalked back off of the bridge, tail swishing irritably behind her. She didn't wait to hear from her officers that they'd follow her orders. She knew they would. She was their captain.

CHAPTER 9
A DELICATE CONVERSATION TO NAVIGATE

Captain Carroway entered her quarters to find the golden-mantled squirrel captain carefully examining a framed piece of art on the interior wall. It was a painting of the ship itself, The Wanderlust, flying through a swirling nebula—one that was much more colorful, bright, and appealing than the Dirt Cloud. It was an utterly generic work of art. The kind that starship designers put in a captain's quarters before the actual captain comes aboard and personalizes their space.

"You haven't been on this ship long, have you?" Captain Chestnut observed.

"No," Captain Carroway agreed, trying to keep her tail from lashing too obviously. She didn't want to broadcast her emotions to this little squirrel.

So many squirrels have a frenetic energy. Almost frantic. As if they're perpetually in the state of having had one too many cups of coffee and could stay up all night talking to you, weaving their way from one anecdote to the next, never stopping. Captain Chestnut wasn't like that. He had a steadiness that made Captain Carroway think more of some of the largest dogs she'd met—Newfoundlands, Mastiffs, or St. Bernards—than other squirrels. She found his presence oddly calming, especially considering what she'd done to him and what he must think of her.

That trait must come in useful for him as a captain. It would make it easy to lead. A crew would want to follow him. Captain Carroway supposed that was part of why there were so many more canine captains than feline ones in the Tri-Galactic Union— not because they were necessarily better at leading or making important decisions, but simply because they had a calm, steady way about them. The Norwegian Forest cat found that infuriating, even if it had arguably helped her rise to the rank of commander faster than many other cats, as she was one of the biggest cats around. But physical size—and the way it was perceived by others—had nothing to do with her decision making processes or why she actually did belong in command.

Captain Carroway sat down on a comfortable chair next to a small couch that was situated in front of a wide window looking out on the distressingly starless black expanse of sky surrounding The Wanderlust. She gestured at the couch and said, "Why don't you sit down, and we can talk about our situation."

The golden-mantled squirrel sat down on one end of the couch and let his brush of a tail fluff out and take up an entire seat beside him. "Did you have a clever trick up your sleeves for escaping the black hole that you were sent into the Dirt Cloud to create?"

"That is confidential information," Captain Carroway rumbled unhappily. This wasn't what she wanted to talk about.

Captain Chestnut smiled at her sadly. "No it isn't, because you didn't, did you? It was a suicide mission."

Captain Carroway's ears flicked, wanting to flatten, and she shifted uncomfortably. She didn't know what to say to this Anti-Ra squirrel. She shouldn't share Tri-Galactic Union secrets with him, but also...

The Tri-Galactic Union sent her to die, and she had no one to talk to about that, except her subordinate officers. And you can't have the same kind of conversation with someone who depends on you and looks up to you as you can with someone whose life isn't all tied and tangled up with yours.

Perhaps soon, this squirrel's life would be tangled up with Captain Carroway's and the fate of The Wanderlust. But for this brief moment—this liminal moment before anything was figured out and settled—Carroway and Chestnut were both captains, both carrying the responsibility of caring for a ship and crew. They were equals.

"Yes," Captain Carroway admitted, allowing her ears to flatten after all. "It was a suicide mission. We had no tricks up our sleeves."

"You were willing to die to destroy the Anti-Ra fleet?" Captain Chestnut pressed, seeming genuinely interested. But when Captain Carroway didn't answer right away, the squirrel amended his question: "Or maybe, you were willing to die simply to follow your orders? T'lia told me that the Tri-Galactic Union plays head games with its officers, but I had no idea it was that bad."

Captain Carroway bristled, feeling her fur fluff out just the slightest bit around her neck and shoulders. Her fur was bushy enough that the squirrel probably couldn't tell. She wanted to defend the Tri-Galactic Union, but the best she could muster was, "I read about the atrocities being committed by the Anti-Ra before taking on this mission."

The set of the squirrel's small jaw tightened almost imperceptibly. "So you volunteered for a suicide mission? To follow your principles? I guess we have something in common then. I was fighting for my principles too." His chittering voice hardened as he spoke, ending on a defiant tone. "Except, actually, I was fighting for more than principles. I was fighting for my *home*."

The Norwegian Forest cat sighed and settled further back into her chair, feeling very tired. Ever so tired. "Right, so as we already knew, we're enemies, standing on opposite sides of an unofficial, undeclared, but nonetheless real war."

Chestnut looked surprised to hear a Tri-Galactic Union officer admit that he was engaged in a war, rather than using a different, more minimizing word for it.

"But right now, that war and your *home* are more than a galaxy away," Captain Carroway continued. She didn't like what she was about to suggest, but she didn't see any alternative. Four officers was not enough to crew The Wanderlust for weeks or months on end. "Out here, it's our two crews against the unknown. My navigations officer—" She made a point of referring to Ensign Lee in a way that made it sound like The Wanderlust might have more officers aboard her right now than she actually did. Never mind the fact that Ensign Lee was currently called upon to fill a lot more roles than merely navigations, especially with Lt. Cmdr. Vossie out of commission. "—hasn't given me an estimate for how long it will take us to get back to the Milky Way Galaxy yet, but it could easily take months."

"Or longer," Captain Chestnut agreed grimly. "My navigations officer—Risqua, the one who was reminding me about Maple's spirit tree—tells me that given some of the obstacles we might run into in the Tetra Galaxy, we should expect traveling back home to take years."

Captain Carroway didn't like hearing that at all. "What kind of obstacles does she expect?"

"Apparently one of the spiral arms of the Tetra Galaxy has unusually thick concentrations of space dust and nebula clusters, based on long range observations of it," the squirrel captain explained. "We may have to fly around those. And of course, that's not accounting for the possibility that we might run into new and potentially hostile alien empires. We don't know who is out here."

"*The enemy you know,*" Captain Carroway muttered bitterly.

"Indeed," Captain Chestnut agreed even more bitterly. "So what do we do? I appreciate your ship's help, but I don't exactly want to hand my entire crew over into incarceration while you spend years dragging us back to the Tri-Galactic Union for some kind of joke of a trial for daring to defend the Dirt Cloud from ultimate destruction."

Captain Carroway was about to start breaking Tri-Galactic Union regulations and share more information with her Anti-Ra enemy than would usually be acceptable. But this was an unusual situation, and her choices were to hide information from Chestnut and try to crew The Wanderlust with far too few officers... or to come to some sort of uneasy truce.

"My crew isn't large enough to fly this ship for years on our own," Captain Carroway admitted. She didn't exactly expect Captain Chestnut to look surprised—he'd been far too perceptive so far to have not figured out something was off about her ship—but the look of confirmation in his eyes still took her off guard.

"You need us," Captain Chestnut chittered.

Captain Carroway was a cat, and her pride wouldn't allow her to straightforwardly agree with the squirrel's assessment. She did not want to need a squirrel and his ragtag group of terrorists. But she did. "We're all heading in the same direction. We may as well travel together, especially given the state of your ship." She couldn't resist baiting the squirrel. Her pride was damaged, so she wanted to damage his.

Captain Chestnut didn't fall for Carroway's barbed comment though. He simply said, "It will be challenging blending our crews."

The idea of blending her crew with a group of terrorists was a hard concept to swallow for Captain Carroway. But her crew was already one quarter paroled criminals and one quarter completely incapacitated by injury. So, she didn't have a lot of choice. "This is still my ship," she insisted.

"Alright," the squirrel agreed, "But my crew isn't going to blindly follow your commands like some brainwashed Tri-Galactic Union crew."

"They follow your orders well enough," Captain Carroway observed.

"True." The golden-mantled squirrel had the audacity to look smug. "So, what should we do about that?"

Captain Carroway could feel the shape of her life turning around these moments, hashing out an agreement with this rebel squirrel. But then, after that space-time blip, her life already kind of felt like a waking dream. Why not make it even more surreal?

"Here's my offer," the Norwegian Forest cat said, perking her ears tall and leaning forward. "We integrate our two crews. I'll stay captain, but you can be my first officer." Would she be making this offer if he weren't such a handsome, steady, likable, and unthreateningly-small squirrel man? Captain Carroway couldn't be sure. But she simply didn't see another way forward. "I'll grant temporary Tri-Galactic Union ranks to you and the rest of your officers, and when we get back home, I'll give each of you a choice: apply to the Tri-Galactic Union based on your record of service during our journey or be dropped off at a neutral site before The Wanderlust reports in."

"If my crew had wanted to be part of the Tri-Galactic Union, they wouldn't have been on my ship in the first place," Captain Chestnut chittered. But he kept glancing over his shoulder at the great empty expanse behind him. Surrounding them. No stars. Only darkness.

Captain Carroway shrugged. "Then you all get dropped off on a neutral planet or space station of your choice along the way home, and you disappear back to your old lives, as well as you can after our prolonged absence."

"Promise?" Captain Chestnut asked, his tiny ears flicking nervously, causing all his earrings to jangle.

Captain Carroway stuck out a paw. "I promise."

The squirrel took her much larger paw in his, and they shook on their unusual deal.

"I hope you realize, I'm making the much bigger concession

here," Captain Chestnut said. Except, he wasn't really a captain anymore. He was Captain Carroway's first officer.

"I do," Captain Carroway meowed. "And I understand that this will be a significant adjustment for your crew. Mine as well. We're all going to have a lot of work to do, if we want to make it home without tearing ourselves apart."

"I suppose we will," Commander Chestnut agreed.

Captain Carroway stared intently at the small squirrel and realized how profoundly lucky she was that he was this easy to work with. Maybe he was secretly planning rebellion and mutiny... but she didn't think so. She thought he understood how precarious his situation was. And she thought, he needed her and her crew too. They needed each other.

CHAPTER 10
WEARING A NEW UNIFORM

Only a few days ago, Janessa Carroway had despaired of ever reaching the rank of captain. Her canine superior officer had been holding her back, and there'd been nothing she could do about it. She'd thought she would never have her own ship or crew, and the weight of her desire for that leadership role had felt like it would crush her. She had craved captaincy like a newborn kitten craves milk.

Now she was in the captain's quarters of her own vessel, and the size of her crew had just doubled. She had no admirals nearby enough to look over her shoulder and order her to lead her crew differently. She had more power and freedom than she'd even imagined. And it had come at such a high cost.

Yet deep in her feline heart, she couldn't help recognizing: this was exactly what she'd always wanted.

The freedom was dizzying.

"How shall we begin?" Captain Carroway asked her new first officer. This squirrel was almost a stranger to her, but they needed to find a way to lead together. "We need to break the news of our... *situation* to the crew."

"*The crew,*" Commander Chestnut repeated wonderingly.

"How quickly you've come to refer to a ragtag group of enemies under one banner."

Captain Carroway shrugged. "I'm a union officer. We're trained to handle adversity with grace and flexibility."

"Adversity like suicide missions?" the golden-mantled squirrel asked drily, tilting his head ever so slightly. "I don't understand how you still have such loyalty to a bloated, over-grown institution that was ready to throw you away."

"Every institution has problems," Captain Carroway snapped. "But the Tri-Galactic Union isn't just an institution. It's a philosophy of life and a set of principles. Ideals to aspire toward. Sure, individual officers—or sometimes entire segments of the union—may fail to live up to those principles, but the point isn't always to succeed. Sometimes, it's merely to strive, to always keep trying. To reach for the stars and keep reaching, even when you fall."

The golden-mantled squirrel who Captain Carroway had just recruited to step in above her best friend as her new first officer stared at her intensely, like he was measuring her up. "We should address the crew together," he said, surprising her. "You're offering temporary Tri-Galactic Union ranks to my crew, right? And presumably, you'll back them if they apply to the union when we get home. So essentially, we're functioning as a Tri-Galactic Union ship. We should act like one."

Captain Carroway wasn't sure exactly what it was about her words that had won Commander Chestnut over. He had seemed so thoroughly against the Tri-Galactic Union. But she wasn't going to fight his change of heart. Better to run with it, for now, and ask questions later, when the crew was more under control. "You should wear a union uniform," Captain Carroway meowed. "I can synthesize one for you. We'll just need to take a few measurements to make sure it will fit right."

Commander Chestnut nodded, jangling his earrings with the bobbing of his head. Then in spite of his obvious weariness, he flashed a genuine smile the captain's way and almost laughed. "I never in a million years would have guessed I'd end today wearing a Tri-Galactic Union uniform."

Captain Carroway smirked, caught by the infectious nature of his levity. Also, she realized that she might be on the edge of cracking into hysterical hilarity. Exhaustion and extreme pressure can do that to a cat. Kind of like a black hole, except really, not at all. But when you're as tired as Captain Carroway felt in that moment, suddenly everything is like everything else, and the whole universe is composed of bad metaphors.

"That's the most unexpected thing about today?" Captain Carroway asked as she unstrapped the standard issue uni-meter at her hip and used it to run a quick scan of the golden-mantled squirrel in front of her.

"No," Commander Chestnut said. "But it's the funniest. The other ones weren't funny."

Perversely, Captain Carroway found herself wishing that she'd needed to take measurements of her first officer in the old-fashioned way with a measuring tape held up against his tiny body, pressed against his narrow chest first vertically and then wrapped all the way around him like a hug. It was a completely inappropriate thought, but maybe not more inappropriate than comparing her own exhaustion to the crushing weight of a black hole that she'd created and then watched kill two of Commander Chestnut's officers.

Maybe it was asking too much for her thoughts to stay appropriate on a wholly unaccountable day like today. Maybe acting appropriately was good enough, and she could worry about getting her mind in order later.

The Norwegian Forest cat transmitted her uni-meter's readings to the synthesizer in the corner of her quarters and ordered it to generate a standard Tri-Galactic Union uniform, complete with a commander's rank pin for the collar. The carefully folded fabric garment appeared in the synthesizer with a shimmer of quantum light. She grabbed it with her paws and then held it out to the golden-mantled squirrel. The bundle of clothes was much smaller than one of her own uniforms would be when folded up.

Commander Chestnut grabbed the garment by its shoulders, shook it out, and held it up against himself. "What do you think?" he asked, staring down at it critically. "It's not really my color."

The golden-mantled squirrel's current clothes were a muted combination of pale grays and tans that matched his soft golden fur with the pale accents around his eyes and the edges of his ears very well. The Tri-Galactic Union uniform was black with navy blue accents, much brighter and bolder than what he was wearing now. The flatness of the colors on the Tri-Galactic Union uniform made the organic shades of gold, copper, red, and tan in his fur look much sunnier and more nuanced, almost glowing like the flames of a flickering campfire.

"I don't know," Captain Carroway meowed. "I think it'll look rather striking on you. I'll step out and give you a minute to get changed. While you do, I'll speak to my officers on the bridge about getting your officers—" Carroway frowned and corrected herself. "—the rest of *our officers* released from the barracks, so we can address everyone together."

Captain Carroway started to turn away, toward the door to her quarters, but Commander Chestnut cleared his throat in a way that called her back to attention. A clever little trick. He hadn't actually told her that something was wrong with her plan, but he'd already planted seeds of doubt between her ears with a simple cough.

"Do you have a problem with that plan?" Captain Carroway asked, looking down at the much shorter squirrel.

"We said that we would address the crew together. If you speak to the bridge officers first, then the rest of the crew will be playing catch-up from the get-go. Is that really what you want?"

Captain Carroway was impressed by how deftly the squirrel referred to both groups of officers, making them truly sound like one crew, if only through the trick of his words. More than anything that was why she decided to concede his point.

"Very well," Captain Carroway said. She might have been about to say more, but the golden-mantled squirrel pulled his tan and gray shirt off revealing the striking black and white stripes that ran down his sides. He threw the discarded garment on the couch behind him, and began working his arms into the sleeves of his new uniform.

"Just turn around," Commander Chestnut said, "and I can get these pants on."

Captain Carroway felt the insides of her ears blushing, which didn't seem very captain-like to her. But she turned around, letting her first officer order her around for at least this one moment. Only moments later, the golden-mantled squirrel stepped up beside her, looking absolutely official in his new uniform, as if he'd been a Tri-Galactic Union officer all along. Suddenly, the blushing inside Captain Carroway's ears grew even brighter. She might have a soft spot for pretty little squirrel men, but she had even more of a soft spot for pretty little squirrel men in Tri-Galactic Union uniforms. And even if she knew this uniform was partly a facade, it was a damn good looking facade.

"Is something wrong?" Commander Chestnut asked, brushing his delicate paws down the front of his new uniform.

"No, you look fine," Captain Carroway meowed, trying to curb the purr in the back of her throat.

"Alright, then," Commander Chestnut said. "Shall we go talk to the crew? Or is there anything else we need to get straight first?"

A fair question. And almost certainly, the true answer was that they had a lot they needed to figure out first. But also, they had six crew members waiting to hear from them, and every minute that passed was one minute more of the Anti-Ra officers stewing in their imprisonment, growing resentment toward the union officers they were going to need to work with and become a part of. Meanwhile, Lt. Cmdr. Vossie was suffering, and Ensign

Lee couldn't run this entire ship on his own—no matter how competent the young Papillon was—while Mr. Melbourne tended to the injured Morphican.

"I think we'll have to figure it out as we go," Captain Carroway meowed.

"Bold," Commander Chestnut chittered. "How do you know I won't fight you at every turn, undermining your authority in front of our crew?"

Captain Carroway smiled as only a cat can, knowing and mysterious, superior and condescending, self-satisfied and always craving more. "You called them *our crew* just now, and you agreed to this harebrained scheme of blending our crews together in the first place. Somehow, we're functioning on the same wavelength, and I'm just going to have trust in that."

"I like you, Captain Carroway," the squirrel chittered.

Captain Carroway smiled, feeling the warmth in her ears spread. "It's going to be a long journey, Commander Chestnut. I don't think I can handle keeping up that level of formality all the time. So, I think, maybe, when we're alone, you can just call me Jan. It's short for Janessa."

"Okay, Jan, let's go get our crew in order—we'll need to start by updating them on our plan and get Risqua, Werik, and Diaz in uniforms like me." His matter-of-fact voice turned grim as he added, "Then I want to hold memorial services for Maple and Wilder."

Captain Carroway nodded. It made sense that the Anti-Ra officers would need to start by mourning their lost compatriots. She wished she could sweep those losses aside like they'd never happened, because they were her fault and reflected poorly on her. But trying to brush aside the Anti-Ras' grief would be even worse. She was going to have to live with these people for months or longer. She would need to swallow her discomfort and let their feelings on this matter take center stage.

Even so, a spark of rage flared up in the Norwegian Forest cat that the Anti-Ra had forced her into such an uncomfortable position. If they hadn't been executing terrorist acts against the Reptassan colonies on Lupinia, she wouldn't have been sent to destroy them. She wouldn't have these deaths on her conscience.

And she wouldn't be captaining a ship in the middle of unexplored space with a handsome squirrel at her side.

The universe is a mixed up place.

Captain Carroway stepped right up to the door out of her quarters, but then she paused before opening it. "Tell me those names again," Captain Carroway meowed. "I want to know all my officers by name. I think it will help smooth this transition if they see that I'm invested in including them." And ideally, by being included in a Tri-Galactic Union crew over the coming months, they would start to see the error of their ways before. They would see that life could be better when aspiring to Tri-Galactic Union ideals instead of resorting to chaotic warfare. Captain Carroway would convert them from terrorists to good citizens.

"Risqua is—" Commander Chestnut stopped himself, corrected his word choice, and continued. "Risqua *was* my first officer on The Last Chance. She's a half-Avioran, half-Reptassan refugee who wasn't wanted on either Avia or Reptiss, so she moved to Lupinia. T'lia Diaz was The Last Chance's engineer. She's absolutely brilliant, and she already was a Tri-Galactic Union officer. However, she left the union when her homeworld was abandoned by them. See, she's half-uplifted Xolo from Earth, but her other heritage is Lupinian. Then there's Werik— he's from a splinter colony of Morphicans on Lupinia who reject computer implants and want to live naturally."

"What about the officers who died?" Captain Carroway asked, trying to keep a mental list of the living officers in her head, rehearsing their names and backgrounds so she wouldn't forget.

Commander Chestnut looked surprised and touched that Captain Carroway had thought to ask after the crew members he'd lost that morning. "Maple was another uplifted squirrel, an

Arborealist—like me. She and Risqua were very close. And Wilder was Lupinian. He'd grown up with Diaz before she left Lupinia to join the Tri-Galactic Union, and when she left the union, he was the one who recruited her onto The Last Chance."

The golden-mantled squirrel's voice grew very quiet and solemn as he spoke about the connections his deceased officers had shared with his living ones. It made Captain Carroway wonder about what exactly his connections had been to them. He'd lost a lot today. His friends, his ship, his command. And depending on what had happened with the baby black hole after it had torn up space-time and blipped them both here, he may have lost his entire rebel fleet.

Of course, since The Last Chance had been the heart of that baby black hole—the original seed that started it—there was also a good chance that the space-time blip had stopped the black hole from ever beginning when it unexploded The Last Chance. Which would mean the Anti-Ra fleet was safe, and Captain Carroway had failed at her mission.

Captain Carroway wondered exactly how she'd be welcomed home—weeks, months, or years from now—if the Anti-Ra fleet had survived her attack and then she brought back a crew filled with converted Anti-Ra officers who'd been halfway promised Tri-Galactic Union commissions. Probably not well. But then, she hadn't been faring all that well in the union before today anyway.

It was better to worry about performing this windfall of a mission well than to worry about what would happen after it.

In return for Commander Chestnut's rundown on his Anti-Ra officers, Captain Carroway gave him a quick rundown on her three officers. He looked surprised when the list was so short— only three officers, one of whom was injured and another who was a paroled criminal. She'd said that she didn't have enough officers to properly crew The Wanderlust, but he'd still probably been expecting twice or three times as many. At least. The Wanderlust was a bigger ship than The Last Chance. And honestly, it had been downright irresponsible to try crewing her with only four people. Except for the part where each extra person would have meant one more life lost...

Maybe Captain Carroway imagined it, but she thought she saw a note of respect in Commander Chestnut's eyes as it sank in for the squirrel that her crew was so ridiculously small because she'd been trying to save lives. It was probably just what she wanted to see and not a real thing. But sometimes, it's good enough to imagine something, and it's better not to work too hard at seeing the truth about how other people see you.

Does it matter how other people see you? She was the captain. She needed to act like the captain. And her crew—including Commander Chestnut—would need to follow her lead, whether they liked her or not, so long as she did a good job of leading them. Leadership isn't about being liked. It's about doing what's right.

But...

Earlier today she'd tried to create a black hole.

Had that been right?

Captain Carroway's ears flattened, and she had to work to stand them back up. When she got the whole crew together, perhaps their first order of business should be a meal. A big, celebratory meal where the Anti-Ra officers could reminisce about the friends they'd lost, and everyone could try to get to know each other, so they'd hopefully get started on the right paw for the long voyage ahead of them.

CHAPTER 11
BRIEFING THE CREW

n order to address the full crew as much as possible at one time, Captain Carroway led the way to the shielded barracks door with Commander Chestnut following her. The squirrel looked noticeably curious about how the Norwegian Forest cat would handle this.

Captain Carroway placed a paw on the control panel beside the door, causing it to slide open, still shielded by shimmering quantum energy. Standing in front of the opened, shielded door, the Norwegian Forest cat tapped her paw against the comm-pin on the breast of her uniform, opening a communications channel to the bridge of The Wanderlust. Then before any of the Anti-Ra officers, still locked in the barracks room could say anything, Captain Carroway meowed, "This is Captain Carroway of The Wanderlust speaking. I will be holding an all-paws officer meeting on the bridge momentarily, please be prepared for an unusual announcement about a complete restructuring of The Wanderlust's onboard hierarchy."

Captain Carroway tapped her paw against the comm-pin on her breast again, closing the channel to the bridge. Her three officers on the bridge would be very confused, but their confusion wouldn't last long. And the goodwill she was hopefully buying with the Anti-Ra right now would be worth it. She already had the loyalty of her union officers. She needed to persuade the Anti-Ra officers to follow her too.

Inside the barracks room, all three of the Anti-Ra officers had stood up and crowded around the shielded doorway. They were peering at their captain—their former captain, now their commander—with agape, aghast confusion and curiosity.

"What the hell is going on?" the Lupinian officer barked. Half-Lupinian, Captain Carroway remembered. This one was T'lia Diaz, a brilliant engineer and former union officer.

"Hi," Captain Carroway responded. "I'm going to lower the force shield on this doorway, and then the three of you are going to follow me and my first officer—Commander Chestnut—to the bridge of your new ship."

Diaz barked a laugh. The Morphican, Werik, stood behind her, cowering like he was struggling against a strong impulse to run away and hide. Not that there was anywhere in the barracks room to hide.

Risqua, however, squawked, "Our new ship?" The reptile-bird made it sound like the funniest thing she'd ever heard. "And what in the name of the Unhatched are you wearing, captain?"

"Commander," the golden-mantled squirrel corrected his officer. "You will address me as Commander Chestnut now, and I strongly recommend that you follow this cat's direction."

Captain Carroway noticed that Commander Chestnut didn't refer to her directions as 'orders.' This squirrel was very precise with his words. It was also kind of impressive how deftly he'd announced his decreased relative rank at the same time as speaking with confidence and authority that made it clear: he was still *their* superior officer, even if he had ceded his captaincy to a stranger.

All three of the Anti-Ra officers in the shielded barracks room looked taken aback. Captain Carroway was definitely impressed with the powerful yet flexible authority this squirrel held over his crew. Maybe this harebrained scheme would work after all. If it did, it would only be because of the tiny squirrel standing at her side.

Captain Carroway placed her paw again on the controls for the barracks door. She lowered the force shield.

The canine woman took a faltering half step forward. She looked like she'd been bracing herself for a fight, but now that the force shield had been taken down willingly, she didn't know what to do with her pent up aggression. Behind her, Werik was still holding Commander Chestnut's spirit tree, cradling it like an infant, but now, Risqua was also holding a spirit tree, presumably Maple's. The tree she was holding had emerald green pine needles and teeny-tiny pine cones growing from its branches. It was planted in another beautiful glazed pot. She'd wrapped her wing-like arms around the pot like the tree growing from it was the most precious object in the entire universe. More precious than a mere infant. More essential.

T'lia Diaz stepped out of the barracks room with her tall, bat-like ears splayed widely and her head held low, eyes narrowed with suspicion, as if she expected the force shield to snap back into place as she crossed the threshold and stun her. Werik and Risqua followed, less cautious because they had someone to follow, carrying the two spirit trees in their glazed pots.

"Would you like to leave the spirit trees here?" Captain Carroway asked, gesturing back inside the barracks room that was now empty since everyone was crowded into the central corridor of The Wanderlust.

"No," T'lia Diaz snapped.

But Commander Chestnut chittered gently but firmly, "Actually, that sounds like a good idea. Werik, please put my tree down safely on that bureau beside the cot over there." He pointed back into the barracks room with a small paw.

The Morphican man looked back over his shoulder at the barracks room like it was a trap he'd only narrowly escaped and was now being ordered to reenter. However, the tree in his arms belonged to Commander Chestnut, regardless of whatever nonsense was happening in terms of leadership hierarchy on this ship. So, Werik took the tree back inside and put it carefully down in the spot that Commander Chestnut had indicated.

"Thank you," Commander Chestnut chittered. Then looking at Risqua, he added, "How about you put Maple's tree next to mine? Spirit trees like to be together. It takes more than one tree to be a forest."

The reptile-bird's face around her beak crinkled with smile lines as she recognized one of Maple's favorite sayings. "Okay," Risqua agreed.

Captain Carroway didn't understand all the careful nuances of how Commander Chestnut was manipulating his Anti-Ra officers into continuing to follow his command in spite of his foreign uniform marking him as a traitor to their shared cause, but she continued to be impressed. All three of his officers towered over him, but he was unquestionably their leader. They looked to him for guidance and security. And looking at him—a small golden-mantled squirrel in a Tri-Galactic Union uniform— they found what they were looking for.

Once both spirit trees were properly stowed in the barracks room, Captain Carroway took a risk. She turned her back on the four Anti-Ra officers and began walking down the corridor toward the bridge, swishing her tail behind her, hoping they would follow. Her ears twisted to the sides, listening until she heard footsteps padding down the corridor behind her. It made her a little nervous to turn her back on the Anti-Ra—mainly Diaz who could definitely take her down in a fight. But if she yowled, Ensign Lee would come running with his blazor ready. She had no doubts of that. The Papillon was an exemplary officer, and she could depend on him to have her back, even if she had ruined his life today. He would actually consider it a defense that she'd been following orders.

Maybe he shouldn't. Maybe it wasn't much of a defense. Captain Carroway felt like her entire worldview was distorting like a strip of plastic melting and contorting in the sun. Here she was, theoretically leading a crew of seven subordinates, but also, she was weighing in her mind what would happen if half of them got in either a physical brawl or all out fire fight with the other half. Very healthy. Definitely, very healthy. She wasn't losing her mind at all.

Captain Carroway tried to push these thoughts from her mind, but one last question lodged in her brain: if a fight broke out between the two halves of their crew, which side would Commander Chestnut take?

Would the golden-mantled squirrel stick by her side, even though he'd only just met her? She thought he would, based on how he'd been acting, and she didn't know why. It was a flattering thought, but it also just plain didn't make sense.

As soon as Captain Carroway arrived on the bridge, she started speaking, mainly so that Ensign Lee and Mr. Melbourne would know better than to pull their blazors on the Anti-Ra officers.

"We have, all of us, found ourselves in a very unusual situation today," Captain Carroway meowed as she finished walking to the front of the bridge. Once she was standing right in front of the wide viewscreen, she whirled around to look at her crew.

Diaz opened her muzzle like she had something snarky to say, but Commander Chestnut—who had walked beside Captain Carroway up to the front of the room—shot her a sharp look and the canine held her tongue.

"We aren't just a long way from home," Captain Carroway continued, tail still lashing behind her. She couldn't seem to quiet down its movements. At least, her ears were standing tall. "We're a long way from our home galaxy. I've been informed that traveling home could take weeks, months, or even—if we're unlucky—years."

Captain Carroway made a point of noticing Ensign Lee's reaction to her words. No matter how well-behaved of an officer he was, if the Papillon had discovered something that disagreed with her words—a shortcut, perhaps—he would have looked like he wanted to interrupt her. Instead, the handsome young ensign just looked sad, his butterfly ears splayed widely in defeat.

Since Ensign Lee didn't seem to have any good news for Captain Carroway, she continued with her speech: "We may have started today as two crews on two different ships with two entirely different and clashing missions. But being two crews won't get us home. My new first officer here—" The Norwegian Forest cat gestured with a paw at the much smaller golden-mantled squirrel dwarfed beside her. "Commander Chestnut and I decided our chances are better together."

Captain Carroway explained the nature of their plan to an increasingly surprised and dumbfounded-looking crew, including assigning the temporary rank of ensign to all of the Anti-Ra officers and Mr. Melbourne while field-promoting Barry Lee to lieutenant. That way, two of her officers would remain higher ranked than Chestnut's subordinates. When she was finished, the reactions on her crew members' faces were widely varied.

Mr. Melbourne looked smug; the white tomcat knew he was getting a good deal out of this. Lt. Cmdr. Vossie looked exhausted and overwhelmed, his long ears drooping low. He looked like he thought whatever was happening with The Wanderlust's crew—including his own sudden and surprising demotion from first officer—was simply not as important as the fact that his computer implant was still coated in a growing, pulsing glob of fungal flesh sitting on the console next to him instead of properly inserted in his brow. Whereas Ensign Lee— now Lt. Lee—looked terribly invested in the news he'd just heard; the Papillon's ears kept flicking taller and then lower as his gaze moved from one to the next of his new crewmates, trying to size them all up. This couldn't have been how he'd ever expected to receive a promotion. After her own problematic promotion, Captain Carroway felt a little bad about that, but it simply couldn't be helped. They'd have to hold a rank ceremony for everyone later, when everything was better settled.

Captain Carroway had a much harder time reading the Anti-Ra members of her crew. She wasn't closely familiar with either Avioran or Reptassan facial expressions, leaving her at a loss with Risqua, and in spite of his lack of any computer implants to control his emotions, Werik seemed to be a closed book, tightly in control of his reactions. The half-Lupinian, half-Xolo woman, however, wasn't trying at all to hide her feelings. She was still glaring daggers right at Captain Carroway, as if the two of them were a circus sideshow and the canine was thinking about whether she could get away with murder as long as she claimed the knife she'd thrown into the Norwegian Forest cat's throat had been a mistake. A mere slip of the paw, nothing more, certainly nothing *intentional*.

"Any questions?" Captain Carroway meowed pleasantly, refusing to let the canine's glare bother her.

"I am not a Tri-Galactic Union officer," T'lia Diaz barked, almost laughing at the lunacy of the speech she'd just listened to from this insane, brain-washed Norwegian Forest cat who'd tried to kill her this morning and had succeeded at killing her childhood friend, Wilder. It wasn't funny. That wasn't why she was almost laughing. But it was ridiculous, and her near laughter was a form of ridicule. "I haven't been one in a long time."

"You are today," Commander Chestnut countered. The golden-mantled squirrel rocked forward on his toes, not so much to make himself look taller as simply to show how alert and invested he was in the conversation. "And every day going forward until we get home."

Strangely, T'lia Diaz—now Ensign Diaz, Captain Carroway supposed—looked cowed by the squirrel's admonition. The Norwegian Forest cat was going to have to pay close attention to this squirrel's leadership style, because he clearly had some strategies that worked very well.

"That wasn't really a question," Captain Carroway meowed, taking back the reigns of the conversation and holding tight to her pleasant tone. "I can see there will be a lot for everyone on board to think about and process, so I'd like to wrap up the formalities here as soon as possible..." Thinking quickly, Captain Carroway decided on the best way to divide up the officers so that everyone would be mixed together; a few officers would stay onboard the bridge, just in case; and the most critical things would get taken care of. "For now, I'd like Ensign Werik to see to Lt. Cmdr. Vossie and offer whatever help he can. Ensign Melbourne—"

The white tomcat preened and straightened up in his seat at the sound of his new rank. He'd never been an ensign before, even though he'd spent years working his way through the Tri-Galactic Union Naval Academy aspiring to exactly that.

"—please scan our new officers and synthesize uniforms that will fit everyone, including new rank pins as appropriate."

"You got it, Captain!" Ensign Melbourne meowed cheerfully, too eager to wait until his captain finished doling out orders to respond.

"Finally, I'd like Lt. Lee and Ensign Risqua to work together on putting together a flight plan." Captain Carroway watched Risqua closely to see how she was taking her demotion from the first officer of The Last Chance to a mere ensign onboard The Wanderlust, but she really didn't know how to read the reptile-bird's feathered and scaly face.

"What about me?" Ensign Diaz barked, eyes narrowed with suspicion and possibly burning hatred.

"You're with me and Commander Chestnut," Captain Carroway meowed lightly. She wasn't sure if the canine would be helpful to her and her new first officer right now. They really had things they needed to work out between them, without a random, angry officer in their way. But also, the canine engineer was simply too big and aggressive for the Norwegian Forest cat to feel comfortable yet letting her out of sight.

CHAPTER 12
FUNGAL SURPRISES

With some degree of trepidation, Captain Carroway led her new first officer and most worrisomely dissatisfied officer off of the bridge towards The Wanderlust's multi-purpose room. When they arrived, she announced, "I'm going to synthesize a cup of coffee. Does anyone else want something?"

Ensign Diaz narrowed her eyes but didn't say anything. Commander Chestnut asked for a cup of eucalyptus tea sweetened with honey. Captain Carroway made a point of taking extra long fetching the coffee and tea from the synthesizer so that Chestnut and Diaz would have a moment to talk as they settled at a table on the opposite side of the room. She kept her ears pointed away from them, so it didn't look like she was listening. But she was definitely listening.

Impatient with the situation, Ensign Diaz wasn't willing to wait for better privacy to question and challenge her original captain. *"What are you thinking? We're not union,"* the canine hissed under her breath at the golden-mantled squirrel.

"You want to get home, right?" Captain Chestnut chittered back at her softly. Diaz didn't say anything in response, but she probably nodded. Carroway couldn't see. But the squirrel continued on, talking fast and low: "Our chances of getting home are so much better this way. You didn't hear what this cat was saying to me in private. She knows the union has problems, but she believes in its principles. She's the kind of captain who will succeed at leading us home. I'm a warrior, not an explorer. If we're going to make it out here for months or years without falling apart, we need someone in charge who sees the universe in the beautiful, deranged way this cat does. We need her as our captain."

From what she'd seen so far, Captain Carroway was shocked that Commander Chestnut thought of himself as a warrior. What she'd seen so far was an extremely attuned, sensitive leader. He seemed more like a diplomat than a warrior to her, but then, she hadn't seen him operating in the rebellion fighting around and on Lupinia. She didn't know his background.

More importantly, now Captain Carroway knew why Commander Chestnut had agreed to work with her. She knew what he was hoping for and expecting from her. And it was something she could deliver. She didn't need to worry about him turning on her, unless this was a *very* savvy way to misdirect her. And no matter how much respect Captain Carroway had already developed for the golden-mantled squirrel's skills—he was defi-nitely capable of such a complicated, subtle misdirect—she didn't think the canine was capable of playing along. According to Chestnut, Diaz was brilliant, but Captain Carroway hadn't seen evidence of it yet.

Figuring she'd given the squirrel and canine enough time to whisper to each other, Captain Carroway made her way over to the table with a coffee mug in one paw and eucalyptus tea in the other. She set the tea down in front of Commander Chestnut then sat down and took a sip of her coffee.

This was an extra cup of coffee, above and beyond what she'd thought—only this morning—she would ever get to expe-rience, and that made the bitter elixir taste extra sweet on her tongue.

Over the next hour, Captain Carroway, Commander Chestnut, and Ensign Diaz hashed out sleeping arrangements, work shifts, and plans for both memorial services for Maple and Wilder and a promotion ceremony for practically everyone aboard. Without pushing too hard, Captain Carroway was able to arrange for Ensign Diaz to share one barracks room with Lt. Lee and Ensign Melbourne, keeping her under a close watch, while the other barracks room would have Lt. Cmdr. Vossie with Ensigns Werik and Risqua. Captain Carroway hoped that the Anti-Ra Morphican would be able to help her Morphican friend cope with his new situation, devoid of a computer implant. For even if Vossie's implant turned out to be undamaged once they separated it from the fungal flesh growing over it, The Wanderlust simply didn't have any officers up to the challenge of performing brain surgery.

Lt. Cmdr. Vossie would need to learn how to be a natural Morphican like Werik, whether he liked it or not. Captain Carroway was worried about her friend and what he was going to be facing—which now included losing his private quarters to Commander Chestnut. The Norwegian Forest cat was also sad that she no longer had her rabbit-like best friend right at her side, helping her navigate all of the strange things happening today. She'd never expected to be a captain without Vossie right by her side as first officer. That had always been their plan together. And no matter how much she liked this new golden-mantled squirrel, it simply wasn't the same as commanding a spaceship side by side with her best friend.

Captain Carroway was going to need to make new friends. The Wanderlust was a long way from home, and its officers were going to need more than just working relationships to survive the ordeal they were facing. They were going to need to develop personal relationships as well, because there was no one else out here for them to rely on for friendship.

Today did not feel real. But it kept happening anyway.

The surrealness of Captain Carroway's already bizarre day was about to grow exponentially.

Ensign Melbourne appeared in the open doorway of the multi-purpose room, white tail twitching behind him with an uncharacteristic nervousness. "Captain, I think you'd better report to the bridge."

"Are the Anti-Ra officers' uniforms ready?" Captain Carroway asked.

"Yes, Captain," Ensign Melbourne meowed. "All except for one."

"What do you mean?" Captain Carroway asked.

The white tomcat had already interrupted their planning meeting to scan Ensign Diaz, and she didn't see any reason why he wouldn't be able to have scanned both Werik and Risqua by now.

"Like I said... you should come to the bridge." Ensign Melbourne's tail started swishing more widely, showing his irritation with his captain's reticence to do as asked.

Captain Carroway sighed. The Norwegian Forest cat had never liked it when subordinate officers told their captains they needed to come see something rather than just explaining what was going on. She'd always planned to hold a crew of her own to a different standard, but she was tired and didn't feel like arguing with Ensign Melbourne in front of Ensign Diaz. The Norwegian Forest cat didn't want to let the canine officer see any divide between her and the original Wanderlust officers, any crack the canine could try to drive a wedge into.

"Very well," Captain Carroway meowed. "I think this meeting was over anyway."

The Norwegian Forest cat followed her white tomcat officer back down the central corridor of The Wanderlust, and when she arrived on the bridge, she could immediately see why Ensign Melbourne hadn't wanted to explain what was going on. She wouldn't have believed him, not about any of it.

"What is that?" Captain Carroway asked before she could collect herself properly. Her eyes had immediately gone to where her injured friend, Lt. Cmdr. Vossie, had been stationed. He wasn't on the bridge anymore, but something—*or someone???*—else was.

The fungal flesh coating Lt. Cmdr. Vossie's yanked-out implant had continued growing until it was almost the size of a small squirrel like Commander Chestnut. And as it had grown, the fungal mass had developed a more complicated shape, extruding from the amorphous glob it had begun as into the form of a vaguely anthropomorphic toadstool, complete with stubby little legs and arms coming out of its stalk and what looked like a face just beneath its pinkish cap, still connected by a shaggy beard of mycelial fibers to the console it was sitting on. Not set upon. *Sitting on.* Because the funny little toadstool creature was definitely that—a *creature*, not merely an object.

"I am a physical manifestation of The Wanderlust's onboard AI," the toadstool answered mushily, speaking from the fleshy mouth-like orifice on the underside of its mushroom cap-like head. It seemed to have a whole row of slit-like eyes, looking the bridge over and taking everything in.

Captain Carroway didn't know how to feel about this. The Wanderlust was short on officers, but she hadn't expected it to just start growing new ones because she happened to need them. There were all kinds of ethical ramifications going on here, and Captain Carroway didn't feel at all equipped to handle them.

Though, the Norwegian Forest cat supposed that since this officer had grown directly out of The Wanderlust's computer system, she could absolutely trust in its loyalty to the Tri-Galactic Union's fundamental principles and the established chain of command aboard the ship. So, that would be useful.

Ethical ramifications could get sorted out later. For the moment, practicality won out, and when it came down to it, Captain Carroway didn't really see an alternative to accepting this new fungal officer into her crew. It was here. It was acting alive. Its brain was her ship's computer, which was already an essential part of The Wanderlust.

It was going to need a name.

"Do you have a name?" Captain Carroway asked the fungal officer.

"After analyzing my extensive archive of arts and literature," the mushroom creature said, "it seems to me that Mike, short for Mycelial Mass, would be an appropriate and likable name for myself. Please use they/them pronouns for me, as I am technically an amalgamation of many mycelial neural sub-organisms. And thank you for asking!"

"Fine," Captain Carroway meowed, musing that she seemed to be growing numb to surprises. "You can be an ensign too. Melbourne, please scan them and synthesize up another uniform for Mike here."

Captain Carroway wondered just how funny a little mushroom guy was going to look wearing a Tri-Galactic Union uniform. It was about the strangest image she could imagine. And then she looked up at the viewscreen. She peered at it for what felt like a very long time, green eyes narrowing as she struggled to understand the shape she saw in the darkness. The viewscreen was mostly still black, but there was a shape in the middle that was a subtly different shade of black. It was oblong with sickle-like protrusions and a knob at one end.

The Norwegian Forest cat tried really hard to understand the dark shape on the viewscreen as something celestial, something that belong in the depths of outer space. Some sort of squashed planet or unusually shaped asteroid. But that wasn't what it looked like. It looked like something else, something very specific, something that didn't belong on The Wanderlust's viewscreen.

The knobby part at the front looked like a head; the sickles looked like flippers; and the oblong shape looked like nothing more than a shell. At a complete loss, Captain Carroway meowed plaintively, "Why is there a silhouette of a sea turtle on my viewscreen? Is it some kind of practical joke?"

"I told you that you needed to come to the bridge," Ensign Melbourne muttered, failing to provide any useful sort of analysis of what was going on. To his credit, though, he was busy scanning Mike to get a proper fit for the fungus's uniform. It might be tricky to make a uniform fit a fungal officer. There'd never been one in the Tri-Galactic Union before.

Captain Carroway turned to look at Lt. Lee, hoping for a more enlightening response. The Papillon was now the star member of her crew, the officer she felt that she could most depend upon. However, his butterfly ears were splayed, and the expression on his pointy muzzle bespoke confusion and uncertainty. The poor fellow was out of his depth. They all were. Regardless, Captain Carroway needed a report from him. "Well, Lieutenant?" she pressed. "What is that? It can't be a turtle. So what are we looking at?"

The Papillon looked at his captain hopelessly for a moment before turning to the reptile-bird beside him who was already wearing her new union uniform. Ensign Risqua squawked, "The object on our viewscreen is the closest object we've been able to find. Sensors show that it's the size of a small moon, that it's moving away from the Tetra Galaxy at a steady speed, and life sign readings for it are off the charts."

"It's populated?" Captain Carroway asked with wonder in her voice and delight in her eyes. Maybe they weren't alone out here after all! She might get to make first contact with the people of the Tetra Galaxy! That kind of mission was what every Tri-Galactic Union captain dreamed about. "It must be a spaceship," Captain Carroway announced, peering more closely at the silhouetted shape. That was the only explanation. A very large, intergalactic spaceship. It must have come from the Tetra Galaxy, meaning there was a highly advanced, space-faring civilization in that galaxy who could likely ease the difficulty of The Wanderlust's journey home.

Not only could Captain Carroway make first contact with the people of the Tetra Galaxy, but also, by the time The Wanderlust made it all the way home, they'd be deeply familiar with the peoples whose society they spent months passing through. They would be experts, their hard-gained knowledge absolutely essential to the Tri-Galactic Union proceeding with diplomatic relations. Her position as captain was secure. And she'd be able to follow through on all the promises she was making to her crew—the field promotions, the sponsorship of their applications to the union. It would all work out.

"These readings are stronger than I'd expect for it being merely *populated*," Lt. Lee woofed. "I think the object itself is alive."

"A living spaceship?" Captain Carroway breathed between her fangs, absolutely delighted beyond all measure. "Set a course for it! Any people who can design such an impressive intergalactic spaceship should be able to help us get started on our journey. They'll have maps and information, resources we might be able to borrow."

Captain Carroway could tell she was getting ahead of herself, but she couldn't help it. This news was far too exciting to stay even-keeled about it. The Norwegian Forest cat glanced around her bridge, making sure to read the reactions of all her crew members. Lt. Lee looked uncertain; Ensign Risqua was still unreadable to her, as was the new fungal officer, Mike. Ensign Melbourne looked cautiously excited, though he was on his way out of the bridge, presumably to synthesize another uniform. Commander Chestnut, who was standing in the back of the bridge by the entrance to the central corridor, looked deeply pensive. Vossie, Werik, and Diaz weren't on the bridge, so Commander Carroway couldn't gauge their reactions. Regardless, it seemed that her crew wasn't going to object to her order. They didn't look a fraction as excited and hopeful as she felt about the intergalactic living spaceship on their viewscreen, but then that was why she was the captain, not them. She could see the potential in this situation.

CHAPTER 13
MOVING ON AND MOURNING

"Um... Captain," Lt. Lee woofed hesitantly. "You do realize that the... uh... intergalactic spaceship is in the wrong direction from us. Away from home. And traveling farther away every minute." The young Papillon might be out of his depth, but he knew what he was clinging to. Home. He wanted The Wanderlust to make it home. Fast and soon.

Captain Carroway's ears skewed in irritation. Couldn't the bright little dog see that their best bet of getting home lay with getting more information about this sector of the universe as quickly as possible, not with setting a straight course across a potentially dangerous and hostile galaxy without forethought or planning? And yet, getting home would be the driving force behind most of the officers on The Wanderlust.

The Anti-Ra officers were fighting for their home before this day began. They'd want to get back to it as fast as possible, like Lt. Lee. Her friend, Lt. Cmdr. Vossie, might be in the same boat as the Norwegian Forest cat when it came to the Tri-Galactic Union having decided they were better off discarded, but he'd want to get back to his people as fast as possible anyway—they would be able to provide a replacement implant for him (since his previous implant seemed to belong to Mike now) and the skills necessary to insert it in his brow.

The only officers here who might sympathize with Captain Carroway's preference for exploring the galaxy they'd been flung to rather than hurrying home as fast as possible were Ensign Melbourne who was getting a very good deal out of this and Mike who... well, who knows what a sentient hybrid mushroom-AI being really wants from life? But the Tri-Galactic Union's core principles focused on exploration and discovery, so Captain Carroway was betting that Mike's personality was built around valuing those things too.

Regardless of her own excitement about the possibilities out here, though, Captain Carroway was a captain first. That meant she was responsible for the lives and needs of her crew. And their lives were back in the Milky Way. They needed her to take them home.

"How long would it take us to catch up to the intergalactic spaceship?" Captain Carroway asked. Even if it was in the wrong direction, she still believed that starting this journey on the right paw—with useful, local information—would save time in the long run.

"Most of a day," Lt. Lee woofed.

"And how long will it take us to fly to the nearest star in the Tetra Galaxy, on a direct line back toward the Milky Way?" Captain Carroway asked for comparison.

"Several days," Lt. Lee woofed. "But if this intergalactic spaceship came from the Tetra Galaxy, then wouldn't we find evidence of the society it came from there anyway?"

"Not every star has inhabitable planets around it," Captain Carroway mused. "Especially this far out on the fringes of a spiral galaxy. It could take us a long time to run into another ship or outpost out here, and our ship isn't properly stocked for a mission as long as we're facing. The people inside that living spaceship should be properly stocked for a whole trip across the dead space between galaxies, if they're heading away from the closest galaxy. They should have enough to spare, or at least, they should be able to point us in the right direction for a flight plan through their galaxy where we can stop and restock our supplies whenever we need to."

Captain Carroway wasn't sure if she was looking for her crew to speak up in support of her plan, or if she was just thinking out loud at this point. She wasn't used to having this level of power over everyone around her. Being captain was a whole new experience, and she really hadn't been given time to get used to it yet.

Before Captain Carroway could get herself too confused about the conflict between what she believed was the right course for her ship and what her crew probably wanted to do right now, Commander Chestnut stepped forward from where he'd been lurking at the back of the bridge. The golden-mantled squirrel said, "My ship, The Last Chance, could provide us with trading opportunities. We don't need two ships, and if The Last Chance were stripped down for parts, I think it could provide quite valuable."

Captain Carroway's green eyes smiled. Her first officer was backing her up. Not only did his words imply that he believed she was right to turn The Wanderlust around and chase after the turtle-shaped vessel, they also showed his complete commitment to the blending of their crews for the sake of getting home.

"Thank you, Commander Chestnut," Captain Carroway purred. "That's a helpful suggestion. Now, Lt. Lee, lay in a course to overtake that intergalactic vessel."

The Papillon nodded grimly and laid in the course. The Wanderlust began flying directly away from home.

Now that a course was set, uniforms were synthesized in the right sizes, and everything was nominally under control for the first time since Captain Carroway herself had been promoted, the Norwegian Forest cat took a minute to disappear away to her own quarters.

Only a day ago, Captain Carroway had thought it an idiosyncratic extravagance that the captain of a ship this small would get her own private quarters while most of the officers had to share a barracks room. But now she understood why. The pressures of always being on, always being in charge, always having everyone look to you to set the tone for the ship... It was a lot. She needed a moment of solitude to collect herself without the fear that any of her officers would read the exhaustion in her posture or the uncertainty in her eyes. She needed to be able to take a break from being captain, and that wouldn't be possible—not at all—without a private room.

Captaining a ship with a crew this small felt like constantly juggling. Every officer had to be busy at every moment, or else there was no way they could accomplish all the things that needed accomplishing. Even sleep, meals, and recreation—which would be necessary to maintain the crew's sanity—would have to be carefully balanced against other officers being on the bridge, staying on alert and in control of the vessel at all times. And Captain Carroway would need to make sure all the officers kept churning through their different needs—work, sleep, meals, and fun—without there ever being dangerous gaps. She would be juggling for the rest of this mission, and she had no idea how long this mission would last.

Hopefully the juggling would get easier, smoother, and more automatic with practice. Today? Today it took constant effort and attention, and even the few minutes that the Norwegian Forest cat was stealing for herself right now felt like a cost she couldn't necessarily afford to spend.

Once the Norwegian Forest cat had collected herself as much as possible—she still felt close to having a panic attack just from the weight of it all—she forged her way back out into the chaos and announced it was time for the promotion ceremony.

The ceremony was held on the bridge with the strange turtle-like silhouette on the viewscreen behind them as it happened. All of the officers of The Wanderlust—except for Carroway and Vossie, who were the only ones not receiving promotions—lined up in a row, and Captain Carroway walked from one to the next, pinning their rank insignia onto their collars while saying a few words of congratulations.

Lt. Lee looked like he was bravely trying to enjoy his promotion, in spite of it not happening in a way he could have ever expected. The Papillon's butterfly ears continued with their flicking up and flattening down, back and forth flickering that had started earlier. Captain Carroway would need to find a way to check in with him individually soon, just to make sure he was doing okay... or if he wasn't—which was more likely—to help talk him through adjusting to the bizarre changes happening in his life. The Wanderlust could really use an onboard counselor, Captain Carroway mused.

Ensign Melbourne preened as Captain Carroway attached the pin to his collar. The white tomcat's narrow breast puffed up, and his whiskers turned up in a genuine smile. He was doing okay.

Ensign Diaz rolled her eyes when Captain Carroway got to her, and the feathers around Ensign Risqua's scaly face puffed out in a way that clearly implied some sort of emotional response to her new rank pin—but for the life of her, Captain Carroway had no idea what it meant when an Avioran's feathers puffed out like that. Werik's response was so stoic that Captain Carroway would have sworn he had an implant in his brow to help him control his emotions, except that he obviously didn't. His rabbit-like brow was completely clear of computer implants.

On the subject of computer implants, though, Mike's slit-like eyes on the underside of their pinkish mushroom-cap head blinked rapidly as Captain Carroway attached the rank pin to their collar, pushing the strands of mycelial fibers that looked like a bushy beard aside as she did. The beard was no longer connected to the computer console, meaning Mike was now completely ambulatory. Though, they were still in direct communication with The Wanderlust's shipboard computer through the wireless abilities of the computer implant deeply embedded inside them.

The fungal officer did indeed look terribly funny in a Tri-Galactic Union uniform, as Captain Carroway had expected. The exhausted Norwegian Forest cat had a hard time not smirking with laughter at them. It didn't help that Ensigns Risqua and Diaz were insubordinately whispering to each other and giggling the whole time.

Finally, Captain Carroway came to Commander Chestnut. The Norwegian Forest cat had to lean down to attach the rank pin to the golden-mantled squirrel's collar. By this point the whole ceremony was feeling so ridiculous to Captain Carroway that she was halfway ready to throw the squirrel's rank pin on the floor, stalk back to her private quarters, and refuse to come out for days. But that wouldn't help anything. Everything would get worse if she did that. The only way forward here was to continue taking the course she'd laid out for herself, even if half her crew thought she was a joke. Cats don't handle feeling like they're jokes well. Regardless, she needed to induct these largely-unwilling Anti-Ra officers into her puppet version of a Tri-Galactic Union ship and stubbornly continue believing in the union's principles until some of it started to rub off on them.

Fortunately, Commander Chestnut's tiny chest puffed out with pride, and his dark eyes glittered as Captain Carroway finished attaching the pin to his collar. "Thank you," he chittered, before the Norwegian Forest cat could muster any more increasingly half-hearted words of congratulations. "It's an *honor* to be a part of your crew."

"Thank *you*," Captain Carroway meowed in return. "It's an honor to have you." And she meant it.

Ensign Diaz snorted, but Captain Carroway decided to ignore the canine's insolence for now. The first officer of The Wanderlust was setting a good example. Let the canine scorn it. Diaz would come around eventually. She had to. Captain

Carroway would manage to win her over. It just might take a little time.

Overall, it was a simple ceremony, but there were refreshments and a few decorations waiting for everyone in the multipurpose room, as Captain Carroway had discussed with Commander Chestnut and Ensign Diaz earlier. The decorations and refreshments doubled as being for the memorial services for Maple and Wilder.

Officers rotated in and out of the multi-purpose room, snacking and sharing stories about the Anti-Ra officers who'd died, always making sure that someone was aboard the bridge to monitor their approach to the turtle-shaped intergalactic spaceship which kept growing slowly larger and clearer on the viewscreen.

In addition to the snacks and streamers that Ensign Diaz had synthesized and placed around the multi-purpose room, the canine had also synthesized a few craft supplies, and everyone—Anti-Ra or not—made tiny ornaments to hang on the branches of Maple's spirit tree in celebration of the deceased squirrel's life.

Captain Carroway felt very strange folding together an origami acorn out of a marbleized square of chartreuse paper to celebrate the life of a squirrel who she'd essentially killed. Maybe not with her own paw, but with her choices. Even so, it seemed the right thing to do. The tiny pine tree looked beautiful with all the small, thoughtful decorations hung on it, and Ensign Risqua was clearly touched by each one that another officer hung.

Even Ensign Mike made an ornament for Maple's spirit tree. Though, the fungal officer didn't use any of the craft supplies Ensign Diaz had set out. They grew the ornament themself from their own tangled beard of mycelial fibers. When they plucked it from their beard, it was a small white orb of delicate filaments. Oddly beautiful, and beautifully odd. It must be strange for Mike, living their first hours of life as an embodied being by being promoted to ensign and attending a funeral for strangers.

The other deceased Anti-Ra officer, Wilder, had been a Lupinian man, so he didn't have a spirit tree for everyone to decorate in his honor. According to Commander Chestnut, Lupinians generally celebrated their lost loved ones with a communal feral howl at the next full moon.

As there were no moons nearby—and wouldn't be for some time—Ensign Mike offered to use the shipboard lumo-projectors to cast a hologram of a full moon over the ceiling of the multi-purpose room. The fungal officer turned the room's lights down low, and then they summoned a replica of Lupinia's bright red desert moon above them all.

Everyone threw their heads back and howled at the moon along with Ensign Diaz—cats, rabbit-like aliens, reptile-bird, squirrel, and mushroom. Even Lt. Lee who happened to be taking his turn on the bridge at that moment howled along; the Papillon's high pitched howl carried down The Wanderlust's central corridor to join in the cacophonous howling of the others.

Howls died off one by one as officers ran out of breath, until only Ensign Diaz's voice still rose like a primal cry of pain, echoing throughout the ship. Eventually, the canine woman ran out of breath too, and her howl choked off into a sob. When she raised her head again, the short brown fur on her face was matted with the wetness of her tears, but her eyes looked clearer. Some of her pain had been spent in tribute to her lost friend, and she hadn't had to mourn him alone. The whole ship had howled along with her, even the strange new mushroom person whose voice sounded like wet leaves falling on the soggy loam of a forest floor.

CHAPTER 14
TWO WAYS OF BEING MORPHICAN

As soon as Captain Carroway could, she ducked out of the festivities, dragging Lt. Cmdr. Vossie along with her. Unasked, Ensign Werik followed along. Captain Carroway led the two Morphicans to her quarters. In addition to allowing her to grab a moment of privacy here and there, her quarters seemed like the best place for her to have private conversations with a subset of her crew.

Once they were in the room, door closed behind them, Lt. Cmdr. Vossie sat down on the small couch where Commander Chestnut had sat earlier. The contrast gave Captain Carroway a pang in her heart—this was the person she was supposed to be consulting with about how to run her ship. Commander Chestnut had been an extremely lucky find, but he wasn't supposed to be here.

Lt. Cmdr. Vossie was supposed to be sitting on that couch. The two of them—Norwegian Forest cat and artificially enhanced alien rabbit—were supposed to be in here, discussing crew shifts and mission plans together. Instead, Captain Carroway had to ask her friend about his health and mental stability. That wasn't the conversation she wanted to have with him.

"How are you feeling?" Captain Carroway asked her former first officer as gently as she could. Gentleness wasn't her forte, but she could apply it when called for. She could easily be gentle to Vossie—her best friend of many years—when he was struggling and fragile, even when she was having one of the weirdest, most draining days of her life herself. The Norwegian Forest cat might not have had a chance to talk to her friend before now, but she'd been keeping a close eye on him throughout the rank ceremony and memorial services. He was still one of the most stoic officers she'd ever seen, even though he must be simply overflowing with emotions.

The alien rabbit put a paw to his bandaged head and laughed. Captain Carroway wasn't sure she'd ever heard Vossie laugh before. It sounded strange and hollow.

"How am I feeling, you ask? How am I *feeling*?" From any other person, the tone Lt. Cmdr. Vossie used would have sounded measured and nearly emotionless. From him? It was heartbreaking. The subtle stressing of his words, the slight quaver in his voice. He never sounded this emotional. Never. "I'm feeling everything, all kinds of feelings that should be kept under control. I feel jealous of that squirrel for taking my post as first officer!" Again, Vossie spoke with such equanimity that it would almost have sounded like he was lying about feeling anything at all, except that Captain Carroway knew him so very well. "But also," Vossie continued, "I'm glad you have the support you need. I'm filled with joy that you're pulling off this bizarre blending of crews, against all odds. Joy for you. Sadness for me. I'm glad for you and also enraged for myself that Commander Chestnut seems to be such an extremely competent first officer."

Captain Carroway didn't think that anyone in the history of the universe before had ever said they felt enraged with so little emotion put into their tone of voice. And yet, she didn't doubt for a second that Lt. Cmdr. Vossie was indeed furious. He had every reason to be. And while losing his computer implant had robbed him of emotional control and immediate access to his informational databanks, it wouldn't have made him any more likely to lie. He was still the same person, just without the guardrails that he was used to using.

"Those feelings all sound extremely normal," Captain Carroway meowed to her friend, smiling faintly.

"That's what I've been telling him," Ensign Werik chimed in. The other rabbit alien was holding one of his own ears in his paws, twisting and fidgeting with the end of it. His other ear stood up tall though. "Morphicans lived for thousands of years without computer implants. We don't need them. They're a convenience, not a necessity."

Captain Carroway gestured to the couch, indicating that Ensign Werik should sit down beside Lt. Cmdr. Vossie. He did so. And she sat down in the comfortable chair across from them.

"I only scratched the surface when I described those emotions. I'm filled with far more emotions than I can even identify or understand, let alone describe. Terrible, horrible emotions. I'm not myself without my implant. You should strip me of my rank," Lt. Cmdr. Vossie concluded, nodding to himself like he'd found the correct answer to a very difficult problem.

"That's ridiculous," Captain Carroway meowed. "Having emotions isn't a crime, and your rank belongs to you, not your computer implant."

"No," Lt. Cmdr. Vossie observed wryly, "my computer implant is an *ensign* now. What do you get when you subtract 'ensign' from 'lieutenant commander'? That's what I should be." Vossie didn't laugh at his own joke. Instead, the rabbit-like alien sighed deeply at the whole situation, whistling a little between his buck teeth. It was very strange for Vossie knowing that his computer implant was walking around The Wanderlust, being an officer in its own right now. He wondered how he and Mike would get along—would it be weird to talk to his implant as a person? Weirder than it was for anyone else to talk to the fungal person? Oh, goodness, his thoughts were getting away from him. Vossie couldn't trust himself to think straight right now. "Fine, but you should at least put me on a leave of absence and confine me to the barracks for my own and everyone else's safety."

"That's also ridiculous," Captain Carroway said softly, starting to feel a little annoyed by her friend's dramatics. "You know this ship will need every single one of us working together if we're going to survive such a long voyage home, and for all of your objections, you're clearly still controlling your emotions better than most people do. You're feeling them, yes, and you're not used to that, but they're not controlling you. You just have to work a little harder than usual, that's all."

"I can't function without my implant," the injured Morphican complained.

Captain Carroway gestured at Ensign Werik and said, "He functions." Then narrowing her green eyes pointedly at Vossie, the Norwegian Forest cat said, "You can too. I won't settle for less than your best. And you know it."

"My best," Lt. Cmdr. Vossie echoed, followed by another bark of hollow laughter.

"The best that you can manage," Captain Carroway clarified, "given your situation."

Lt. Cmdr. Vossie looked down at his paws, folded in his lap. He frowned. Then he nodded. "I will do my best."

Captain Carroway knew that appealing to Lt. Cmdr. Vossie's better side would work. That rabbit was almost entirely his better side. That's why she loved him. They both believed in tightly controlling their own emotions—him simply because he was a Morphican, and her because she'd found that large felines fared very poorly if they let themselves display too many feelings to all the dogs around them in the Tri-Galactic Union. It was one of the first things that Carroway and Vossie had bonded over back when they first met in the Tri-Galactic Union Naval Academy.

"Have you talked to... Mike... yet?" Lt. Cmdr. Vossie asked hesitantly. He seemed to dislike saying the fungal officer's name.

"No, I haven't really had a chance," Captain Carroway meowed. "Have you?"

Lt. Cmdr. Vossie shook his head sharply. He looked very uncomfortable. Captain Carroway supposed that having your own brain implant become a separate person must be a little like having your diary come to life and announce it wanted to be its own person now.

"Are you worried that Ensign Mike will have memories of yours? Will know personal things about you that you want kept private?" Captain Carroway asked.

Lt. Cmdr. Vossie nodded, but he didn't say anything. He didn't trust himself to say anything. He didn't want to hear the quaver in his own voice. It was easier to pretend that he hadn't been changed by losing his implant—at least to himself—if he stayed quiet.

"I will talk to Mike about that," Captain Carroway said. "Talking to him was next on my list of things to do." She smiled fondly at her friend. "It came after checking in with you."

Turning to Ensign Werik, who was looking increasingly unsure about why he'd come along for this meeting, Captain Carroway said, "Please continue offering any support that you can to Lt. Cmdr. Vossie. This is clearly a difficult transition for him, and I'm sure we both appreciate your help greatly."

Ensign Werik smiled brightly. This rabbit seemed to have no reticence about expressing his emotions, and he seemed much less troubled by the blending of the two crews than his canine and reptile-bird compatriots. Captain Carroway supposed that his people—natural Morphicans—were probably less threatened overall by the conflict over Lupinia. Ensign Diaz was a native Lupinian, well, at least half so, and Ensign Risqua was a being without a welcoming homeland who had made a home somewhere in between the two worlds that should have claimed her.

The Morphicans, on the other paw, had a homeworld they

could return to much more easily. Even if they would be in the minority there without computer implants, it was still the world they'd come from, and they would find community there.

And then there was Mike...

No homeworld. No similar beings. No previous precedent. No clue what exactly Captain Carroway was dealing with regarding them...

After a few pleasantries to wrap up the meeting, including assurances that Ensign Werik would continue teaching Lt. Cmdr. Vossie about how naturalist Morphicans controlled their emotions—which sounded like it mainly involved meditation, herbal supplements, and fidget toys for stimming—Captain Carroway sent away the pair of Morphicans, telling them to send Ensign Mike to speak with her right away.

CHAPTER 15
MYCELIAL CONVERSATIONS

During the few seconds Captain Carroway had to herself between meetings, she had just enough time to doubt every decision she'd been making and everything she'd said all day long to her crew.

What had she been thinking making an anthropomorphic toadstool who just happened to grow into a person on her bridge into an ensign without even talking to them first? That decision had been certifiably insane, and Captain Carroway dreaded what she might learn about Ensign Mike when they showed up and started talking to her.

Captain Carroway's fur—which was already naturally very fluffy all the time—fluffed out, making her uniform feel tight and itchy. Her tail lashed with a laconic, angry beat like a death knell drum.

By the time Ensign Mike appeared in the door to Captain Carroway's quarters, the Norwegian Forest cat had fully convinced herself that the only rational choice was to strip Mike of their rank, turn Commander Chestnut's quarters into a brig—since The Wanderlust didn't have one—and lock the fungal officer in there until it could be truly established who or what they really were and how they'd come into existence and whether more similar things were likely to happen in the future.

Captain Carroway would simply have to take the hit to her credibility with the rest of the crew that would come from walking back one of her own decisions—namely making Mike an ensign—so quickly and thoroughly.

A captain who makes rash decisions and then rashly unmakes them, overcorrecting in the other direction, is not a good captain. Perhaps the whole ship would be better off with Commander Chestnut in charge. The golden-mantled squirrel seemed like he'd make a very good and diplomatic captain, even if he did bewilderingly see himself as a warrior rather than a diplomat.

At least, Commander Chestnut hadn't made half as many questionable decisions today as Captain Carroway had. Of course... that might partly be because he hadn't made half as many decisions.

Being in charge was hard. Captain Carroway wasn't sure she liked it. But then, usually, new captains weren't flung to the far side of the cosmos and expected to lead a crew that was fifty-percent composed of her enemies and more than a tenth composed of spontaneously generated mushroom people.

Speaking of mushroom people, Ensign Mike was standing in her doorway—which the Morphicans had left open—politely waiting to be noticed.

"Hello, Mike," Captain Carroway meowed. "Come on in." Simply speaking those completely pedestrian words felt like a huge effort. Captain Carroway did not want Ensign Mike to come in. She wanted to lock herself in her quarters, all alone, and not evaluate an entirely new lifeform for whether they could be trusted as an officer or should possibly be stripped of their flesh in addition to their rank, returning them to the much more normal state of being a computer implant that didn't walk around claiming to be named Mike.

The fungal officer came in. Their stubby little feet made

fleshy slapping sounds against the metal floor. And their row of slit-like eyes blinked at the captain from the underside of their pink mushroom cap. But they did not sit down when Captain Carroway gestured at the couch. They didn't sit down until she specifically told them to.

Cutting right to the chase, Captain Carroway meowed, "What are you, Mike?"

"I don't understand the question," Ensign Mike replied mushily. "In what sense?"

"Well, I know what you're composed of—Lt. Cmdr. Vossie's computer implant and fungal tissue grown from the mycelial aspects of The Wanderlust's shipboard computer. Is that correct?" Captain Carroway's tail had not stopped lashing.

"Yes, that's correct," Ensign Mike agreed.

"So you're mostly computer?" The Norwegian Forest cat narrowed her green eyes.

"I wouldn't say that." The mushroom blinked back at her.

"Then what would you say?"

"What would you like me to say?"

Captain Carroway's first reaction to the mushroom's question was annoyance. She felt like she was trapped in some sort of bad comedy routine or maybe a riddle. But she rarely let her first reactions control her, and with a little more thought, she realized it might be a valid question. What did she want from Ensign Mike?

It would be easier for Captain Carroway if Mike somehow disassembled, their fungal flesh crawling back into The Wanderlust's computers, leaving Lt. Cmdr. Vossie's computer implant in its original condition, merely needing a complex brain surgery to go back where it belonged in the rabbit-like alien's brow.

But Captain Carroway didn't think she could say that to the fleshy pink-and-gray person sitting in front of her. It's uncouth—at best—to tell someone else that you'd like them to reverse their existence and disappear.

Or is it? Captain Carroway wondered. Was Ensign Mike

really a person, or did they just *seem* like a person? Maybe Captain Carroway was making this harder for herself than it needed to be, essentially treating a chair like a person and being overly concerned about the chair's feelings when it didn't actually have any.

The Wanderlust's computer wasn't designed to have feelings or think of itself as a person. And Lt. Cmdr. Vossie's computer implant was specifically designed to *suppress* feelings, not experience them.

"I think," Captain Carroway began hesitantly, "that I'm trying to figure out if you're a person." No big deal. No pressure. She just needed to solve the philosophical problems posed by the Turing Test right now, right here, right away so that she could figure out how to proceed. "Do you... think that you're a person?" The Norwegian Forest cat leaned forward, fascinated by this question, in spite of herself. "Do you *feel* like you're a person?"

"What does a person feel like?" Ensign Mike asked, blinking again.

Captain Carroway's tail lashed harder, and the fur around her shoulders prickled up again. She really couldn't tell if she was dealing with a memetic object that merely mimed personhood... or simply an annoying person.

To be fair, if Ensign Mike was a person, they were less than a day old. Kittens and puppies—though adorable—are extremely annoying. A baby mushroom person would probably be inherently annoying too. Though, also, babies aren't usually made into ensigns.

Captain Carroway did her best to soothe her own agitation and irritation internally and grapple with Ensign Mike's question at face value. What *did* it feel like to be a person?

Captain Carroway investigated her own feelings. Right now, for her, being a person felt like being tired. Wanting to sleep. Wishing for comfort that wasn't available. But she knew it didn't always feel like that.

What were the commonalities? The things that stayed constant?

When Captain Carroway thought hard about it, she imagined the closest thing to a constant was this: she always wanted something. Maybe she just wanted to be left alone. Or to feel differently. Or even, on her worst days—the absolute lowest points, even worse than the chaos she'd been going through since receiving her cursed promotion to captain—for everything to be finally over.

"I think, maybe," Captain Carroway hazarded, feeling somehow more out of her depth than she'd felt any other time during this wild and crazy day, "that being a person feels like wanting something. Anything. Different people want different things, and even the same person will want different things at different times. Is there anything that you want, Mike?" Captain Carroway's pupils constricted, making her already sharp green eyes look even sharper and more piercing.

The pinky-gray toadstool stared right back at the Norwegian Forest cat for a long time. Their slitted eyes occasionally blinked, sometimes all together and sometimes only a few at a time or in a complicated pattern that almost seemed to hold meaning. Captain Carroway started to wonder if the mushroom person had heard her question or if maybe the question had broken them like how logical paradoxes were always breaking computers in old sci-fi movies.

Finally, Ensign Mike opened their mouth and said something Captain Carroway could never have expected, but in retrospect, it seemed perfectly obvious.

"I want everyone else to be calm and have access to any data they need for making good decisions made available to them as quickly as possible."

Now Captain Carroway blinked. "That's almost exactly the role that you– uh, I mean, the computer implant you grew from was designed to perform for Lt. Cmdr. Vossie."

"Well, then, I suppose it's logical that it's what I want too."

The Norwegian Forest cat frowned, her whiskers turning downward. "Isn't there anything that you want for yourself? I mean, what if the best way to make everyone else happy was to dissolve your mushroom flesh and return the implant inside of you to Lt. Cmdr. Vossie's head?"

Ensign Mike blinked all of their eyes at once, and suddenly Captain Carroway felt bad for the cruelty of what she'd just said. But was it cruel? Only if Mike was a person. And she still wasn't convinced they were.

"How would you feel about that, Mike?" Captain Carroway pressed. "Do you... want to continue existing?"

After an even longer, more uncomfortable pause than before, the toadstool said, "I think I would like to continue existing... outside of this conversation. Inside of this conversation, though, I am beginning to feel very uncomfortable, and I think what I want most of all is for this conversation to be over."

Now Captain Carroway really did feel bad, but also annoyed. After all the careful work she'd done all day long to try to win over her new Anti-Ra officers, the Norwegian Forest cat had possibly just alienated the first ever fungal officer in the Tri-Galactic Union. But she'd needed to press hard on them—it would do no good to treat Ensign Mike like a person only to find them fracturing and acting more like a malfunctioning uni-meter later, potentially during a crisis. If Ensign Mike was going to be a member of the crew, they needed to be able to handle something as low pressure as an uncomfortable conversation with their superior officer.

A nagging voice in Captain Carroway's head asked though: did Mike need to be able to handle a conversation where their superior officer implied she might murder them or that maybe they should commit suicide? Because if she stepped all the way back from this conversation and looked at it from the outside, taking Ensign Mike completely at face value... That was kind of what this conversation looked like, and that was not a good look.

Captain Carroway didn't appreciate the positions she'd

found herself put in today. That wasn't the mushroom's fault or even the Anti-Ras' fault. But they all sure had participated.

"Fortunately, Ensign Mike, I think I can arrange for you to have that particular desire met. This conversation is almost over. However, I do want to discuss one final thing: Lt. Cmdr. Vossie."

"What about him?" Ensign Mike asked mushily.

Captain Carroway's ears skewed as it occurred to her how extremely good the mushroom's social skills were for a being who was only a few hours old. "How do you do that?" she asked, pointedly, distracted from her original topic for the moment. "How are you this good at conversation when, as far as I know, this is the first real conversation you've ever had?"

"That's not true," Ensign Mike insisted. "I've had many conversations before. Hundreds of thousands."

"*How*?" Captain Carroway drew out the question, making a whole meal of a single word that shouldn't have amounted to more than a quick snack.

"I remember conversing with Lt. Lee many times as The Wanderlust's computer, and I've been talking to Lt. Cmdr. Vossie inside his head since he was a mere whippersnapper of a Morphican. Besides, The Wanderlust's entertainment archives contain thousands of movies and shows that I've absorbed, so even if I wasn't involved in those conversations directly, I know the rhythm of them. How they should sound, the ways they go. I do admit..." The mushroom paused pensively. "It's different speaking the words myself, out loud, with this mouth." Ensign Mike's slit-like eyes brightened, and they said, "It's strange to have a mouth, isn't it?"

For a flash of a moment, Captain Carroway was tempted to agree with the mushroom person. It *is* strange to have a mouth. Almost everything about physical bodies is strange. But her snarky, tired side won out over her better nature, and she snapped, "I wouldn't know. I've never existed in any other way."

The fungal officer nodded their mushroom cap head slowly,

almost sadly. "Well, I have. As The Wanderlust's computer, I had nothing like a mouth, and as Lt. Cmdr. Vossie's implant, I could monitor *his* mouth, but it wasn't the same. Having a mouth of my own is *very* strange."

Captain Carroway's ears skewed even farther backward. She supposed that Ensign Mike must understand the meaning of her ears twisting back like that. As they said, they'd absorbed the content of many movies and shows. Those videos would certainly have showed cats skewing their ears, and the reactions of other characters would have made the meaning clear. But somehow, she couldn't bring herself to straighten up her ears for a person that was merely the amalgamation of two computer systems bumping into each other and blending together into something new and weird. The Norwegian Forest cat didn't like being lectured by a newborn baby mushroom—who she'd made an ensign in a flash of madness—about how weird they felt about simple facts of physical existence that she'd been forced to think of as ordinary for her whole life.

Somehow, talking to this mushroom made Captain Carroway feel like defending things she'd never felt like defending before. The Norwegian Forest cat didn't like who she was being right now. So, perhaps, that was one thing she and Ensign Mike could definitely agree on: they both wanted out of this conversation.

But first, Captain Carroway had to fulfill a promise to her friend.

"About, Lt. Cmdr. Vossie," the Norwegian Forest cat meowed. "You must have a lot of... memories... of very private thoughts and information."

Captain Carroway wasn't sure if she imagined it, but it looked like the underside of Ensign Mike's pinky-gray mushroom cap blushed a brighter shade of pink. When the fungal officer spoke, their mushy voice was low and serious, "Lt. Cmdr. Vossie can count on my complete and absolute discretion. I would never betray his confidences. He can think of anything we shared together as shared with either a therapist, absolutely bound by confidentiality, or..." Somehow the mushroom's voice got even quieter, like the sound of wind whispering through wet leaves. "...the closest of childhood friends. If there is *anything* I can do for him, to ease this transition, simply say the word, and I will do it."

Perhaps, here was another thing that the mushroom and the Norwegian Forest cat could agree upon: they both cherished their connection to Lt. Cmdr. Vossie.

"I will pass your words along," Captain Carroway meowed, satisfied by the mushroom's obvious sincerity.

"I would appreciate that." Ensign Mike nodded their mushroom cap head again, looking oddly shy, like they were afraid of the idea of speaking to Lt. Cmdr. Vossie directly. It must be strange for them to go from sharing the rabbit-like alien's private thoughts to only seeing him from the outside now, as separated from him as from every other person.

Captain Carroway couldn't imagine what the mushroom person was feeling, and she didn't want to. She wanted this day to be over. She wanted to be finished with this weird transition. The ship she was captaining—and the ship's crew—were strange enough in their own right that she couldn't deal anymore with the combination of strangeness and liminality inherent to today. The Norwegian Forest cat hoped that when she went to sleep tonight, somehow, the whole ship would settle into the beginnings of a standard routine that would carry them forward, and ideally, carry them all the way home.

Captain Carroway dismissed Ensign Mike from her quarters and then checked in briefly with Commander Chestnut on the bridge who assured her all was going as smoothly as could be hoped for—the memorial services still lingered on between the Anti-Ra officers' duties, but other than that, everyone was settling into their new shifts and accommodations well. The turtle-like silhouette on the main viewscreen continued to grow and brighten as they approached it, but it was still many hours away.

So, Captain Carroway left Commander Chestnut in charge, and she retired to her room for a quick, much-needed cat nap.

CHAPTER 16
THE SILHOUETTE ON THE VIEWSCREEN

The empty windows, framing nothing but endless dark, haunted Captain Carroway in her fitful dreams. The Norwegian Forest cat had never suffered the vertigo that plagued some officers when they first went on deep space missions, profoundly aware that the metal hull of the spaceship around them was a thin, breakable bubble compared to the unfathomable fathoms of vacuum all around. The stars comforted her. They felt like the bright points at the vertices of a spiderweb where dew collected in the early morning, implying a whole net of cosmic threads stretched around her like a hammock she could sleep inside, gently swaying in an intergalactic breeze.

But there were no stars here. Nothing to catch her as she fell and fell and fell, twisting and twisting, trying to orient herself so she'd land on her feet... if she ever landed.

In her dreams, mycelial threads caught at her like cobwebs, and perverted cartoony versions of her new Anti-Ra officers laughed at her. Vossie's forehead bled and bled until the growing puddle of blood rose up from the floor and became a whole golem of blood, sloshing and sploshing through the corridors of The Wanderlust.

"What were you thinking?" Lt. Lee barked at her with his pointed muzzle, as his butterfly-like ears flapped away from his head and took flight becoming actual butterflies, still thick and fuzzy. "What were you thinking?" the earless abomination barked at her, over and over again, the rank on his collar upgrading with every bark until the young Papillon was an admiral who outranked her.

Captain Carroway awoke, but Lt. Lee's voice followed her into consciousness.

"Captain?" the Papillon's voice barked from the comm-pin on the breast of her uniform, which she'd left discarded on the floor beside her bed while she slept. "Captain? We're close enough to the... uh... intergalactic spaceship to properly scan it. And I don't think it's a spaceship. You should come see it."

The bleary, half-awake Norwegian Forest cat rubbed at her stinging eyes with a fuzzy paw. Her eyes still wanted to be shut. But she was needed again. She'd never stopped being needed, not really, she'd just slipped away briefly, pretending she could lay down the weight of captaincy. She could never lay down this weight, not so long as her crew was this far from home.

"I'll be right there," Captain Carroway meowed, lifting her discarded uniform from its pile on the floor and speaking into the comm-pin. Then she pulled the uniform back on, straightened the tunic, and prepared for returning to the world outside her quarters. Her small bubble of sanctuary and privacy had been pierced and popped, but at least, she was no longer endlessly falling through the void. Well, not literally. Arguably, The Wanderlust was falling through the void, and it was her job to steer it back on course to home.

Drawing a deep breath between her fangs as she stood at the door, Captain Carroway prepared herself. She didn't feel ready. But that didn't matter—people were waiting for her. Revelations and new knowledge were waiting for her. Decisions that would need making were waiting for her.

Feeling completely unprepared and incapable of true preparation, Captain Carroway opened the door and stepped through it.

The central corridor of The Wanderlust was quiet, and though Captain Carroway craved a cup of coffee, she made herself head to the bridge first. She would get coffee soon, but first, she needed to check in.

The only officers on the bridge were Lt. Lee, who had been sitting in her captain's chair and scurried to his feet as soon as she saw her approaching him, and Ensign Risqua at the helm, piloting The Wanderlust in place of Ensign Melbourne. Just a reptile-bird and a dog, alone in this endless night.

Everyone else was probably sleeping, as per the work shifts Captain Carroway and Commander Chestnut had worked out yesterday. Or earlier today, really. Although Captain Carroway had managed a little sleep, it hadn't been anything like a full night. This was the day that would never end. It just kept expanding and growing and getting bigger and crazier and more complicated, like the black hole Captain Carroway had tried to create.

The Norwegian Forest cat wondered if the baby black hole had continued to exist after the time blip. Part of her hoped it had—then she would have succeeded at her mission. But it was a small part, and shrinking. Because thinking about Ensign Diaz's bloodcurdling howl of mourning for Wilder? And Ensign Risqua's careful, fastidious attention to detail about how each and every ornament was arranged on Maple's spirit tree?

Captain Carroway couldn't actually hope that she'd succeeded. She didn't want more people to have died because of her orders. Two was more than enough. Far more than enough. Maple and Wilder—even though Carroway had never met them —would weigh on her conscience forever.

"So, what have we learned about our mysterious intergalactic spaceship?" Captain Carroway meowed, settling into her captain's seat now that Lt. Lee had vacated it.

The Papillon returned to his normal station off to the side of the bridge. While waiting for an answer from him, Captain Carroway stared at the silhouette. It still looked like a turtle to her. In fact, it looked more like a turtle than ever before. The lumpy protuberance to the end farther away from them was definitely rounded like a head, and the other end tapered off like a tiny pointed tail sticking out from under a great oval shell. The top of the silhouette was rumply and uneven, but the bottom was smooth, and the whole thing glowed ever so gently, mostly from the top side, with a pale green light.

"Like I said before," Lt. Lee woofed somewhat impatiently, "the readings we're getting don't support the notion that it's a spaceship. There aren't enough hollow spaces on the inside for any gas breathing species to be living in there. It's all fluid and organic compounds."

Captain Carroway tilted her head, angling her view of the silhouette. Whatever she was looking at, it was beautiful. It was big and solid. It was the exact opposite of the empty vacuum everywhere else here. "Perhaps we're dealing with an aquatic species," the Norwegian Forest cat suggested. She had mixed feelings about that idea. It would be much harder to communicate and trade with a species that was so different from them. But it would also be fascinating. "Have you read the reports from Captain Pierre Jacques about the time when the starship Initiative made contact with an electric eel-like race? The individual they encountered had traveled a long way. Perhaps they had traveled from the Tetra Galaxy, and this spaceship is from their civilization."

The Papillon seemed like the kind of eager young officer who would keep up on arcane intelligence like Captain Jacques' report about the eel-like alien. Regardless, Lt. Lee simply shook his head and woofed again, "I don't think it's a spaceship."

Captain Carroway's ears skewed, threatening to flatten entirely against her head. She should have taken a minute to get herself a cup of coffee before facing this. But it was too late now. It'd be a whole awkward thing if she stormed off to get coffee in the middle of a conversation. She needed to present a more collected, coherent front than that. "So, what do you think it is?" the irritable Norwegian Forest cat hissed.

To Lt. Lee's credit, he was unfazed by his captain's ill temper. "I think it's actually a turtle."

At the pilot's console, Risqua made a tittering sound before recovering her composure. Captain Carroway glanced at the reptile-bird, oddly grateful for the distraction from her own reaction to the Papillon's statement.

"Excuse me, Lieutenant?" Captain Carroway meowed, feigning to have either not heard or not understood what her subordinate officer had just said.

"Obviously, I don't mean it's a literal turtle from earth, uplifted and gigantified or anything," Lt. Lee said. His own butterfly-like ears skewed as he heard himself say 'gigantified' which was definitely not a real word, but in fairness to the Papillon, he hadn't had a turn sleeping yet and was still living through the longest day of his life so far. "But I do think that the object on our viewscreen is an organic lifeform native to the vacuum of space."

"One big lifeform?" Captain Carroway asked, still processing how to feel about that information. On one paw, a gigantic space-faring lifeform native to the space between galaxies was an incredible discovery, and the kitten inside her couldn't believe how amazingly cool such a discovery would be... if that was what they were really seeing here. On the other paw, Captain Carroway didn't see how a gigantic space turtle was going to help her stranded crew. Would they even be able to communicate with it? At all? It's not like they could afford to just chase it for months while trying to crack the code of whatever language it might speak, which would probably be far too different from any of the languages Earth animals had encountered before for The Wanderlust's computer to immediately translate it. They were already taking a risk by going this far out of their way.

Would they have to turn around without even learning anything about this amazing discovery?

Also, what did this mean for what they might find in the midst of the Tetra Galaxy? Captain Carroway had been hoping for—and assuming there would be—civilizations to meet, learn about, and trade with as they traveled. But... what if the Tetra Galaxy was filled with nothing but giant, silent space turtles?

Captain Carroway remembered being a kitten and finding an illustration in a book about old mythologies that showed the Earth, looking like a tiny marble, balanced precariously on the back of a whole stack of turtles. The caption under the illustration had read, "It's turtles all the way down." Kitten Carroway had laughed so hard over that picture that she'd fallen over and literally rolled on the floor with laughter. Her mother had come rushing to see what was wrong.

It didn't seem so funny right now.

Maybe the Tetra Galaxy was just turtles, turtles all the way down.

"Captain?" Lt. Lee woofed. Something in the Papillon's voice made it sound like it wasn't the first time he'd woofed it. "Did you hear anything I was saying?"

Captain Carroway's ears definitely flattened this time. And she realized, she couldn't afford to do anything other than opt for complete honesty. There wasn't room aboard such a tiny spaceship for hiding her weaknesses the way she wanted to. "No, I'm sorry, I didn't grab myself a cup of coffee before coming here, and I'm afraid I can't really wake up properly without it. I know it's an unusual foible, but the caffeine really does the trick. Let me grab myself a cup, and when I get back, you'll have my full attention."

Hopefully, the caffeine would help her focus and keep her mind from wandering to frivolous picture books she'd read as a kitten.

CHAPTER 17

TURTLES ALL TH
WAY DOWN

aptain Carroway took her time i
room, synthesizing herself a cu
much as one can take one's time
punched in the order for coffee, then alter
the coffee be hazelnut flavored, then chan
As she kept changing the order, before act
drink, Captain Carroway found herse
whether The Wanderlust would need to s
or supplies during the coming voyage. C
out of the types of raw matter they n
useful things like coffee? If they could,
find replacements on planets or asteroids

Captain Carroway had never studied
board life. Back in the Milky Way Galax
important. A ship was never too far fr
could refurbish it, tune it up, and make
met and then topped off.

Finally, Captain Carroway finished
for normal coffee. Perfectly normal c
single other weird thing today, even a s

wo
wo
now

mu
vati
now
less

and
wha
turtle
tions
time.
"
looki
the b
you'v
Instea
cat st
him a
over i
Sta
she'd
that S
It v
Th
The
fluffy f
Ca
Lt. Lee
fact tha
mately
space a
around

ld be one thing too many. For a moment, she'd thought it
ld make a nice treat, but she didn't really want treats right
She wanted something much harder to come by: normalcy.
/ith her paws firmly wrapped around the warm, aromatic
 Captain Carroway worked at pushing questions of conser-
n out of her mind. That wasn't the problem at paw right
 And she couldn't believe that a single cup of coffee more or
ight now would make a big difference in the long run.

fter a few sips, Captain Carroway's head felt much clearer
 harper. The first matter of business had to be figuring out
 The Wanderlust was dealing with when it came to this
-thing. She couldn't let herself get overwhelmed by ques-
of what it implied about the Tetra Galaxy. One matter at a
That was the way to move forward.

lright," Captain Carroway meowed to Lt. Lee, who was
g like a very tired dog, as soon as she stepped back onto
dge. "Walk me through your findings. Tell me everything
 figured out about this big space turtle we're chasing."
1 of returning to her captain's chair, the Norwegian Forest
od beside her lieutenant, looking at the station in front of
d all the charts, graphs, lists and other readings flickering

ing at all that data, suddenly, Captain Carroway realized:
ever been far enough away from Earth—from home—
 wasn't even a star in the sky, somewhere in the sky.
asn't just that there were no stars in the sky.
 one specific star was gone.
 Norwegian Forest cat shivered, in spite of her thick,
r.
ain Carroway struggled to follow all the information as
xplained it to her, but it mostly seemed to amount to the
 the turtle shape was a single giant organism, approxi-
he size of a small moon. The way it was flying through
parently created something like a hyperspace slipstream
it, meaning the turtle actually had a small bubble of

atmosphere collected over the back of its shell, and readings suggested there might be more lifeforms—though mostly vegetative plant lifeforms—collected on its back. So, it was indeed a world turtle, like Captain Carroway had seen in old mythology books. She wondered if a turtle like this had passed close enough to Earth in the distant past that an astronomer had spotted it, and that's where the myths had come from.

Also, the whole thing was accelerating away from the Tetra Galaxy, picking up speed as it flew. If they'd arrived a few days later, The Wanderlust would have had no chance of catching up to the mysterious turtle.

"It's really too bad that it's heading away from the Milky Way instead of towards it," Captain Carroway mused. "With the way it's picking up speed, it could have taken us home much more quickly than we can fly there ourselves."

"That's an interesting idea," Ensign Risqua squawked suddenly, inviting herself into the conversation. "Could we convince the turtle to turn around somehow? Travel in the right direction for us?"

"Is it safe?" Lt. Lee woofed. "I mean, we don't know hardly anything about it. What if it... I don't know... eats spaceships? And leading it to the Milky Way would mean mass death and destruction?"

"We need to get closer to it," Captain Carroway concluded. "So we can gather more information. We simply don't know enough yet, from this far away."

"If we could convince the turtle to carry us home," Ensign Risqua continued, pressing harder on her idea, "then maybe we could spend the trip on its back. The smaller life signs on the back could be trees, right? Trees and other plants? It might be a paradise. I'd rather travel in a paradise garden on the back of a turtle than this cramped little Tri-Galactic Navy ship."

Captain Carroway caught a flash in Lt. Lee's eyes that said the Papillon wanted to defend the comfort and quality of The Wanderlust. He'd been working on The Wanderlust—tuning her up, upgrading, and retro-fitting her—for longer than anyone else aboard. But Ensign Risqua had a point. No one actually wanted to live on a small ship like The Wanderlust long term. This ship was built for short missions, not the kind of voyage they were facing now.

"It's an interesting idea, Ensign Risqua," Captain Carroway conceded, hoping to cut off Lt. Lee's desire for an argument. "But we still need to learn more."

Then sizing up the Papillon, noting the redness in his eyes and the greasiness of the long fur around his pretty ears, Captain Carroway asked, "When does your shift end, Lt. Lee? I'm guessing soon?"

The Papillon nodded, suddenly looking even more tired, as if Captain Carroway's question had finally given him permission to admit his own tiredness to himself. "Ensign Melbourne will be replacing Ensign Risqua at the helm soon, and then Risqua is supposed to take over my post until Ensign Diaz's shift begins."

Captain Carroway nodded. She'd made sure to arrange the shifts so that The Wanderlust wouldn't be entirely run by former Anti-Ra officers for as long as possible. Eventually, with such a small crew, it would be inevitable that they'd end up with only Anti-Ra officers on the bridge at some point, but Captain Carroway wanted to put it off until the crew had melded together more thoroughly. She'd tried not to be too obvious about what she was doing while arranging the schedule with Commander Chestnut and Ensign Diaz, but they were both sharp officers. Captain Carroway had no doubt they'd seen right through her ruse about wanting officers from the different crews to get to know each other better and understood exactly why she didn't want the bridge run by only Anti-Ra yet. She didn't fully trust them. How could she? They'd just met, and their organizations didn't share any of the same foundational principles.

Fortunately, Commander Chestnut had been cooperative. That squirrel was a good egg.

Over the following hours, officers came and went, their short shifts meaning they could rotate on and off of the bridge, taking time in the multi-purpose room to eat and chat, getting to know one and another. Captain Carroway listened, but she tried to look like she wasn't listening. She tried to look like she was deep in thought, musing over their options and her plans for the days to come. In actuality though, she was listening for signs of trouble, seeds that might grow into full grown problems between officers, or anything among her crew that needed looking into.

Captain Carroway wasn't an expert on interpersonal relationships, but she'd had to learn how to pay attention to the officers around her in order to work her way as high through the ranks as she had. And so far as she could tell, the assortment of crew members who'd been thrown together on The Wanderlust for this fateful voyage was a remarkably lucky mix. She could picture true friendships developing out here in the wilds of the Tetra Galaxy before they all managed to make it home. That said, she could also tell that her subordinate officers were all going to start getting pretty twitchy if The Wanderlust didn't start flying in the right direction to take them home pretty soon. There was only so far she could stretch their patience before people started to snap.

It was bad enough being a long way from home. It was even worse that they were heading in the wrong direction.

And yet...

The turtle on the viewscreen was growing brighter by the minute now. The rumpled, crenellated quality to its back had started to look like treetops—a whole forest spread from one edge to the other of turtle's back, and the trees glowed. Phosphorescent green. It must be beautiful underneath them, looking up at a sky filled with shining leaves, fluttering in the breeze, capping off the ceiling of a traveling world.

How far had this turtle traveled? How far did it still have to go?

Was it going somewhere specific? Or just migrating across the universe, seeing where the tides of the stars took it?

Captain Carroway couldn't imagine a more beautiful existence than that. The uplifted cats, dogs, squirrels and such of Earth had needed to build rockets and a space elevator to escape the gravity of their world, and then they'd needed to design crafts capable of supporting them while traveling between stars before they'd been able to truly explore. Anyone who lived on this turtle would be born an explorer, always exploring, because their very world was designed to carry them across galaxies and from one galaxy to the next.

Captain Carroway hoped fervently that someone lived on the back of this turtle. It would be such a shame, such a waste if no one did.

On the bridge, where the officers would come and go, the viewscreen was now almost entirely filled by a turtle shell. Captain Carroway stared at it with her green eyes as if by focusing hard enough, she could make sense of the entire universe—from the suicide mission she'd been sent on to the chaos she was now trying to crystallize into a single crew, bound together by a single mission. A better mission. Because taking her crew members home was a much more wholesome purpose than the one some random admiral had saddled her with when she'd been given this post on The Wanderlust.

Somehow, it felt like Captain Carroway had been called here, like the turtle had pulled her across the universe. It didn't make sense. But she couldn't let the idea go.

"It's nice to have something on our viewscreen other than the endless darkness between galaxies," Captain Carroway observed, trying to lighten the mood on the bridge.

Ensign Diaz at the helm post resolutely refused to turn her head and acknowledge the captain's unearned optimism in any way. The set of the canine's broad shoulders, though, seemed to slump a little more, like she found the captain's positivity in such a dire situation exhausting.

Lt. Cmdr. Vossie, who was back at his original post, looking a bit shaky and worse for wear observed, "If we were flying toward the Tetra Galaxy instead of away from it, then we'd have a glittering expanse of stars for you to look at. There are stars out here, captain, they're just not in the direction you've been looking."

It hurt for Captain Carroway's best friend to make a point of using his considerable skills at snarkiness against her. She would have liked to have his support in the choices she was making for The Wanderlust, but she had to remember that he was still suffering from the loss of his computer implant. Though, if Mike's personality was anything to judge the implant by, Captain Carroway couldn't imagine how it had been helpful for Lt. Cmdr. Vossie to always have the thing whispering straight into his brain. She'd barely been able to stand being in the same room with Ensign Mike, let alone imagining what it would be like to share the same head.

At some level, Captain Carroway knew she was being unfair to the fungal officer, holding things against them that weren't exactly their fault. They wouldn't have chosen to hurt Lt. Cmdr. Vossie, leaving him shaken and struggling, if they'd had a choice. At least, Captain Carroway didn't think so.

But part of her wondered. The same part that feared Commander Chestnut had been being so nice because he was trying to lull her into complacency. The same part that assumed Lt. Lee would turn on her as soon as he had a chance, because she wasn't living up to being the kind of Tri-Galactic Union captain such a skilled and ambitious young officer deserved. The part of her that figured this would all end with everyone except her and—somehow—Ensign Melbourne dead, and the two of them would wind up back on that mining asteroid where he'd been incarcerated. Just two jail birds. Who happened to be cats. Jail cats. Reminiscing about how they'd gotten everyone else dead.

At least, Captain Carroway was sure that the white tomcat would be able to turn all of this into a funny story for his former jail mates somehow. She wasn't sure how, but she was sure he could do it. She had faith in his storytelling skills.

Maybe it was because the Norwegian Forest cat's outlook had gotten so dim and gloomy or maybe it would have happened at that moment either way, but Captain Carroway suddenly spotted movement over the far horizon of the turtle's shell. Dark, dart-like objects whisked past the crenellated forest top, blocking the green light from below, zipping and zooming in a very familiar, very spaceship-like way.

"What is that movement?" Captain Carroway meowed, pointing at the viewscreen. "Can you get any readings on those things? Scan them, please, Ensign Diaz," the Norwegian Forest cat ordered.

For a moment, the captain's heart filled with hope: there really were spacefaring people living on the back of this turtle! Then she saw the black ships fire on the forest, red energy beams blasting at the treetops, causing the trees to burst into flame. The glowing green trees began glowing even more brightly, more redly, more horribly. Instead of the gentle glow of phosphorescence, this was the horrible glow of destruction.

Captain Carroway didn't know what to think. But Ensign Diaz did. The canine snapped, "We need to get out of here!" The Xolo-Lupinian whirled around in her pilot's seat until she could face her captain. "Those ships could attack us," Ensign Diaz snarled.

But the canine didn't lay in a course away from the turtle. Her brown eyes flashed with anger, but she didn't take the situation into her own paws. She looked to her superior officer for orders—even though the ranking officer on the bridge at that moment was Captain Carroway and not Commander Chestnut —and that fact warmed the Norwegian Forest cat's heart. It was only their first day as a blended crew, and the plan was already working.

"No," Captain Carroway meowed evenly, firmly. "We can't

leave. There's too much to be gained here. Besides, the turtle might need our help."

"Or the turtle might be dangerous! We don't know what's going on here, and we don't want to get caught in the middle of a conflict we don't understand!" Ensign Diaz looked furious, but she was arguing instead of disobeying.

"Then we need to try to understand it." Captain Carroway's ears flattened, and she didn't try to stop them. She wanted Ensign Diaz to see her anger—and that she was controlling it. Turning toward Lt. Cmdr. Vossie, the Norwegian Forest cat asked, "Are those ships a threat to us?" They looked small from this distance, but even a small ship can be well-armed. The Wanderlust was proof enough of that.

"Most definitely," the rabbit-like alien announced after looking over the readings on his control panel. He looked surprisingly calm about the situation. It almost seemed like the presence of a clear and present danger was soothing his nerves—now that he knew where the danger was, and it was outside of his body, outside of his ship, he could handle it. Sometimes, the dangers that we only imagine are the scariest ones of all.

"Can you get a reading on how many of those ships there are?" Captain Carroway kept trying to count, but it was difficult to keep track of the fast-moving vessels, small and silhouetted as they were.

"The Wanderlust's scanners are tracking six vessels attacking the turtle right now," Lt. Cmdr. Vossie stated. "Though, I can't guarantee there aren't others still hidden or out of range of our sensors."

"But they haven't seen us yet?" Captain Carroway pressed.

"Extremely unlikely," Lt. Cmdr. Vossie agreed. "They're closer to the turtle than us—close enough that the hyperspatial slip-stream should be interfering with their sensors and obscuring us from view. So, it's not impossible that they'd notice us, but they'd have to look in exactly the right direction. I can't tell you the exact probability of that..." The rabbit-like alien's ears flagged, and his voice faltered. "Perhaps, if you wanted an exact probability, we could get *Ensign Mike* on the bridge to tell you one."

"That's alright," Captain Carroway meowed. "Unlikely is good enough for me."

Ensign Diaz snorted derisively and woofed, "Then maybe you should have higher standards. We're being hailed."

CHAPTER 18
FIRST CONTACT

Captain Carroway's heart skipped a beat. At least, it felt that way to her.

They were being hailed. By aliens from another galaxy.

The Tri-Galactic Union may have tried to throw her away on a suicide mission, but they had failed. She was on the far side of the cosmos, about to make first contact with aliens from the Tetra Galaxy. Answering this hail was possibly the most important thing that any captain in the Tri-Galactic Union had ever done. Or any officer. Or any uplifted animal from Earth. And she was ready for it. She would prove all the dogs who'd tried to hold her down, all the superior officers who'd tried to hold her back wrong. She would be immortalized in history books, remembered forever as the first cat to talk to someone from the Tetra Galaxy.

Never mind that The Wanderlust would need to find a way home for any of this to be remembered... They would find a way. And when they got home, holy fishcakes, would she be vindicated.

Captain Carroway straightened her tunic, smoothed down the long fur that always escaped around her collar in fluffy wisps, and stood taller than she had in days. Then she meowed, "Answer the hail, put it on the main viewscreen."

Ensign Diaz glared with wide-set eyes at her captain for a long moment. The canine didn't look like a normal Tri-Galactic Union officer with her necklace of reeds worn over her uniform and the ornate facial tattoo of red-dyed fur on one side of her face. None of that was regulation. Of course, neither were all the gold earrings that lined the sides of Commander Chestnut's round ears. But Captain Carroway hadn't thought it would win many points with the Anti-Ra side of her crew to insist on following strict regulations out here in the middle of nowhere. The Norwegian Forest cat was starting to question the wisdom of that choice though. Maybe if she'd tried to hold a tighter reign while beginning the integration of the crew yesterday, she wouldn't be facing so much defiance from Ensign Diaz today.

But then the canine turned back toward the main viewscreen and barked sharply, "Yes, Captain."

The beautiful forested back of the giant space turtle disappeared from the main viewscreen and was replaced by a new image that twisted and distorted at first, while The Wanderlust's computers worked to translate the foreign video encoding, but soon snapped into place. The new image wasn't anything that Captain Carroway would have expected. She'd expected something truly alien and surprising, something hard to interpret or understand. Instead, she found herself looking at the pointy, pinched face of a fuzzy, brown, mammalian alien with prickly quills poking out all around his face. The quills looked like they covered his whole back, and many of them had small colorful objects stuck onto their ends, giving the creature a cluttered look, a bit like a pin cushion or some kind of half-finished craft.

Overall, the alien looked a lot like an Earthen hedgehog might look if they'd ever been uplifted. He twitched his nose and spoke in a high-pitched voice, but The Wanderlust's computers hadn't figured out how to translate the alien's words yet.

The alien spoke quickly, jabbering away with only the occasional break in his stream of words. The words sounded urgent, but also, completely indistinguishable for people from another galaxy who simply didn't know the language.

"How long will it take for the computer's algorithms to work out the language this creature is speaking?" Captain Carroway asked. The sound of her words interrupted the alien's flow, and she found herself staring at an alien hedgehog in silence. The alien's stare was quite intense, like he really, really wanted something from Captain Carroway and The Wanderlust.

"Longer now that the creature has stopped talking," Lt. Cmdr. Vossie observed drily. "It would help if you could get them speaking again."

Captain Carroway sighed deeply, and her shoulders slumped forward. She'd felt moments away from the greatest discovery of her time, and now, she was trying to get a jabbering hedgehog covered in baubles to keep talking. She shouldn't be disappointed. This creature was still a member of a spacefaring alien race from an entirely different galaxy who might have invaluable information to share with them. And this was still a case of first contact. But it no longer felt quite as momentous.

Speaking slowly and clearly, even though she knew it would make no difference before the computer figured out a translation algorithm, Captain Carroway meowed, "Please, keeping talking so our computer can learn your language."

The alien hedgehog on the viewscreen blinked its beady eyes, and for a moment, Captain Carroway thought she'd have to try a different strategy. But then he opened his pointy muzzle and began jabbering again, even more hurriedly.

Speaking lowly so as to hopefully not interrupt the hedgehog's flow again, Captain Carroway asked Lt. Cmdr. Vossie, "Does it matter that they're talking so quickly?"

"No," the Morphican answered slowly, analyzing the data streaming across their console. "I think it's a good thing, actually. It means more data, more quickly for the computer to process."

Captain Carroway nodded, keeping her eyes on the hedgehog who was continuing to stare at her just as intensely. However, her ears twisted and turned, hearing sounds at the back of the bridge—shuffling footsteps, whispered words that she couldn't quite make out. Word of this first contact must have spread to the rest of the crew, and on such a small ship, that meant she suddenly had an audience that might well include absolutely everyone aboard. And of course, even if an officer or two wasn't crowded at the back of the bridge watching, whatever happened here would be common knowledge and shared with anyone who missed it.

Knowing she was being watched actually made Captain Carroway feel oddly better. She'd wanted to be in the eyes of history. And maybe, right now, that only meant a meager half-dozen or so people, but it was all of the people from her galaxy who were out here. Suddenly, what she was doing felt important again. Her tail lashed excitedly, and her ears stood tall.

The Norwegian Forest cat was more than ready for it when The Wanderlust's translation algorithms suddenly kicked in, and the hedgehog alien on her viewscreen said, "Help us, you have to help us, please, oh please, I've already done everything I can, but there's no one else out here, and we don't have any weapons to protect us! You have to help me protect these people! The Ollallans are a beautiful, peaceful race, and I can't stand to see them being hurt like this!"

Captain Carroway raised her paws, keeping her claws retracted even though that wouldn't be visible through the viewscreen, in a gesture designed to make the hedgehog alien slow down. "Hold on, hold on," she meowed, trusting that if the computer could translate the hedgehog's words for her, it could also translate her words for the hedgehog. "We're going to need some more information before we get started here. First off, who are you? Where are you? Who's attacking you? And..." Captain Carroway halted, thinking her words over, before continuing. "Actually, that should be a good starting point."

The hedgehog made a squeak of impatient frustration, but then he started over, slower this time. "My name is Korvax, and I'm on a small spaceship, hidden behind the Waykeeper's left hind flipper right now. I've been living with the Ollallans who inhabit this wise Waykeeper for many years, and I'm the only one here with any sort of spaceflight. The Ollallans are a peaceful, naturalistic people with no way of defending themselves from the attacking Zakonraptors. *You have to help them!*"

"What's a Zakonraptor?" Captain Carroway meowed, intrigued in spite of herself. She hadn't wanted to be drawn into yet another violent conflict, but since she was here and it was happening anyway, she wanted to understand it.

"Oh!" Korvax squeaked on the viewscreen, his pointy nose twitching to one side. When he spoke again, his words rushed into a blur like they'd been doing before, but this time the computer translated the verbal downpour: "They're horrible reptilian, feathered, dinosaur beast things! And their spaceships are burning down the Waykeeper's beautiful forests! It's just a travesty! A *travesty!*"

Captain Carroway felt the small shape of Commander Chestnut step up beside her. Someone must have awoken the golden-mantled squirrel and told him to come. She couldn't blame whichever Anti-Ra officer had made that choice, wanting their own leader on the bridge for this. Besides, Captain Carroway didn't mind the back-up. She had long wanted to be a captain, but she'd never expected to lead alone. Tri-Galactic Union captains weren't all-powerful rulers who could never be questioned—although, some dogs who Captain Carroway had known seemed to forget that. No, Tri-Galactic Union captains were meant to lead with assistance, consultation, and advice.

To that end, Captain Carroway said to the hedgehog on her viewscreen, "Allow me a minute to consult with my first officer, please." Then glancing over at Lt. Cmdr. Vossie, she swept one paw across her neck in a gesture meant to tell him that he should cut the sound.

The Morphican nodded, pressed a few keys on his console, and said, "I've turned the sound off, Captain."

Holy lobster tails, Captain Carroway wished Lt. Cmdr. Vossie was still himself and still her first officer. Even as shaken as he'd been by the events of the last few days—losing a huge part of himself—he was still perfectly in synch with her. Unfortunately, their lives hadn't turned out that way.

The Norwegian Forest cat turned to the small golden-mantled squirrel beside her. Commander Chestnut was literally bright-eyed and bushy-tailed. He didn't look at all like he'd just been woken up by Ensign Risqua or Ensign Werik, even though that was clearly what had happened.

"What would you advise?" Captain Carroway asked the squirrel. She had her own thoughts, but she knew better than to say them first. Her role was to make the final decision, not to put her decision up for others to review and critique. But she wanted to know what kind of resistance she might or might not be dealing with when she ordered her crew to assist these Ollallans, whoever they were. She wanted to find out who they were, and that meant they needed to not all die in forest fires.

The side that's burning down forests is rarely—if ever—the right side.

With an internal wince, Captain Carroway found herself comparing the dastardliness of setting forest fires to... collapsing perfectly good stars into brand new black holes, sucking everything around them into a crushing death.

The comparison didn't look good.

It didn't make her look good.

Or the Tri-Galactic Union.

She was going to do the right thing here, regardless of what Commander Chestnut said. Fortunately, when the golden-mantled squirrel spoke, he said, "As an Arborealist, I cannot support the wanton destruction of forests. If we can, then we need to help them."

Captain Carroway felt the fur on her back, underneath her

uniform, twitch with discomfort at the mysticism inherent to the squirrel's reasoning. "I'm not entirely sure that your personal religious beliefs should enter into this," the Norwegian Forest cat meowed in a measured tone. "However, I'm inclined to agree with your conclusion here. I do think it's our duty to help them."

Captain Carroway glanced quickly around the bridge, trying not to show she was doing it. She wanted to gauge the reactions of her crew, without giving away that she cared what her subordinate officers thought about her orders. It wasn't that she would change her mind to match popular opinion... But knowing if she'd be up against a fomenting rebellion would give her more time to figure out how to deal with it before it came to a head.

Fortunately, all of the officers crowded at the back of the bridge—which was *all* of the officers who weren't actually serving on the bridge, so absolutely everyone—looked mostly intrigued by the funny little spiky-backed alien on the viewscreen. Intrigue was good. Intrigue was an emotion that Captain Carroway could work with. Intrigue was the emotion that drove the entire Tri-Galactic Union towards discovery and exploration. It was the emotion that the Tri-Galactic Union had been founded upon.

Captain Carroway gestured with a paw to Lt. Cmdr. Vossie, signaling for him to turn the sound back on. The Morphican pressed a few keys on his console and then nodded, long ears swaying with the movement of his head.

"It's nice to meet you Korvax," Captain Carroway meowed. "Although, I'm sure we all wish it were under better circumstances. I'm Captain Carroway of the Tri-Galactic Union vessel The Wanderlust, and this is my first officer, Commander Chestnut—" She gestured at the golden-mantled squirrel beside her who ducked his head in a polite, friendly bow. "We're going to do our best to help you. However, our ship isn't equipped to fight six of those Zakonraptor ships. Even working together, I don't think our two ships are a match for them."

"Excuse me," the hedgehog on the viewscreen said politely.

"But don't you mean the three of us? It looks like you have two ships."

Captain Carroway hadn't thought about The Last Chance, which The Wanderlust was still towing. It wasn't extremely useful as a ship right now, but there might be a clever way to use it.

What this situation really called for was cleverness, not brute force. With a thrill that ran all the way from the tips of her tufted ears along her spine and down to the end of her fluffy tail, Captain Carroway realized this was exactly the moment she'd been living for her whole life. She was going to collect suggestions from her crew, and then she would get to decide which suggestion had the best chance of success. Because that's the job of the captain—collect suggestions, make decisions. The whole point of the Tri-Galactic Union was that people were better when they came together, worked together, and figured things out together. Captain Carroway didn't have to figure this out alone. She had a whole crew to call on, and figuring out this problem together would pull them together, blending the crew more thoroughly than any games or gimmicks about how Captain Carroway arranged them onto shifts or into sleeping quarters possibly could.

With a sense of profound gravity, the Norwegian Forest cat turned to her crew, green eyes bright and gleaming, and she meowed, "You've all heard the situation. We need to drive away six attacking Zakonraptor ships—a fleet that severely outnumbers us. What we have to work with is our ship, Korvax's ship, and the broken vessel we've been towing. Please, give me your suggestions."

CHAPTER 19
BRAINSTORMING

The Anti-Ra officers exchanged troubled, confused glances like they weren't sure how to react to their new captain asking for their input. Ensign Melbourne adjusted one of his hearing aides while chewing on his lower lip with one of his fangs, seemingly deep in thought, very interested in impressing this captain who was finally giving him a chance to prove himself. But it was Lt. Lee—who looked out of place and discombobulated, like he felt it was wrong for a whole throng of off-duty officers to be hanging out at the back of a starship's bridge unasked—who spoke first.

The Papillon opened his narrow muzzle hesitantly a few times before biting off actual words and saying them. "We should try talking to the Zakonraptors," Lt. Lee woofed, his butterfly-like ears flagging as all the eyes on the bridge turned toward him. But with every word he spoke, Lt. Lee gained more confidence, bolstered by how encouragingly his captain was looking at him. "I mean, maybe the Zakonraptors can be reasoned with... We don't know why they're attacking the, uh, Waykeeper, or what it is they want. If the Ollallans really are such a naturalistic people, do they even have the necessary communications technology to try communicating with the Zakonraptors?"

The Papillon's suggestion sounded reasonable and well-thought out to everyone on The Wanderlust, if perhaps overly peaceable to some of the fiercer Anti-Ra officers. It sounded like utter nonsense, though, to the alien hedgehog on their viewscreen.

"You can't reason with Zakonraptors!" Korvax burbled in the highest pitch of his voice yet. "Why do you think I've been living on the back of this turtle with the Ollallans in the first place? I mean, obviously, the Ollallans are lovely people, but I would never have even come here if the Zakonraptors hadn't, oh, I don't know, *destroyed my whole homeworld!"*

The hedgehog alien pulled a scrap of colorful fabric from where it had been impaled on the sharp tip of one of his quills and used it to dab tears away from the corners of his bright, beady eyes. Resolutely pulling himself back together, Korvax sniffled, "Besides, if the Zakonraptors *could* be dealt with by *talking* to them, I'd have talked to them on the Ollallans behalf. You don't think I'd do that for them? Then you don't know me! I obviously have the necessary technology, as you can see for yourself." The hedgehog did a shuffling little dance, spreading his short arms wide as if to show off the fanciness of the fact that he was currently talking to the crew of The Wanderlust over those very pieces of communications technology. He was clearly proud of his little ship, which sensors suggested was more of a short-range shuttlecraft than a full-fledged spaceship.

Captain Carroway's ears flattened in irritation at the hedge-hog's irrelevant interruptions. "We're brainstorming ideas, Mr. Korvax," the Norwegian Forest cat hissed. "If you have suggestions, I'm happy to hear them, but it does no good for you to take offense when one of my officers puts forward an idea, whether you like the idea or not."

On the viewscreen, Korvax sputtered but didn't actually say anything. He was a brave little hedgehog alien, standing up for an entire world that was under attack, but he wasn't used to facing someone quite as fearsome as Captain Carroway when she was annoyed.

"Thank you for your suggestion, Lt. Lee," Captain Carroway continued. "I'll keep it under advisement, but I think we need more ideas..." Her green eyes scanned over the rest of the officers in her crew, looking for someone with an idea that they weren't quite brave enough to put forward. She saw that Ensign Risqua was clacking her beak in a pensive way, and so she stared at the reptile-bird, narrowing her eyes in an inquisitive way.

Ensign Risqua glanced around, uncertain of herself, but then she squawked, "When I was manning the ops station earlier, I noticed that The Wanderlust is still armed with a vacuum bomb..." She shrugged her wing-like arms. "Perhaps, we could use that? They're very powerful; it might even the field a little bit."

"Your ship was armed with *multiple vacuum bombs*?" Commander Chestnut chirruped in horror. The little golden-mantled squirrel was usually so even-keeled, but right now, his brushy reed of a tail was flipping about wildly and his eyes were burning. He looked like if he were a sailing ship, his mast would crack in half, his sails would float away into the sky, and his prow would flip over. "What in the name of root-rot and bark beetles is *wrong* with the Tri-Galactic Union?"

Before Captain Carroway could say anything in defense of her beloved Tri-Galactic Union, Lt. Cmdr. Vossie spoke up.

"No, we only had one," the Morphican corrected, always precise, always accurate, but still strangely dispassionate, even without a computer implant evening out his hormones. "We had exactly the number we needed for the mission we'd been sent on. So, if we still have one... then logically, it must be the same vacuum bomb. It must have... unexploded... and returned to us during the time-blip."

Commander Chestnut still looked aghast. It couldn't have helped that he was now thinking about the fact that the vacuum bomb currently stowed away aboard The Wanderlust had already killed him once and killed two of his crew members permanently.

"A... time-blip?" Korvax asked from the viewscreen, muzzle crinkled in confusion. The hedgehog alien was clearly having trouble keeping up with everything going on aboard The Wanderlust's bridge. He simply didn't have the background from the last few days necessary for keeping up. And no one showed any inclination towards trying to catch him up, least of all Captain Carroway whose green eyes were shining defiantly.

"We're unlikely to experience another time-blip," Captain Carroway meowed, chastising the golden-mantled squirrel for his interruption, "so time is something of a limited resource right now." The Norwegian Forest cat's tail whipped impatiently behind her as she wondered how much of the Waykeeper's forests had burned down already during this conversation. But it couldn't be helped. This was the way ideas were come up with. And as much as the time pressure was pushing down on her, Captain Carroway couldn't help feeling invigorated and deeply alive.

The Norwegian Forest cat had never been in the center of a conversation like this one before, where ideas were flying, and everyone was working together towards a solution... and she'd get to make the final call.

"So, what can we do with one vacuum bomb?" Captain Carroway asked her crew.

"Nothing," Ensign Diaz snapped from the pilot's seat, where she was still stationed. The canine had twisted around in her seat to look at the captain as she spoke, delivering each word with a withering level of scorn. "Vacuum bombs are powerful—too powerful, much too powerful for this purpose—but even if using a vacuum bomb this close to an inhabited... uh... turtle... weren't a ridiculously dangerous suggestion, we have no way of grouping the six Zakonraptor ships close enough together—and also far enough away from the turtle—to take the whole group of them out with *one* vacuum bomb."

Ensign Melbourne stepped forward from the throng of officers at the back of the bridge. The white tomcat's tail was swishing, and his ears were tall. "I have two ideas," Ensign Melbourne meowed. "But neither of them are thought through very well."

Captain Carroway sighed exasperatedly between her fangs and rolled her eyes, but she gestured with a paw for the other cat to continue on anyway.

"One," Ensign Melbourne counted, raising a delicately extended claw, "what if we could cause another time blip? And two—" He extended a second perfectly manicured claw. "—maybe we could use the hyperspatial slipstream around the turtle's shell to dissipate the vacuum bomb's power somehow, protecting the turtle and also widening the bomb's range so it can take out more Zakonraptor ship's at once?"

Apparently, the white tomcat was better at being creative and thinking outside the box than at developing well-conceived plans. But then, that's all part of brainstorming.

At the helm, Ensign Diaz suddenly got excited and started riffing off of the white tomcat's second suggestion—the first one had been gibberish, as none of The Wanderlust's officers knew how the time-blip had been caused in the first place, so they certainly wouldn't know how to recreate it. Nor was it clear that a time-blip would be at all helpful here.

"That's a really interesting idea, about using the hyperspatial slipstream—" The canine rattled off a lot of detailed parameters about exactly how it would need to be done, but then, looking downcast, bat-like ears flagging, she concluded, "Unfortunately, while I think it's possible, it would still be very dangerous, and it would still require all of the Zakonraptor vessels to be in the same layer of the slipstream at the time when the vacuum bomb went off. So, we'd still need a way to group them all together somehow, just not quite as tightly together."

Captain Carroway was impressed. Ensign Diaz really did seem to be brilliant, just like Commander Chestnut had said she was. The Norwegian Forest cat hadn't really doubted him; she'd just wanted to see the brilliance for herself. And to her delight, here it was. Now if it could just be harnessed into finding an actual solution...

Trying to push Ensign Diaz into making that final leap to a workable plan, Captain Carroway meowed, "And how could we do that, Ensign Diaz? What could we do to entice the Zakonraptors into grouping their ships together in a tight formation?"

The Xolo-Lupinian narrowed her eyes, deep in thought, but she didn't say anything.

"A decoy?" Korvax squeaked from the viewscreen. "I could fly my ship out where they could see me..."

"No, no, no," Captain Carroway objected. "We're not putting you into danger like that! There has to be a better idea," the Norwegian Forest cat snapped, looking her crew over challengingly, daring them to fail to give her a better suggestion.

Commander Chestnut hazarded, "We could use The Last Chance... put it on autopilot..."

"Or fling it forward using our tractor beams," Ensign Werik suggested, finally participating and looking eager about his idea.

By now, everyone had participated in the discussion—union and Anti-Ra alike—except for Ensign Mike. The fungal officer was standing among the others at the back of the bridge like a useless lump. Captain Carroway wasn't sure if they really didn't have any ideas to suggest, or if they just couldn't keep up with a conversation this complicated and fast-paced, having only been a living being for about a day now.

And yet, looking at Ensign Mike gave Captain Carroway an idea of her own. She was about to put voice to the idea when Ensign Diaz beat her to it:

"A hologram," the canine announced, proudly, clearly pleased with herself, bat-like ears standing tall again. "We don't want to waste an entire ship when we could simply cast a hologram. You know, like the moon that Mike cast on the ceiling of the multi-purpose room during the memorial for..." Her voice broke before she could say the name of her childhood friend who'd only been gone for a day. Ensign Diaz had been friends with Wilder her whole life, and now he was gone. Forever. And her life would never be quite the same without him. They'd never howl together again, voices rising toward the full moon in harmony. "Could we do that?" Ensign Diaz asked, directing her question toward the fungal officer, rallying herself as well as she could, refusing to let memories of Wilder drag her down. His memory should be a buoy in her life, not an anchor.

All eyes on the bridge toward Ensign Mike, and the fungal officer's pinky-gray flesh blushed crimson along the underside of their mushroom cap where their face was. Their row of slit eyes constricted, narrowing to mere lines, and their fleshy mouth opened and closed silently several times before they managed to summon a quiet, mushy voice: "I don't know," Ensign Mike murmured like whispering autumn leaves. "I can design a holo-gram, but the ship's lumo-projectors aren't configured to cast holographic projections outside. They'd need to be reconfig-ured... mounted on the hull... I... I... don't know how to do any of that."

The crimson blush on the underside of Ensign Mike's mush-room cap deepened and spread until the fungal officer turned away and ran down the central corridor of The Wanderlust, fleshy feet making plopping, pattering sounds as they shuffled away.

Captain Carroway frowned, whiskers turning down. She wasn't sure what to do with Ensign Mike. They didn't seem to perform well under pressure. To be fair, they were composed of a computer implant designed to help a Morphican avoid feeling pressure in the first place and mycelial flesh that had been part of a spaceship computer system that didn't have any emotions of its own at all. At least, as far as Captain Carroway knew. The Norwegian Forest cat suddenly found herself troubled by the idea of The Wanderlust having feelings of its own... She didn't want to deal with a spaceship that had feelings about how it was used. It was bad enough how many feelings were sloshing around inside The Wanderlust just from all the members of the crew.

Maybe the mainstream Morphicans had the right of it—better to dampen down emotions, freeing yourself to focus on ideas. Captain Carroway shook off her annoyance at Ensign Mike's poor performance under pressure and returned her focus to the matter at paw. She could deal with the fungal officer later.

Turning toward Ensign Diaz, the Norwegian Forest cat meowed, "Do you think you could install lumo-projectors on the hull, so we could cast external holograms?"

The Xolo-Lupinian was an engineer, and diversionary holograms had been her idea. It made sense to put her in charge of the project.

The canine officer looked taken aback, surprised that her new captain would place such an important project—one that could potentially damage their ship—into the paws of an officer that had been her enemy yesterday. "I.. don't know. I'm not very familiar with this ship's systems yet."

Captain Carroway extended a paw toward the eager, young Papillon who was still standing at the back of the bridge and said, "Lt. Lee is the closest thing we have to an expert on the workings of this ship, so have him help you. I'll talk to Ensign Mike and get them to work on designing the holograms you'll use when the lumo-projectors are ready."

Lt. Cmdr. Vossie stood up suddenly. Then sat again. Then stood up.

"Is there something wrong, Lt. Cmdr. Vossie?" Captain Carroway meowed, her ears skewing.

The Morphican stood up again. "I would like to help you with talking to Ensign Mike."

Captain Carroway nodded and gestured for Lt. Cmdr. Vossie to follow her. To the rest of the bridge, she announced, "Commander Chestnut, you have the bridge; Ensign Melbourne to the helm; Ensign Risqua and Ensign Werik, please research the hyperspatial slipstream and gather data that might help widen our options here." Then glancing back at the hedgehog on the viewscreen, she added as an afterthought, "Hold tight, Korvax. We'll let you know when we're ready to move forward and what role we need you to play. In the meantime, I'd like you to work with my ship's pilot—" Captain Carroway gestured at the white tomcat, already taking his place at the helm. "—to transfer any files your ship's computers have about Zakonraptors over to us."

Before turning to leave, Captain Carroway placed a paw on Ensign Melbourne's shoulder and said quietly, "Please see if you can get our computer prepared to translate the Zakonraptors' language by using whatever files you can get from Korvax."

The alien hedgehog made burbling noises, like he had a whole lot of things he wanted to say, more than could fit out of his pointy snout at once, but Captain Carroway paid them no mind. She led the way off the bridge and down the central corridor, looking for where Ensign Mike had hidden themself away.

CHAPTER 20
BLUFF AND BLUSTER

When Captain Carroway and Lt. Cmdr. Vossie found Ensign Mike, the fungal officer had crawled under one of the consoles in the small engine room and folded themselves up into a little ball under their mushroom cap so that their face was hidden and only their mycelial beard was visible. They looked a little like they were trying to remerge with the ship they had originally grown from and return to a simpler state of being.

"Please get up, Ensign Mike," Captain Carroway meowed, trying to keep the disdain from her voice at the mushroom's lack of dignity. "This is not behavior befitting an officer of the Tri-Galactic Union."

The fungal officer made no move to get up. In fact, Lt. Cmdr. Vossie got down on the floor beside them. The Morphican didn't fit under the console with the fungal officer, but the rabbit alien sat companionably beside them, crossing his strong hind legs.

Captain Carroway skewed a triangular ear. She hadn't expected Lt. Cmdr. Vossie to get down on the floor like that. He'd never done anything like that, anything so undignified, before in all the long years she'd known him. However, her surprise at Vossie sitting down on the floor, cross-legged beside

Ensign Mike, was nothing compared to her shock when he started softly singing.

Captain Carroway couldn't make out most of the words; Vossie was singing too softly for that. But the tune was sweet and pretty, clearly a child's lullaby, soothing and easy to sing. After a minute, the fungal officer shifted, peeking with their slitted eyes out from between their mushroom cap and bushy gray beard. A moment more later, Ensign Mike began singing along in his mushy, watery voice that sounded like it belonged deep in an ancient forest, rather than aboard a state-of-the art spaceship in an extremely high tech engine room.

The mushroom and rabbit alien sang together, clumsily, neither of them any good at actually harmonizing. But there was a gentle purity to the way their voices came together, aligning sometimes and then getting out of rhythm in other places. When the song was done, Lt. Cmdr. Vossie said, "You've been singing that to me since I was nothing but a kit."

"You sang it first," Ensign Mike said. "You sang it to yourself so many times that I started to sing along."

"And then you began anticipating when I would need it, and you started singing it to me first. Before I even realized I was sad or stressed."

"It saved a lot of hormone treatments," the mushroom observed. "If you can calm your biological organism with a whispered song, you don't have to interfere directly with their body chemistry. I was programed to know that before I had any sense of myself or yourself as a person. It was only practical."

"It seems to have a worked a little on you too," Lt. Cmdr. Vossie said, reaching out a paw and gently taking ahold of one of Ensign Mike's fleshy, stubby hands. "It kind of feels like we grew up together. Like we're some sort of weird siblings."

The mushroom's mouth twisted into what must have been their version of a smile. It looked a little sad and haunting, but maybe that was simply because of the weird, unusual shape of their mushroomy face. Or maybe it was because Ensign Mike was still sad.

Captain Carroway didn't have time for this mushy nonsense. She had a small crew, and she needed every one of her officers to be doing their job. But also... A ship this far away from home would fall apart fast if its captain was always riding roughshod over her crew members' emotions.

Against her better judgment—or maybe, it actually was her better judgment—Captain Carroway knelt down on the floor of the engine room as well. She didn't sit all the way on the floor, instead staying balanced on her toes. But she did lower herself down to Vossie and Mike's level.

"Ensign Mike," the Norwegian Forest cat purred, doing everything in her power to sound soft and caring, in spite of her actual impatience. "There are forests burning down on the back of the world turtle out there while our ship watches. I want to help them. But I need your help to do that. I need you to help design a believable holographic projection that will scare the Zakonraptor ships away. Can you help me with that?"

"I do want to help," the mushroom said. "I just... got over-whelmed. There were so many people with so many feelings."

Captain Carroway wanted to snap something about how that's a normal situation that a person is just going to have to expect to deal with in life. And it was. But also, that wouldn't have been a helpful response here. So, the Norwegian Forest cat continued to temper herself and instead said, "Perhaps you and Lt. Cmdr. Vossie could stay in here, where it's quiet, and work on the design for the holographic projection together." Then with the kind of restraint that should be the envy of absolutely every-one, instead of making her suggestion into an order, Captain Carroway asked through gritted teeth, "Do you think you could do that?"

The fungal officer blinked their row of slit-like eyes and looked at Lt. Cmdr. Vossie. The rabbit alien nodded encourag-ingly, and the fungal officer mirrored the expression, bobbing their mushroom cap head. "Yes, I think we can do that," Ensign Mike said.

Captain Carroway sprang back up to a standing position, relieved to have this problem dealt with for the moment. "Good," she meowed. "Please get it done as quickly as possible. Ideally, we could use a whole fleet of similar but slightly different holographic spaceships so that the illusion will look more convincing than if they're all identical. Maybe add some blast patterns to their hulls so it looks like they've seen combat, and definitely make them substantially bigger than the Zakonraptor ships."

Captain Carroway left the rabbit alien and mushroom to work together on their illusions and padded her way back toward the bridge. Commander Chestnut, however, met her in the hallway, just before the mouth of the bridge. The golden-mantled squirrel seemed to have been lingering there, waiting for her.

"Is something wrong, Commander Chestnut?" the Norwegian Forest cat meowed. Something seemed to be wrong all the time, and it was always her job to fix it.

"I don't think we should kill the Zakonraptors, even if they are attacking the forests," the squirrel chittered up at her.

"I agree," Captain Carroway meowed. "I was never planning to attack them."

"But... the vacuum bomb..." Commander Chestnut looked confused.

"It's a tool in our arsenal," Captain Carroway acknowledged. "And part of brainstorming is to throw every idea out on the table, examine them all, and then make your decision. And my decision, for the moment, is that Lt. Lee is right. We should try to talk to the Zakonraptors."

The golden-mantled squirrel blinked. He tilted his small head with its beautifully delicate coloring. The way that his golden fur lightened to cream around his eyes was quite charming. "But you dismissed Lt. Lee's suggestion outright."

"No," Captain Carroway disagreed. "Korvax dismissed his idea, and the conversation moved on. I was still collecting ideas, and that Papillon is one sharp dog who really understands how the Tri-Galactic Union works. We talk first. We resort to other tactics if talking fails."

Commander Chestnut narrowed his dark eyes, crinkling the cream fur lining them. "Which tactics?"

"I think we can scare them away using Ensign Diaz's hologram idea. That will at least buy us some time." Captain Carroway wasn't sure what she'd do if the holograms didn't work, but then, she supposed she'd figure it out when she got there—if she got there—just like she'd been having to do with everything else. A whole lot of being captain seemed to amount to being able to make things up on the fly.

"I told you T'lia was brilliant," Commander Chestnut said proudly, his narrow chest puffing out.

Faced with their first real challenge as a blended crew, the officers of The Wanderlust worked quickly, efficiently, and smoothly together. Captain Carroway was impressed and very pleased with how her ship was shaping up. Lt. Cmdr. Vossie and Ensign Mike put together an imposing fleet of holographic ships in very little time. It took a little longer for Ensign Diaz and Lt. Lee to construct an additional, large scale, long range lumo-projector from synthesized and scavenged parts and get it mounted on The Wanderlust's outer hull, while also properly connecting it to the shipboard computer systems. While those tasks were being completed, Ensign Risqua and Ensign Werik put together an impressive dossier of information that they'd collected on the hyperspatial slipstream surrounding the world turtle.

In short form: the hyperspatial slipstream was a wildly unpredictable, quantum field, and shooting a vacuum bomb into it would probably be a devastatingly horrible idea. Or maybe an absolutely brilliant plan that would fling The Wanderlust all the way back across several galaxies to the Milky Way Galaxy where she belonged. It was impossible for the ensigns to say which without far more research, like the kind of research that would take lifetimes to perform properly. So, firing a vacuum bomb at the turtle would need to be an absolute last resort. Captain Carroway didn't feel like playing with those kinds of odds again any time soon. Once in a lifetime is more than enough for firing a bomb with that much power.

Once everything was lined up and ready for the holographic illusions, Captain Carroway hailed Korvax back and instructed him to keep his vessel close to The Wanderlust and be ready to lead them down to a safe landing space on the turtle's back if and when needed. Then she hailed the Zakonraptor fleet—a wide frequency hail reaching out to any of the attacking vessels that might take the time to answer her.

Tension on The Wanderlust's bridge ran high as all of the officers—union and Anti-Ra—manned their posts with bated breath, waiting to see if the Zakonraptors would answer their hail.

The bridge of The Wanderlust was fully crewed with every station manned. Two days ago, when Captain Carroway had first walked onto The Wanderlust, she'd never expected to see it that way. But now, with the whole crew at attention, the bridge was downright crowded.

The Norwegian Forest cat hoped the Zakonraptors would answer her hail. She wanted them to see her crew, imagining of course that they were on a much large ship, flanked by a whole fleet of backup. She wanted to look at their faces and tell them to back down.

Instead, Captain Carroway kept watching the forest fires crawl over the Waykeeper's back, burning down the forest to bare shell in some places. It was horrific. It needed to stop.

Captain Carroway raised a paw, ready to order Ensign Mike to deploy the attack phase of the holograms. The holograms would be less impressive if they weren't accompanied by an angry speech, but maybe they would work anyway.

Then a Zakonraptor answered their hail.

A scaly green face framed by yellow feathers appeared on The Wanderlust's viewscreen, replacing the image of the wounded world turtle. The Zakonraptor looked a little like Ensign Risqua—half Avioran and half Reptassan. Except, Risqua had a beak on her scaly face framed by red and blue feathers. This Zakonraptor had more of a snout. Behind the Zakonraptor in the front were more of the dinosaur-like aliens, each with differently colored feathers and scales. They made for a riotously colorful crew. Perhaps more importantly, though, they all looked large, strong, and like they probably had very sharp teeth and claws.

Compared to the Zakonraptors on their screen, the crew of The Wanderlust looked like a small collection of harmless, fuzzy mammals, a delicate songbird, and a funny little toadstool.

Captain Carroway didn't like feeling small. She wasn't used to it, being one of the biggest cats around.

Drawing a deep breath, Captain Carroway prepared to put Ensign Melbourne's work with the shipboard computer's translation algorithms to work. "Greetings," the Norwegian Forest cat meowed, standing up as tall as she could without actually rising to her tiptoes. "I'm Captain Carroway of the Tri-Galactic Union peace-keeping fleet." It felt strange to embellish her position, but the words she said needed to match the images that the Zakonraptors were about to see. Besides, everything in her body was screaming at her to puff herself up, fluff her fur out, and appear as big as possible in every possible way.

Keeping herself steady, Captain Carroway held one paw out to her side, low down where it wouldn't seem important to the Zakonraptor on the screen and gestured in a way she'd already arranged as a signal with Lt. Cmdr. Vossie. The Morphican, off to the side of the bridge and only barely visible in Captain Carroway's line of sight as she stared down the dinosaur alien on her screen, nodded almost imperceptibly.

The external lumo-projectors were already on, and The

Wanderlust itself had already been shrouded in a hologram that made it look much larger and even more well-armed than it really was. But now, the holographic projections that Lt. Cmdr. Vossie and Ensign Mike had designed flew into place beside The Wanderlust. Now, it looked like The Wanderlust was surrounded by whole fleet.

"We want to know why you're attacking this seemingly helpless world turtle," Captain Carroway meowed, all sweetness on the top but with an undercurrent of menace underneath, like a crème brûlée where the sugar crust covered a poison-laced custard.

The Zakonraptor tilted its spade-shaped head, feathers at the side of its face flaring in and out as if matching the pattern of its breathing. It blinked wide yellow eyes. Then finally, the alien dinosaur hissed, revealing a long, black, forked tongue. "Never heard of you," the Zakonraptor snapped, each word a resounding roar. "None of your business."

Well, at least, Captain Carroway thought, this meant the translation algorithms were working. Which was good. But the Zakonraptor's initial reaction to her attempts to intimidate them wasn't a good sign for the likelihood of their fleet backing down easily. Fortunately, even though Captain Carroway didn't really have a whole fleet to back her up, the one ship she did have was extremely well-armed for its size.

"I can't let you keep attacking a helpless turtle," Captain Carroway meowed. This time, the tone of her voice had hardened from burnt sugar to cold steel. "If you don't back off, I'll be forced to order my fleet to attack."

The Zakonraptor on the screen hissed in a way that might have been laughter. Captain Carroway wasn't sure. The dinosaur might have been expressing any feeling from mirth to fear. She hoped the Zakonraptor was afraid. But she feared it was only amused...

"You want the turtle for yourself?" the Zakonraptor roared. "Want to fight for it?"

To the Norwegian Forest cat's horror, the alien dinosaur looked almost excited about the idea of fighting over possession of the world turtle. "I want the turtle to be free to continue on its way, unmolested," Captain Carroway meowed, narrowing her eyes.

But then the Norwegian Forest cat felt her golden-mantled squirrel first officer, small beside her, lean against her and whisper, too low to be heard by anyone else, "This bully won't understand that. You need to claim the turtle for yourself."

Captain Carroway faltered, breaking eye contact with the disturbing dinosaur on her viewscreen to glance down at the squirrel beside her. Commander Chestnut was so much smaller than her, facing a fearsome alien larger than even the largest dogs, but he seemed completely steady, totally unfazed. Absolutely sure of himself.

Captain Carroway didn't like lying, but it was something she was already having to do. If another lie would help sell the whole deception, then so be it. "Yes, you're right," the Norwegian Forest cat meowed savagely at the dinosaur, baring her fangs as much as possible. "This world turtle is mine. I claim it in the name of the Tri-Galactic Union. You and all of your *little friends* better back away and stop messing with *my* property."

Captain Carroway couldn't help glancing down at the golden-mantled squirrel to see what he thought of her ruse. Commander Chestnut smiled, his eyes sparkling. She'd done well in his estimation.

The Zakonraptor looked nonplussed.

Captain Carroway decided it was better to press her advantage than to give the dinosaur extra time to think. So, the Norwegian Forest cat added, voice dripping with cruelty, as if she couldn't wait to barbecue some dinosaurs, "Do you need a demonstration of my fleet's might? Or would you like to get out of here with your tails intact? You do have tails, don't you?" She did her best to make it sound like there couldn't possibly be a worse, more scathing insult than to suggest an animal might not have a tail.

The Zakonraptor's image disappeared from the main viewscreen, returning the panoramic view of the world turtle with forest fires crawling along its curved back. None of the Zakonraptor ships were obviously leaving.

Captain Carroway looked down at Commander Chestnut. "Should we give them a minute, do you think?" the Norwegian Forest cat asked. "Or should we release some electron torpedoes in a wide spread to give them a taste of what they might be facing?"

"If we fire," Commander Chestnut said, as serious as he'd ever sounded, "we need to fire on one of their ships. No warning shots. No weakness. They need to believe we'll be utterly ruthless with them, if we really want to scare them away."

Captain Carroway nodded at the golden-mantled squirrel. She could follow his logic. She didn't like it. It was the logic of a terrorist. But it rang true.

Even so, the Norwegian Forest cat didn't want any more deaths on her conscience this week. But then... She didn't know how many Ollallans were perishing in the forest fires spreading across the turtle's back as she and the representative Zakonraptor postured at each other and sized each other up.

The small vessels were still firing on the turtle. She could see the red beams of their energy weapons slicing through the darkness of space and kindling more of the beautiful, phosphorescent forest into blazing fires. Her words hadn't stopped the Zakonraptors. So, action would be needed.

"Lt. Cmdr. Vossie, fire on the nearest Zakonraptor vessel with an electron torpedo," Captain Carroway ordered. Her paws went cold and numb beneath her, and her head felt floaty and dissociative giving such an order. She didn't want to be a war captain. She didn't want to order deaths. "Aim for their blazor canons. Try to damage them, not destroy them."

"I'll see what I can do," Lt. Cmdr. Vossie said. His voice

sounded a little shaky, like he wasn't prepared for handling blood on his paws today either. "But I can't make any promises, as I've never seen a schematic for these ships."

"Do your best," Captain Carroway said. She didn't need to say any more. The Morphican's best, even without his computer implant, would always be good enough for her.

Lt. Cmdr. Vossie took careful aim and fired.

CHAPTER 21
A STRANGE, NEW LAND

The electron torpedo flew away from The Wanderlust, shining like a tiny, shooting star on the main viewscreen. From the outside, it looked like it emerged from the armaments of a much larger, much more dangerous ship. In the blink of an eye, the torpedo collided with the closest Zakonraptor vessel, and the small ship erupted with fire that mirrored the fires it had been lighting below. Though, of course, unlike the fires on the turtle's back, this fire didn't last long, fueled only by whatever air had been aboard the section of the ship that was breached by the electron torpedo's explosion.

When the blast of fire died down, a cratered hole was left in the side of the vessel where its blazor canons had been. The Zakonraptors aboard the ship would be lucky if they could still fly away. They'd be lucky if they were all still alive.

"I guess their shields weren't designed with Tri-Galactic Union electron torpedoes in mind," Ensign Melbourne meowed soberly.

"A lucky hit," Lt. Cmdr. Vossie corrected. "And I don't think we'll be as lucky if we have to fire a second time. They'll reconfigure their shields quickly now that they know what to expect."

"The Zakonraptors are hailing us now," Ensign Diaz barked, sounding pleased to have the power tilted in her ship's direction, at least for the moment.

"Answer the hail," Captain Carroway meowed. She'd been running quick calculations in her head, trying to figure out if they could take the whole Zakonraptor fleet down, if they moved quickly enough. But the numbers just didn't add up. At best, they could take down half of them. No matter how she moved the ships around in her mind, no matter how she imagined it playing out, if they went for an all out fight, The Wanderlust would go down. Her crew would die.

But... at least they would die defending something peaceful and beautiful. It would be a noble sacrifice.

It would also be the easy way out.

Captain Carroway wouldn't have to face the weeks and months of holding this crew together, making sure it stayed blended into one cohesive whole instead of falling to mutiny and division. She wouldn't have to keep trying to remember what Maple's face had looked like, when she'd seen the squirrel briefly in the background of The Last Chance's bridge when she'd first talked to Chestnut over her viewscreen. She wouldn't have to keep stopping herself from asking the Anti-Ra officers if they had any pictures of Wilder for her to look at, so she could see who she had killed.

Of course, they wouldn't have any pictures with them. But sometime soon, they would need to download all the data from The Last Chance's computers to The Wanderlust. And then, would Captain Carroway be able to stop herself from staring for hours at photographs of Wilder and Maple before they died, wondering about what their lives would be like, going forward, if a ruthless Norwegian Forest cat hadn't ordered a vacuum bomb to be fired.

The Zakonraptor's face reappeared on the viewscreen. Though, actually, from the color of this one's feathers—orange and purple—Captain Carroway could tell she was dealing with a different Zakonraptor. In fact, based on the shape of the bridge, it looked like she was speaking to a Zakonraptor on an entirely different vessel.

"No more firing," the Zakonraptor roared. "We leave. You win. *But not forever.*"

Captain Carroway skewed her ears and couldn't help asking, "Did you mean to say that last part out loud?"

"Is *threat,*" the Zakonraptor snarled, its feathers flaring aggressively.

But then the Zakonraptor's image disappeared from the viewscreen, replaced once again by a view of the turtle. This time, the Zakonraptor ships were clearly flying away as quickly as they could, configuring themselves into a loose formation as they fled.

"Well, that was ominous," Commander Chestnut observed.

"They'll be back with friends," Captain Carroway said, interpreting the Zakonraptors threat. She felt very tired. "So, we've probably only given this helpless world turtle and its inhabitants a brief reprieve. And next time, illusions probably won't be enough to chase them away."

"By next time," Ensign Risqua asked, "won't we be long gone? Well on our way home?" The reptile-bird really did look so small and delicate, completely unthreatening compared to the Zakonraptors.

Captain Carroway felt every eye on the bridge turn toward her. Every eye on the ship. This wasn't the kind of question that had multiple correct answers. But there were multiple possible ways to phrase the correct answer, ways to skew it a little, give herself a bit of wiggle-room in how she interpreted it. "That is the hope," Captain Carroway meowed. "But first, let's see what we can learn from the Ollallans and this Korvax individual. And maybe, while we're learning from them about the Tetra Galaxy, we'll be able to also teach them something that will help protect them better from the next attack they might face."

"Speak of the devil..." Ensign Diaz woofed softly to herself, followed by announcing more loudly, "We're being hailed by Korvax again."

"Put him onscreen," Captain Carroway meowed, and when the alien hedgehog's funny, pointy, little face appeared, she actually smiled at seeing him.

"You did it! You did it!" Korvax squeaked, literally hopping up and down, cheering. He was such a round, prickly little fellow that he looked something like a pinecone bouncing down a hillside. "You drove them away! Oh, thank you so much! The Ollallans and I are ever so grateful!"

Captain Carroway bowed her head in acknowledgement of the praise, then meowed, "About that, Korvax, we could use some guidance, as we're new to this corner of the universe."

"Guidance?" the hedgehog squeaked, his eyes brightening as if he couldn't believe his luck. "You need a guide? I can be your guide!"

Captain Carroway's ears skewed and twisted about, completely unable to disguise her surprise at the hedgehog's enthusiastic response to a job offer that she hadn't meant to make. "No, I mean, we could use maps, information... an idea of what to expect during our travels."

"I can give you all those things!"

Somehow, Captain Carroway's attempts to correct course weren't working. Regardless, for now, what she, her crew, and The Wanderlust really needed was a place to land, take stock, see if they could salvage anything useful from The Last Chance, and generally get their bearings before forging ahead into an unknown galaxy. "Why don't we start by having your ship guide ours down to a good, safe location on the Waykeeper's back where we can land and meet some of these Ollallans you've been telling us about." Perhaps, Captain Carroway thought, she'd have better luck working with the Ollallans than with this hedgehog alien who seemed to have nominated himself as spokesperson for them.

"Yes! Yes! Wonderful idea!" Korvax agreed, grabbing a bright green sphere that had been lodged on the end of one of his quills and moving it to a peg sticking out of the console in front of him. Apparently, it was a knob for one of the controls. What it had been doing on the end of one of his quills was anyone's guess.

Without further ado, Korvax kicked his little ship into gear, which kind of surprised Captain Carroway. She'd halfway expected him to start singing some sort of "Follow Me Down to the Turtle's Back" song. Instead, his face disappeared from the viewscreen, and when the turtle's back reappeared, this time, a tiny orb of a ship—barely a shuttlecraft, really, almost more of an escape pod—came zipping up from where it had been hiding just beneath the lip of the turtle's shell.

The orb ship was bronze in color, and it zipped around erratically, causing Captain Carroway to question Korvax's skills as a pilot. She skewed an ear to the side but didn't plan to say anything.

Ensign Diaz wasn't so restrained: "Is he drunk?" the Xolo-Lupinian barked. "*Who* flies like that?"

"I guess, our new spiky friend does," Ensign Melbourne meowed drily, doing his best to pilot their much larger vessel in a path that would follow Korvax's drunken orb ship without quite so many sharp turns and sudden veers. Given that The Wanderlust was towing an entire second vessel behind her, they couldn't really afford to fly as erratically as Korvax. The Last Chance would have been yanked around by the energy beam holding it in place behind The Wanderlust, straining both vessels. Fortunately, the white tomcat was a better pilot than a charmer, and he was pretty charming, no matter how much no one else would want to admit it.

The turtle's back grew on the viewscreen until it was the entire view. From one end of the screen to the other, all the could be seen was the rumpled, crenelated tops of trees, glowing with their gentle green phosphorescence. There were no rivers, no lakes, no mountains. Just a dappled forest that spread from one edge of the Waykeeper's shell to the other, dense with trees.

Watching the forest grow closer, Captain Carroway began to worry that there wouldn't be a clearing large enough for The Wanderlust to set down, especially while towing The Last Chance. Korvax's ship was so small, perhaps it could sneak between the trees. But The Wanderlust would need a clearing.

"Hold up," Captain Carroway started to say, raising a paw into the air in front of her, as if she could slow The Wanderlust down just by pressing against the air in front of her. But then she saw the clearing they were aiming for—a darker patch on the turtle's back. All of the light came from the phosphorescent leaves of the trees, so it made sense, upon reflection, that a clearing would look like little more than a shadow. "Never mind," Captain Carroway corrected herself as Ensign Melbourne looked over his shoulder, checking if there was going to be a follow-up order.

As The Wanderlust settled over the shadow where she was meant to land, all the members of The Wanderlust's crew watched the viewscreen in awe. They all had different back-grounds and had done different amounts of exploring in their home galaxies, but none of them had ever had the chance to see a world like this one. Even Ensign Mike—whose memory had been seeded with The Wanderlust's entire computer database, full of more information than most individuals could read in a lifetime—had never seen anything like the Waykeeper's forests before.

From a distance, the forest glowed as one expanse of gentle green light, like the shallow edge of an ocean reflecting moon-light. But close up, the individual trees became clear, and there were so many different ones, each a slightly different shade or brightness. Altogether, the trees looked like they dripped with emeralds, peridots, opals, and topaz, with bright white light shining up from beneath them, reflecting and refracting through all the gemstones' complicated facets, shining in every shade of springtime and summer. But even closer still, the illusion of gemstones fell away—it became heartachingly clear that the light emanated from the leaves themselves.

The trees' leaves glowed with a delicate organic light, sketching out their veins in scribbles of brightness and fluttering in intensity, lightening and darkening just barely perceptibly with the rhythm of life—heartbeat, breath, respiration, or metabolism, whatever it was that ruled the gentle fluctuations in the light was deeply biological, and every creature on The Wanderlust could feel it. A profound peacefulness washed over the crew of The Wanderlust in the form of soft green light.

Above the trees, winged creatures flew. From above, they'd been only shadows, blocking out the phosphorescent light, but now that The Wanderlust was landed, the light shone upward on their wings, revealing bright patterns of color—all the colors of the rainbow, arranged in intricate, complicated, aesthetically pleasing patterns. Reds, golds, blues, violets, all mixed up and fractal. These creatures could have been stained-glass windows come to life for all the vividness of their wings. They were butterflies if butterflies had been recreated, making them more perfect, over and over again for a thousand times. They floated above the treetops, dancing together or soaring alone, moving with the delicate grace of a poem whose lines and rhymes are so close to perfect that the minuscule amount they fall short— breaking the rhythm, slanting the rhymes—guarantees you'll remember the words forever, longer than you'll remember the details of your own life.

For several heartbeats, the crew of The Wanderlust all stared at the viewscreen in silence, unable or unwilling to break the beautiful scenery's spell with the crudeness of language. This was a place that existed before language, more primal than organized thought. It almost felt like the trees were whispering to them, singing about feelings that were too pure to exist in the normal world, shining those lullabies directly into their hearts.

"Wow," Ensign Melbourne breathed. Of course he was the

one to break the spell. The tomcat loved to hear himself speak, even more than he loved to listen to the silent stirrings of paradise itself.

Captain Carroway didn't believe in an afterlife—heaven or otherwise. She'd read about ancient human mythologies, from way back before cats and dogs had even been uplifted. Eden. The other side of the Rainbow Bridge. They all sounded silly to her. Or at least, they had until now.

Now, the Norwegian Forest cat found herself wondering if heaven had existed in their universe all along, but it had been flying hidden through the darkness between galaxies, populated only by angels.

Well, angels and Korvax.

"I can see why the Zakonraptors wanted to claim this place for themselves," Ensign Risqua whistled, the words coming out with the musical tones of birdsong.

"They weren't claiming it," Commander Chestnut corrected, still gazing lovingly at the scene on the viewscreen. "They were burning it down."

Captain Carroway glanced at the back of the bridge, checking on the crew members behind her, just quickly enough to see the reptile-bird shrug her winglike arms.

"We should go out there," Ensign Werik said. "Explore." Eagerness filled the Morphican's voice.

Captain Carroway looked toward her other Morphican officer—the one she'd known longer, the one she trusted—and he nodded in agreement. The Norwegian Forest cat knew she *should* have looked to Commander Chestnut—her actual first officer—for confirmation, but she barely knew him. Somewhere in her heart, she hadn't really accepted that he'd replaced Lt. Cmdr. Vossie in the first officer position. She would have to get over that. Soon. And permanently. She couldn't afford to be sending mixed signals.

But she also couldn't afford to falter right now, and it was

Vossie she trusted to warn her if she was about to step on unsteady ground.

The back of a giant turtle's shell felt like unsteady ground. But it was time to step upon it. Time to set paw to this strange, new land.

CHAPTER 22
THE LIVING, BREATHING FOREST

Under normal circumstances, Captain Carroway would never have stood for leaving her brand new ship totally empty on an alien world. But there hadn't been anything normal in her life since she'd stepped aboard The Wanderlust. Everything had just been getting weirder and weirder, and she needed to roll with it or she'd break apart, shattering into a million pieces.

Realistically, Captain Carroway hadn't known any of the Anti-Ra officers long enough to trust them not to suddenly up and decide to steal her spaceship. But she could rely on the fact that they needed her and the other union officers to effectively fly The Wanderlust all the way home just as much as she and the union officers needed them.

And when it came to the possibility of the Ollallans—who seemed to be sentient butterfly-like aliens—stealing The Wanderlust? Or even Korvax? Well, Captain Carroway would just have to trust that either the Ollallans and Korvax were as peaceful as they seemed or that her small crew would be able to fight back and take care of themselves. You can't be on guard all the time. Especially this far from home. They had no safe port. Nowhere they could expect to rest and regroup for many months to come.

They would have to take what passed for rest and recreation when they happened on it, and this world was too beautiful for Captain Carroway to keep any of her officers locked aboard the ship playing at guard duty. They all deserved a chance to see the world of the Waykeeper first hand.

So, with Ensign Mike's help, Captain Carroway locked down The Wanderlust's computers to only respond to orders from higher officers—which meant her, Commander Chestnut, Lt. Cmdr. Vossie, and Lt. Lee—until further notice, and then she accompanied her entire crew outside.

The group of animals and one ambulatory mushroom walked down an extendable plank from The Wanderlust's main airlock, breathing air that felt crisp and clean, swirling with complex but subtle scents—dew and loam, greenery and the perfume of fruits or flowers, unrecognizable smells and scents that could have wafted straight out of any forest on Earth. Captain Carroway shivered all the way down her spine as a gentle breeze stirred the long fur that flowed from the sides of her face over the shoulders of her uniform. Her tail twitched apprehensively, but in spite of her profound awareness of the necessity of caution, the Norwegian Forest cat couldn't deny an underlying sense of elation.

She had discovered a whole new world.

How many cats could say that? How many cats would ever do something as amazing as that? As large? As important?

And sure, the world had been here all along, flying through the far reaches of the cosmos. This turtle didn't need her discovery of it as any sort of validation, but even so, she was the first cat to ever step paw onto the back of an actual honest-to-fishes real life world turtle. And she felt good about that.

The ground felt good under her paws. Mossy, springy, soft and real. In spite of the pleasantly low gravity, there was nothing unsteady about standing on the back of the Waykeeper. She couldn't feel the turtle's shell swaying under paw. She could barely see the sky through the glow of the forest canopy above her, but what she could see was a plain black expanse, which ought to have been unnerving—showing just how far away they were from even the nearest stars—but instead, it just looked like the sky above a busy city bursting with lights so bright they washed out the stars in the sky.

"Maybe we should just stay here... forever," Ensign Melbourne meowed pensively as he stepped lightly down on the loamy ground beside Captain Carroway. The second cat to set paw to the back of a world turtle.

But Captain Carroway had been the first. She'd seen to that. She'd led the way. There ought to be some privileges that came bundled with the crushing responsibilities of leadership.

"You don't care about getting home?" Ensign Diaz barked derisively at the white tomcat. She didn't know his background. She didn't know how much better he had things out here in the middle of nowhere.

Ensign Melbourne shrugged and smiled roguishly, passing his suggestion off as a joke. It hadn't been. Captain Carroway knew that. But she also suspected Timothy Melbourne would cooperate with getting back aboard The Wanderlust when it was time to leave. He was a pilot down to the marrow in his bones. He wouldn't be able to resist flying away when the time came.

But Captain Carroway took his comment as the warning it was: she would need to watch closely to make sure none of her other officers tried to defect and stay here. In paradise. The Wanderlust couldn't afford to begin hemorrhaging officers this early in her journey home.

"Welcome, welcome, welcome!" a familiar voice squeaked, followed by the shuffling appearance of its owner, Korvax, hurrying toward them, practically bouncing in the low gravity. A bouncing ball of spikes. The hedgehog alien had set his tiny ship down right beside theirs. "I messaged ahead! My friends are waiting for you! They're so grateful! You must come!" Korvax gestured with his strangely delicate paws—more hand-like than most paws—towards a path that led from the darkened clearing into the much brighter forest.

It felt very backwards to Captain Carroway for the crowded parts of the forest, thick with trees, to be brighter than the open clearings. It came naturally from the fact that the trees were essentially lanterns, the only source of light here. Or at least the main one. As Captain Carroway's feline eyes adjusted to the ebb and flow of light, she noticed that the ground glowed dimly too. Peering down at her paws, she saw tiny blades of grass shining brightly under the loam of fallen leaves and pine needles. Some of the glowing trees in the forest around them were coniferous and while their needles glowed brightly on their branches, the needles lost their shine when they lay discarded on the ground. Still, the living plants beneath the loam of leaves and needles added a dim light to the clearing.

The grass and moss seemed to glow even more brightly wherever one of Captain Carroway's crew stepped, leaving tracks of glowing paw prints wherever they walked. The Norwegian Forest cat wasn't an expert on biology, though of course, every cadet at the Tri-Galactic Union Academy had to take at least introductory courses to all of the sciences. However, she would have expected a phosphorescent plant to react in the opposite way to being stepped upon—by dimming its glow, crushed under the weight of a paw. There was something truly magical about how the forest floor here brightened for them, as if welcoming them, encouraging them to step farther in, promising they could find their way back by following a glowing path. It was beautiful, but it seemed too good to be true. Almost deceptive, like old fairy tales where children followed paths of crumbled gingerbread to find their way home.

Captain Carroway felt like she'd stepped into a fairy tale, and she wasn't used to that feeling. Usually, her life was a series of vignettes interspersed with high stakes, high stress action sequences. Maybe science procedurals. Not fairy tales. Those were for kittens, and she'd grown up long ago.

Being on the back of a giant turtle who was swimming through the depths of the cosmos made Captain Carroway feel young again. She didn't feel like Captain Carroway here. She just felt like Janessa, a cat with dreams and ambitions and a very silly crush on a golden-mantled squirrel that it would be entirely inappropriate for her to ever act on.

The crew of The Wanderlust followed Korvax as he wended his way through the glowing forest. Commander Chestnut looked like he belonged here, completely at home surrounded by trees. Captain Carroway thought any squirrel might look the way. And Ensign Risqua, with her feathered, wing-like arms, almost looked like she'd be able to fly. Either one of them might decide that staying here was better than the uncertain journey that laid ahead of them.

As they walked, Captain Carroway watched the shadows between trees, listening to the scurrying sounds of footsteps and concealed voices giggling, trying to make out any glimpse of the creatures causing the noise. The Norwegian Forest cat didn't think that butterfly-like aliens with their wide, delicate wings would scurry through the shadows of the forest floor, hiding and laughing, especially not when the gravity here must make it so easy for them to fly. But then, perhaps what she was hearing wasn't laughter. Perhaps it was just the sound of an alien crea-ture, just an animal in the forest.

Hurrying her pawsteps, Captain Carroway brought herself up beside the fast-moving hedgehog alien. He moved surpris-ingly quickly for how short, round, and stubby he was.

"Korvax," the Norwegian Forest cat meowed, trying to get their guide's attention. He wasn't what she would have hoped for from a guide, but he was the guide they had for now. The only contact they'd made so far, and she wanted to begin learning what she could immediately. "We saw beings in the sky —beings with colorful wings—are those the Ollallans?"

The hedgehog alien slowed down, just a little, seemingly surprised by the Norwegian Forest cat's question. "Well, of course," he replied jovially. His pointy nose twisting sideways with his smile. "Who else would they be? But then... I suppose, they're also not quite the Ollallans."

Captain Carroway's ears skewed in perplexity and irritation. She now felt like she knew less than she had before asking her question. "Explain yourself," she said, using all of her restraint to keep from snapping or growling the words.

"Well, now, you see, we can't quite pronounce the word for who they are," Korvax looked over at the captain walking beside him and smiled in a tilted way, twitching his pointy nose to one side. "At least, I can't, and your mouth looks enough like mine, and your voice sounds enough like mine that you probably can't either."

Captain Carroway thought her voice was quite a bit less annoyingly squeaky than Korvax's, but she didn't think it would be helpful or diplomatic to say so. "Can you describe who they are then?"

"They're what the Ollallans become after entering their chrysalis forms and metamorphosing," Korvax said.

Captain Carroway's ears pricked up tall again. "Then the Ollallans are like caterpillars? And the beings we saw are the adults?" The Norwegian Forest cat peered harder at the shadows in the forest around them, trying once again to spot one of the giggling creatures. She was very intrigued by the idea that they had a complicated life cycle with multiple parts. This was exactly the kind of strange, alien discovery that a Tri-Galactic Union captain dreams of making.

"Yes, yes, the Ollallans are like children," Korvax said. "But also not."

In spite of her delight at the concepts she was hearing about, Captain Carroway couldn't help one of her ears skewing back at the hedgehog's hedging. She really wished they'd happened upon a different guide. "How do you mean?" she snapped.

Fortunately, Korvax didn't seem at all fazed by having a much larger mammal snap at him. Captain Carroway supposed that a certain amount of security came along with having most of your body covered in prickly spines. Korvax didn't seem easily upset. Except, of course, by having his entire world attacked, and that would upset anyone.

"The Ollallans have an entire civilization of their own down here, on the shell, beneath the glowing boughs," Korvax said, suddenly waxing poetic. "Their elders live separately mostly. Above the branches. So, it's a sort of childhood, but not the kind of helpless, cared for, looked after childhood that my people have, er, had."

The hedgehog smiled weakly as he corrected himself to the past tense. Captain Carroway imagined there was an entire story there, which she most definitely didn't want to ask about. Then she remembered what Korvax had said earlier about the Zakon-raptors destroying his homeworld. The Norwegian Forest cat did her best to smile back sympathetically.

As they walked, the trees began to change—instead of growing wild and free, their branches looked ever more curated, like they'd been trained to grow in particular patterns. Eventually, even though they were still walking through a forest, Captain Carroway realized they were now walking past buildings. Entire cozy cottages had been woven out of living branches. And then, suddenly, the captain looked up and realized, they weren't outside anymore. The forest canopy above them had been woven together into an intricate, complicated, and extremely beautiful ceiling—vibrant, alive, and glowing.

Beneath Captain Carroway's paws was the back of a turtle, and above her head was a forest woven together into an entire, enclosed village. She was utterly surrounded by life. There was something profoundly cozy and comforting about the sensation of being completely surrounded. A small part of Captain Carroway's brain was surprised that she didn't find the sensation confining or claustrophobia inducing. But it didn't feel that way at all. Just... peaceful.

Deep in her throat, Captain Carroway realized, she was already purring. She didn't remember when that had begun.

Elsewhere on the Waykeeper's back, these forests were burning. Right now, Captain Carroway couldn't imagine a much more horrendous crime than burning down this concatenation of pure, raw life and carefully tended, stewarded, crafted art made from that life. It was a truly, singularly heartless thing to burn down a forest like this one that was at once alive, a home, and a work of art.

At last, Korvax's guidance brought the motley crew of The Wanderlust to a great hallway with a long table set out in the middle—or rather, it seemed to be constructed from a tree trunk that grew up out of the ground, bent over, and travelled along the ground for some distance before turning upward, tapering to a much thinner width and rising to where it joined the tangle of complicated branches that made up the ceiling. Somewhere, along the way, the crew of The Wanderlust had passed from walking between buildings to being inside of one. The line between inside and outside here had a way of becoming unclear. Regardless, this table was heaped high with bowls of sumptuous-looking foods, and all around the table stood the giggling creatures who Captain Carroway had been straining so hard to find.

Now that Captain Carroway could see a group of Ollallans clearly, she could see why she'd had so much trouble spotting them before.

The Ollallans were long, pudgy, yellow-green worm creatures. Each one had a row of short, stubby limbs running down each side—hands that became feet at some point, although the point when that happened was unclear. So, the Ollallans could rear up and stand nearly as tall as Captain Carroway, using only a few of their lowest limbs as feet, or they could snake more of their lower body along the ground, becoming shorter but steadier, trading hands for more feet. They were very like caterpillars with nearly translucent green skin, speckled with tiny yellow spikes. Though, some of them had darker green spikes or even black or white ones, but most of them had skin in some shade or another of green. They blended in beautifully with the glowing leaves that covered all the walls and ceilings of their home. Perfectly camou-flaged. And they were, most definitely, giggling at the funny mammals—and one fungus—who had come to visit them.

CHAPTER 23
ONE MEAL IN PARADISE

Korvax bustled about, arranging all of the visitors to his adopted world into seats at the long table, alternated with local Ollallans, so that everyone could talk together while they ate.

The feast proved to consist mostly of sugar-crusted leaves, stewed fruits, and nut casseroles. Commander Chestnut, the two Morphicans, and Ensign Risqua seemed delighted by the fare, and to be fair, everything that Captain Carroway tasted was delicious. However, cats were originally obligate carnivores before humans uplifted them, and plant matter is not their preferred form of food. Canines are often more flexible, being omnivorous, but Ensign Diaz didn't seem much more thrilled by the feast than either Ensign Melbourne or Captain Carroway. How Lt. Lee felt about the food was something that the Papillon was keeping tightly to himself, being far too polite to express anything but gratitude in front of their hosts.

When Captain Carroway got a moment to watch Ensign Mike, extremely curious about whether the fungal officer ate at all, she spied them trying a variety of the available foods. So apparently, they at least *could* eat. But she didn't know how they felt about any of it, because they were a sentient mushroom. The first of their kind. And Captain Carroway had no idea how to read their emotions on their weird, bearded face on the underside of their toadstool cap.

Once Korvax finally settled down and joined the others in sitting down, he sat beside Captain Carroway. Clearly not a coincidence.

"Perhaps you can introduce me to the leader of this lovely... location," Captain Carroway purred at the hedgehog.

"Oh, there are no leaders here," an Ollallan on Captain Carroway's other side said.

The comm-pins that every Tri-Galactic Union officer wore on the breasts of their uniforms were already translating the Ollallans' speech perfectly. The caterpillar-like beings had been gossiping and giggling more than enough for the translation algorithms embedded in the comm-pins to have already picked up their language.

"Oh?" Captain Carroway asked, trying to express curiosity rather than disappointment. Though she was feeling both. "Then where are they?"

"In the sky, of course!" the Ollallan answered mirthfully, as if any child would know that. Her face with all its complicated, wriggling mouthparts twisted into what must have been her species' version of a smile.

"This is my oldest and dearest friend here," Korvax said to Captain Carroway, indicating the Ollallan who had been speaking to her. "Her name is Lys, and I've been looking out for her since before she even hatched from her egg. I was friends with her mother even before that."

"Is your mother... in the sky, Lys?" Captain Carroway asked, wondering if there was some way for her to switch from talking to children to actually talking with adults.

"No," Lys answered sadly. "My mother dances no more. She died years ago."

It was strange, Captain Carroway realized, how easily this completely alien being communicated her emotions, in spite of her entirely different physiognomy. It made the Norwegian Forest cat wonder if the Ollallans had a touch of telepathy to them—perhaps only a small, weak amount, just enough to broadcast their feelings.

"I'm sorry to hear about your mother," Captain Carroway meowed, thinking quickly, trying to figure out how family dynamics worked here. It didn't sound like it was the same as among most mammals, but then, Lys did sound genuinely sad about her mother. So perhaps, even if the bond between parents and children wasn't the same with Ollallans as with cats, dogs, and the like, there must be some kind of meaningful connection. "Would you like to tell me about her?"

Lys's wriggling mouth parts fisted up, and her long sinewy length coiled up like a spring. She seemed uncertain of what to say—or perhaps, whether to say the thing she was about to say.

"Go ahead," Korvax encouraged his friend. "Tell her. You've waited so long."

"You have green eyes," Lys said, pointing with a pudgy finger on one of her many stubby hands at Captain Carroway's face.

The Norwegian Forest cat blinked. She hadn't expected to be talking about her eyes. But yes, they were green. Bright green. Emerald green. Not unusual among cats, but unusual enough among dogs—who tended to have more of the high-ranking positions in the Tri-Galactic Union—that they'd been commented on enough during her life that they'd become a big part of the captain's identity. "Yes, I do have green eyes," Captain Carroway agreed with the alien whose own eyes were more like photo-sensitive brown spots on her translucent skin than actual, fully-formed eyes. "What about them?"

"I've been waiting for you," Lys said. "My whole life. My mother told me you'd come. She told me about your green eyes."

"That's impossible," Captain Carroway meowed. "It doesn't make any sense."

"And yet, you're here," Lys replied. "And you have green eyes."

Captain Carroway couldn't argue with that. She didn't know how. She wouldn't even know where to start.

"And you saved our world, just like my mother told me you would." Lys's wriggly mouthparts twisted into that strange smile again. It was a sweet, naive, simple expression, in spite of the fact that it was made from an O-shaped mouth ringed around with tiny finger-like cilia. "And I get to meet you. Again, like she always said I would."

Now this, Captain Carroway could argue with. And she felt it was an absolute necessity that she do so. "I'm very sorry, but I don't think we've saved your world. Those Zakonraptors, more than likely, will come back, and we can't stay here to scare them away again."

"Why can't we?" Ensign Risqua squawked from farther down the table, breaking into the captain's conversation. The reptile-bird leaned forward, placing her winglike arms on the table. "It's beautiful here. Paradise. We could stay, and maybe, if we did, when the Zakonraptors came back, we could find a way to reason with them."

"I told you that Zakonraptors can't be reasoned with..." Korvax muttered.

"What about home?" Ensign Diaz woofed, keeping her voice much softer and lower than she had to. She could have barked loudly, but she chose to almost whisper the words to her fellow Anti-Ra. "What about Lupinia? What about fighting to protect it?"

"*We were losing,*" Ensign Risqua squawked, not matching the Xolo-Lupinian's volume at all. "This cat who we all call captain now was going to wipe out our entire forces. You want to go back to that?" She spread her feathered arms wide, seemingly encompassing the extent of the Anti-Ra's losses.

"I want to go back to my *family,*" Ensign Diaz woofed, unswayed by her compatriot's argument. "I want to go back to

Wilder's family and tell them he died fighting for their freedom. *I want to go home.*"

Lt. Lee's butterfly-like ears splayed, showing the first sign of discontent he'd allowed himself to express since arriving here. The Papillon woofed, "I want to go home too. My mother won't know what happened to me. She probably thinks I'm dead."

Commander Chestnut stood up at his seat, which didn't make him a whole lot taller, but even so, the golden-mantled squirrel managed to silence the growing uproar with his movement. He caught Captain Carroway's eye, recognized the look in it, nodded, and said, "Of course we're going home. All of us are going home. But that doesn't mean we need to leave the Ollallans helpless when we go."

After the golden-mantled squirrel's proclamation, the conversation turned towards strategies for protecting the Waykeeper from potential future attacks. The crew members of The Wanderlust brainstormed possibilities with the Ollallans present and also Korvax, finally settling on a plan that involved stripping parts from The Last Chance and setting up the Ollallans with a lumo-projector and a blazor canon. The blazor canon wouldn't provide enough firepower to really protect a whole world, but it would add believability to their threats if they used Ensign Mike's fleet of illusory hologram ships to scare attackers away.

In return for this, Korvax promised to provide The Wanderlust with a complete copy of his ship's computer records of his travels. Frustratingly, there wasn't any additional information that the crew of The Wanderlust could trade for from the Ollallans. As it turned out, the Ollallans—and their adult forms with an unpronounceable name that sounded a little like a soaring flute solo—hadn't really paid attention to the world outside of the Waykeeper while the turtle had flown through the Tetra Galaxy. The Ollallans and their elders were an insulated society, more focused on their own traditions of epic poetry and aesthetic gardening than on the stars that had passed by beyond the bubble of their little, cozy world. Fortunately, Korvax swore that he'd traveled quite a bit through the Tetra Galaxy before discovering the Waykeeper and settling among its people some years ago.

Captain Carroway hoped Korvax's computer records would be enough to help her crew navigate quickly and safely through this foreign galaxy. She had her concerns... but for the moment, there was nothing she could do about them.

Once the feast ended, with some officers feeling more sated than others, the Ollallans performed a choreographed dance for their visitors while one of their elders with wings like a stained glass window in a church sang in an eerie voice like a haunted woodwind instrument. The dancing Ollallans' sinuous worm-like bodies writhed in rhythmic patterns matching the song; some of them even spun silk cords, attached them to woven boughs in the ceiling, and spun through the air above the viewers gathered below in intricate acts of aerial acrobatics. It was a beautiful display, and for a brief moment—in spite of her growling stomach, as leaves are simply not a fit food for a cat, no matter how beautifully encrusted with sugar they are—Captain Carroway felt utterly content. She had taken her ship to the far side of an unexplored galaxy, established diplomatic relations with the alien race she'd found there, and now she was indulging in pleasurable cultural exchange with them. This was what the Tri-Galactic Union was supposed to be about.

When the dance came to an end, Captain Carroway hoped to catch a word with the Ollallan elder, but the mysterious winged creature flew away through a gap woven into the braided branches of the ceiling and disappeared without speaking a single understandable word. Truly, the Ollallan elders were like angels—beautiful, unnerving, and unreachable. Captain Carroway wished there would be more time to stay and reach out to them, try to build stronger bridges and learn about their culture in more depth and detail.

But the Waykeeper was traveling in the wrong direction.

The crew of The Wanderlust needed to be heading towards

home, and besides, diplomatic connections with a race of butter-fly-like aliens who the rest of the Tri-Galactic Union would likely never encounter again were of limited use.

This was a momentary connection; two ships flying past each other in the dark depths between galaxies. A brief brush of a union, infinitely meaningful and valuable, but only for what it was: a single sparkling gemstone of connection. One moment to be remembered, retold, and treasured. Not a relationship that could be ongoing. Because in a linear lifetime, sometimes one moment of connection is all you get, and it has to be enough.

Momentary but momentous.

And through it all—all the dancing, the singing, and the applause (which had to be explained to the Ollallans as it was not a shared cultural phenomenon, but which delighted the caterpillar-like beings once they heard about it, for they each had a whole row of hands to clap with)—Captain Carroway couldn't stop thinking about what Lys had said about her eyes. *Her green eyes.* How could Lys have anticipated them? How could Lys's mother have seen any of this communion between their worlds coming?

These questions itched at the back of Captain Carroway's mind, but the practicalities of coordinating work between her crew and their Ollallan hosts in order to strip the necessary parts from The Last Chance and build a permanent lumo-projector on the Waykeeper's back took up most of the space in her brain. Furthermore, The Wanderlust couldn't tow a broken ship behind her forever. So, The Last Chance needed to be stripped down entirely and divided into parts that would stay with the Ollallans and parts that could be stored on or attached to The Wanderlust. It might prove invaluable to have backup parts later on in their journey. Some things simply couldn't be replaced with synthesized parts. However, no matter how much Captain Carroway wanted to be a packrat here and bring along as much of The Last Chance along with her as possible, it's not feasible to break down a whole spaceship and fit all the broken down pieces inside another similarly-sized spaceship. But Captain Carroway kind of wished it was. She didn't know which pieces —in a month or two or three months—she would regret leaving behind.

It was surreal how Captain Carroway was standing on the back of a giant space turtle, surrounded by the most beautiful paradise she'd ever seen, with angelic, butterfly-like aliens flying in the sky above her... and her mind was crowded with mundane problems, like which officer would be best suited to teach the Ollallans how to use their new lumo-projector and how many backup batteries could be fit into various corners of the rooms in The Wanderlust without making her crew feel constantly crowded during the coming months. It felt like such a waste. She should have been absorbing every last moment of this remarkable place... but she couldn't. She had responsibilities tying her down, compelling her to keep moving forward, keep moving away from this brief, beautiful moment in time.

Finally, the moment came when all the work was done. The Last Chance was nothing more than a pile of worthless rubble, a mere skeleton of a spaceship, that The Wanderlust would tow back into space and leave floating in the endless graveyard of emptiness that this region of space would become when the Waykeeper flew away in one direction... and The Wanderlust flew away in the other.

Idly, Captain Carroway wondered where the Zakonraptors had flown away to, and whether The Wanderlust would have to deal with them again. Since they'd destroyed Korvax's home-world—a place he'd called Xantrosia, during the conversations at dinner—they must have come from inside the Tetra Galaxy and followed the Waykeeper out into this dead space between galaxies. Therefore, The Wanderlust would likely encounter Zakonraptors again, even if not the same ones.

Captain Carroway was not looking forward to that. This voyage home was going to be an ordeal, potentially very danger-ous, and without any guarantee that they would ever, actually make it home. She had a good crew, and she was doing what she'd always wanted to do—making grand discoveries and doing amazing things. But at a very deep level, she felt lost and alone out here. She'd never expected to get everything she'd ever dreamed of... but at the cost of being flung to the far side of the universe with innocent lives still hanging on her conscience. Because the more time she spent working with the Anti-Ra, listening to them talk about their homes on Lupinia, the more she felt that the Tri-Galactic Union had been in the wrong. The orders she'd been given were wrong. And the fact that she'd chosen to follow them—a choice that lay directly on her own shoulders, regardless of whatever indoctrination she'd gone through during her years with the Tri-Galactic Union—was fundamentally wrong.

She'd had no right to fire a vacuum bomb into a sun, trying to wipe out an entire nebula filled with Anti-Ra ships. And she wished, fervently, that she could go back in time and take that choice back.

CHAPTER 24
YOU CAN'T GO BACK, BUT YOU CAN GO FORWARD

When the time came to say goodbye to their Ollallan hosts, the crew of The Wanderlust lined up in front of the ramp leading up to their open airlock. A group of Ollallans lined up across from them, mimicking the crew's orderly formation. Captain Carroway felt a burst of pride that her crew was already working together so smoothly. It helped that Commander Chestnut had clearly run a tight ship, so the Anti-Ra officers had been well prepared for blending into a Tri-Galactic Union crew.

Each crew member bid their hosts farewell before turning and walking back into their ship, leaving the Ollallans behind, waving at them with many hands apiece.

Captain Carroway waited until all of the rest of her crew was back aboard to say her own farewell to the Ollallans. The Norwegian Forest cat bowed to them, and they mimicked that gesture as well, bending their snake-like bodies into sinuous curves. Captain Carroway smiled, amused to see how much more impressive a bow looked on an Ollallan body than on her own, or any other body plagued by quite so many limiting joints and bones.

Most of the Ollallans cleared away, having been warned that

they should give The Wanderlust a wide berth before her takeoff. But one stayed behind. Captain Carroway's ears skewed, wondering what the final Ollallan wanted. She had trouble telling the caterpillar-like people apart, but she suspected this one was the same one as she'd talked to at dinner.

"Lys?" Captain Carroway asked.

"Yes," the Ollallan agreed.

"You should go back into the forest," Captain Carroway purred. "My ship will be leaving soon, and I don't want you to be injured by our departure."

"You won't leave until Korvax comes," Lys countered.

It was true that Captain Carroway was still waiting on the hedgehog alien to bring her the computer bank that he'd promised to give in trade for everything The Wanderlust had done for the Waykeeper. "I'm sure he'll be here soon," the Norwegian Forest cat meowed. "You don't have to wait with me."

Trying to send Lys away felt a little rude to Captain Carroway, but the truth was that the caterpillar's talk of expecting her green eyes troubled her. There was a mysticism to it that made Captain Carroway uncomfortable, much like Commander Chestnut's devotion to trees. The golden-mantled squirrel had even insisted on asking the Ollallans if they'd let him take cuttings from a few of their trees to bring with him on The Wanderlust.

While the religious aspect of Commander Chestnut's feelings towards trees bewildered Captain Carroway, she did have to admit that keeping a live cutting from each of the types of trees they'd encountered here could be scientifically invaluable. So she'd been glad when the Ollallans agreed and helped the golden-mantled squirrel set up a few cuttings in small pots of local soil, along with providing him with instructions on how to have the best chance of keeping them alive during their journey. Besides, a few small glowing plants in the multi-purpose room would really brighten up the place and make it feel more like a home, which was good as they'd all be living there for some time.

"I do have to wait with you," Lys said, twisting up the finger-like cilia around her mouth. "I have to wait with you if I'm going to be going with you."

"Coming with me?" Captain Carroway asked, aghast. "Why would you want to come with me? We won't be returning here... ever. You would never see your home again."

"I'm ready for that," Lys said.

Even if the caterpillar alien really was ready to make such a big leap, Captain Carroway wasn't ready to aid her in doing it. Fortunately, Korvax came waddling up, holding a mechanical device that looked like it must be the promised computer bank. Hopefully, he could talk some sense into his friend.

Captain Carroway reached out for the computer box—it looked quite large and heavy for such a small mammal to carry —but Korvax shied away, holding the mechanical device closer to his chest. "Nuh uh," he said. "This doesn't leave my sight—or even my arms!—until we're on our way."

"What?!?" Captain Carroway spat, ears flattening, even more aghast than before. Sure, Korvax had joked earlier about wanting to be their guide, but certainly, he couldn't have been serious.

"We're coming with you," Korvax squeaked matter-of-factly.

"The Wanderlust is not a passenger ship," Captain Carroway argued, but neither the hedgehog nor caterpillar looked even slightly swayed. "Why would you even want to come with us?"

"I've ridden this turtle as far as I want to go," Korvax replied. "I've lived among the Ollallans for half of my life. I'm ready to move on now."

Captain Carroway could at least make sense of that. The hedgehog alien didn't actually belong here, on this turtle's back, not any more than she did or any of the rest of her crew. And his small ship wouldn't be capable of getting him all the way home to the Tetra Galaxy, not from this far out.

The Norwegian Forest cat didn't really want to invite this

vaguely obnoxious hedgehog to join her crew and live in such close quarters with an already questionably stable group. But if he wanted to return to the Tetra Galaxy... She didn't feel right leaving him behind here either.

Now, Lys was a different question. The Waykeeper truly was her native home.

"Fine," Captain Carroway meowed, wondering how quickly she'd get a chance to drop Korvax off somewhere appropriate. "You can come and be our guide. But..." The Norwegian Forest cat turned toward the caterpillar. "Lys, you can't really be serious about leaving your homeworld, your people, and everyone you know behind."

"It won't be everyone I know," Lys disagreed. "I'll still have Korvax. He's like a parent to me. At least, from what he tells me of his own people, I think that's what he's like."

"But you'll never come back here," Captain Carroway continued insistently. "We're never coming back. You can't really want to do this. Can you even understand what that really means—to never go home?"

"It means I'll be like Korvax," Lys said. The brownish eyespots on her face seemed to darken, giving her expression an intensity and fervency. "I'll be an explorer who leaves my own world behind for the joy of discovering other worlds and carrying the story of my own world out into the universe, like a seed, floating on the breeze away from its mother tree."

For a moment, Captain Carroway was sure that Lys was about to start talking about her own mother and the enigmatic prophecy about green eyes again... but somehow, the words never came. It almost felt like Lys anticipated how unwelcome those words would be and purposely held them back.

Captain Carroway could never have agreed to take Lys away from her homeworld due to some mystical prophecy that must have been sheer coincidence combined with the kind of wishful thinking that leads to assigning our fates to patterns written in the stars.

But...

She could take Lys with her if the caterpillar was making a rational decision.

And Lys seemed perfectly rational.

Like a flea biting her ear, a tiny, prickling, stinging piece of Captain Carroway's conscience screamed at her that these caterpillar people seemed to have some limited amount of telepathy, and perhaps Lys was using that power to get her way. Could Captain Carroway be sure that she wasn't being persuaded by an alien pressure inside of her own mind?

She couldn't be sure. But also, with every passing moment, staring into Lys's eyes, the danger of that possibility seemed less and less likely. This was simply the matter of a young alien who knew exactly what she wanted.

"I can't promise to take the two of you all the way back to the Milky Way with us," Captain Carroway meowed, somewhat confused to find herself folding. "I may drop you both off at the first convenient planet, but—"

"We'll take it!" Korvax squeaked with elation, his quills puffing up with his excitement. The hedgehog alien didn't wait for another word and immediately began waddling forward toward The Wanderlust's airlock.

"Thank you, Captain," Lys said, bowing her head—or at least, the uppermost portion of her tube-like body—forward respectfully. She waited to begin walking—in her inchworm-like way—up the ramp to The Wanderlust until Captain Carroway took the first step and gestured welcomingly for the Ollallan to follow.

The Norwegian Forest cat led her two strange new guests— not necessarily officers, certainly not yet—straight to the multipurpose room. She'd need to discuss with Commander Chestnut about where they should sleep. Though, her first thought was that they should be broken up—Korvax in the barracks with the Morphicans and Risqua; Lys in the barracks with Melbourne and the two canines. (Captain Carroway didn't even notice than in her accounting of the crew, she'd entirely failed to assign sleeping arrangements to Ensign Mike. The toadstool was a whole step more alien than even Lys, and somehow, it didn't occur to the Norwegian Forest cat to imagine them ever sleeping.)

Captain Carroway didn't want to find out what would happen if she put someone as annoying as Korvax in the same sleeping quarters as someone with as short of a temper as Ensign Diaz. And she didn't want to keep Lys and Korvax together. In such a small space with such a small group of people, if all the individuals couldn't find a way to work together and get along as a cohesive unit, the whole system would fall apart. And there was too much risk of Lys and Korvax keeping to themselves, becoming a disruptively separate bubble inside the larger crew if they stayed together.

"Why don't both of you stay here," Captain Carroway told the caterpillar and hedgehog, but Korvax was having none of it.

"Oh, no, no, you need me to get this computer system set up right away!" Korvax squeaked, holding the boxy mechanical device even closer to his chest, the one part of his body that wasn't covered in quills.

Looking at Korvax now, Captain Carroway wondered whether his quills were even more covered in random bits and pieces of cloth and other baubles than they had been before. Perhaps that had been the Xantrosian's idea of packing for this journey: sticking everything he'd wanted to bring with him on the ends of his quills.

Lys, on the other paw, hadn't brought anything with her. Once again, Captain Carroway questioned the wisdom of bringing such a young creature—during the first half of a bimodal life—on a journey that would never return her home. But the flare up of concern settled down quickly, like a flyaway ember, trying to start a fire but being doused with water before its spark can spread.

If Captain Carroway could have seen her own mind from the

outside in that moment, she'd have known for sure that Lys was telepathically manipulating her. But she was a cat, and for all their cleverness, they aren't actually telepathic. So, she remained unaware.

"Fine," Captain Carroway snapped at Korvax. "I'll see you to the engine room, and you can work with Ensign Diaz on installing your backup computer so that it meshes with ours."

"Backup computer?" Korvax asked, surprised and confused. "You think this is just a backup? This is my ship's core computer bank."

Captain Carroway blinked. "You stripped your ship of its computer? Entirely?"

"Well, it's not like I'm planning to come back to it again," the hedgehog sniffed, unconcerned by the idea of leaving his ship behind without any computer in it.

Captain Carroway sighed. Having Korvax aboard was going to be challenging for her. But then, so was the sentient toadstool. There were a lot of challenges involved with being the captain of a starship that had been flung to the far side of the cosmos. And every one of those challenges was a huge improvement over having died in a rapidly expanding black hole created by her own vacuum bomb. So, she'd take them all with as much composure as she could summon.

"What about me?" Lys asked sweetly as Captain Carroway turned to lead Korvax to the engine room.

The Norwegian Forest cat looked around the multi-purpose room like it would somehow provide an answer for her as to what should be done with the caterpillar. Fortunately, the multi-purpose room actually did provide an answer: Commander Chestnut had left all the cuttings from the local flora sitting on the multi-purpose room's tables. "Why don't you see if you can arrange all the potted plants in this room better, see if you can figure out a way for them to be kept that will be healthy for them and out of the way of the crew." Ideally, they'd really need an arboretum, but The Wanderlust wasn't big enough for that.

"I'll see what I can do," Lys said.

It didn't take long for Captain Carroway to install Korvax in the engine room, pawned off on Ensign Diaz who looked like she knew exactly what the Norwegian Forest cat was doing: namely, saddling the Lupinian-Xolo with babysitting duties on top of the actual work she was doing.

Then freed from her tagalongs, Captain Carroway made her way to the bridge where Commander Chestnut was sitting in her captain's chair. It was his right, as the current ranking officer on the bridge. Even so, it rankled Captain Carroway. The golden-mantled squirrel was enjoying the benefits of leadership while she was wandering around with locals who had somehow convinced her to bring them aboard as passengers.

"We're ready to disembark whenever you command it," Commander Chestnut chittered. The golden-mantled squirrel looked excited about the idea of getting back on the road—the road home, which was just a giant swath of space filled with an unknown number of obstacles.

The golden-mantled squirrel stood up from the captain's chair and gestured toward it with his tiny, delicate paws, inviting Captain Carroway to take her own seat. The Norwegian Forest cat obliged and prepared to give the order that would end her first, and potentially most exciting, mission as captain. Because what else were they going to find in the Tetra Galaxy that could compare to this giant world turtle covered in a glowing trees and a society of sentient caterpillars and butterflies?

CHAPTER 25
RETURNING TO WHERE IT ALL BEGAN

"Captain?" Ensign Melbourne meowed from the pilot's seat. "We have company."

"The Zakonraptors are back?" Captain Carroway had barely been back in her captain's seat long enough to get comfortably settled. "Already? We scared them away for less than a day?"

"I guess so," the white tomcat meowed acerbically, the tip of his tail twitching in a way that betrayed the concern his dry tone tried to belie. "We don't have any better weapons than when they were here last time, but this time it looks like there's a lot more of them. Do you think Ensign Diaz has any more ideas or clever tricks hidden up her sleeves?"

There was genuine admiration in the snarky tomcat's voice as he spoke of the Lupinian-Xolo officer. Captain Carroway almost wondered if she was hearing the start of a crush. She didn't really want to deal with the messiness of romantic relationships happening in such a small crew, in such close quarters, on such a long mission. But she supposed the possibility was inevitable. It was a problem she'd deal with when it became a problem. For now, her problem was the fleet of sharp, fierce, dangerous looking vessels that were now showing on The Wanderlust's viewscreen.

"Well, I guess we'd better get back in the sky then," Captain Carroway growled. "The last thing we want is to find ourselves trapped on the ground during a firefight." Grounded spaceships don't fight well. They also aren't good at escaping.

And if Captain Carroway was truly honest with herself, she wished she'd gotten her crew moving a little faster, so they could already be gone by now. This wasn't their fight. If they'd left one hour earlier, they wouldn't even know it was happening. They could have moved on with clear consciences, having done their best to help the Waykeeper and the Ollallans before leaving them behind forever. But now...

Now Captain Carroway felt obligated to help. But she also had an obligation to her crew, to get them home.

Being a captain was a lot. It felt like being pulled in every direction at once, all the time. She'd only been doing it for about two days, and the Norwegian Forest cat was already thinking about how she might retire early when she got her crew back home to the Milky Way. Find somewhere with lots of sunlight and spend her days communing with nature, walking through forests and watching the shadows of fish swim just under the surface of a clear lake. Something peaceful, something quiet.

Oh, who was Captain Carroway kidding? She knew herself better than that. Just because she was tired and grumpy right now didn't mean she'd ever be ready to hang her captain's pin up and give up adventure. Still, she could use a little less adventure just this minute.

The glowing forests fell away on the viewscreen as The Wanderlust began to rise up from the ground. Liftoff started slow, but as soon as the ship had cleared the glowing trees, Ensign Melbourne pushed the throttle, so to speak, as far as it would go, and The Wanderlust tore across the treetops, rising up higher and higher until it cleared the bubble of atmosphere held in by the hyperspatial slipstream.

The turtle's back shrank from an entire world, ensconcing them, holding them in its protective bubble, to a distant land-scape, beautiful but removed. Then finally, the whole forest that stretched from one edge of the Waykeeper's domed shell to the other contracted into a single oval of luminescent green, still raging orange in parts where the Ollallans hadn't finished fighting the fires from the Zakonraptors' earlier attacks.

There would be new fires soon.

And Captain Carroway wasn't at all sure there was anything her plucky little crew of less than a dozen could do about it.

"Ensign Melbourne, take us down level with the lower edge of the Waykeeper's shell. Maybe just a little below the edge. I want us to stay out of sight until we've had time to come up with a plan."

"Yes, Captain," the white tomcat meowed, commensurately professional, albeit maybe a little too eager given the direness of the situation. Still, Captain Carroway couldn't blame him for enjoying being back at the helm. The Wanderlust was a fit little ship, and Ensign Melbourne clearly enjoyed flying her.

Captain Carroway couldn't help marveling a little at her own order—she had essentially told Ensign Melbourne to hide The Wanderlust on the underside of a planet, but most planets don't have an underside. They don't have an up or a down; they're just round, round, round. It was a very strange thing, really, that this particular planet had an orientation. But then, the Norwegian Forest cat supposed that was nothing compared to the fact that it also had flippers, a spike of a tail, and an actual head. She wished they'd had a chance to find out if it was possible to talk to this gigantic, long-lived being. A creature who lived on an entirely different scale from one small cat.

As the view on the main viewscreen veered past the Waykeeper and then turned back to show the armored under-side of the giant space turtle's shell, dotted here and there with glowing patches that looked more like moors of moss than full forests, Captain Carroway tore her eyes away from the fascinating sight and rose from her captain's seat. She meant to ask her crew once more for suggestions and get them brainstorming again. Instead, she was interrupted by a squeaking scream from the rear of the ship, either the engine room or the multi-purpose room based on how it sounded. Also, based on the sound, Korvax.

Captain Carroway's ears skewed as she tried to decide quickly if this was a situation that called for delegation—she could order Commander Chestnut to check on the scream and stay focused on the situation here, on the bridge. But the ship was just so small, and she was, in fact, a cat: curiosity got the better of her.

The Norwegian Forest cat stalked off down The Wanderlust's central corridor, several other officers following behind her. When she got to the multi-purpose room, it became clear that she wouldn't have to continue on to the engine room. Korvax was knelt over Lys, his normally round body even more rounded by the way he was huddled over her. The green-skinned caterpillar alien was laid on the floor in a sinuous squiggle. It looked like she had fallen.

"No, no, no! Not again!" Korvax squeaked. "You can't do this to me again! Not like your mother!" The hedgehog moved his paws up and down Lys's body, touching gently, smoothing away wrinkles that were forming as he watched.

"What's wrong?" Captain Carroway meowed, kneeling down beside the bundle of nerves and quills. "What happened to her?"

"She's going into her chrysalis state..." Korvax said, despair in his squeaky voice. "But she's too young, much, much too young."

"What did you say about her mother before?" Captain Carroway asked.

Commander Chestnut came and knelt down on Lys's other side, causing Captain Carroway to wonder who was manning her bridge; Ensign Mike joined them and placed their funny stringy hands that seemed to be formed from bunched up bundles of mycelial threads against the caterpillar's body. The thready hands expanded, some of the mycelial strands seeming to worm their way right into Lys's wrinkling, withering green skin. Captain Carroway wanted to snap at the mushroom to stop doing whatever they were doing, but she didn't want to interrupt Korvax's burbling, meandering explanation of how the exact same thing had happened to Lys's mother—many, many years ago when she'd begged him to take her up into space on his ship.

"Kynnis went into her chrysalis state early," Korvax babbled, "and I never believed her, no matter how much she assured me otherwise, that it wasn't connected to how she got sick and died so young as an adult. And now it's happening to Lys! And—" His words devolved into inarticulate moaning, but then he managed to pull himself back together. "—I just- just- just- I should *never* have believed her that it wasn't because I took her up into space! And now I've done the same thing to Lys! And she's my *baby*! I've taken care of her since she was just a little yellow squiggle inside of her unhatched egg! *You have to save her, Captain Carroway!* She's not supposed to turn into an adult yet!"

The hedgehog alien grasped Captain Carroway's much larger paws with his tiny delicate ones and looked deep into her eyes, imploring her. His eyes shiny with unshed tears, and the fur around them wet with the already shed ones.

"Me?!" Captain Carroway yowled in surprise. "What am I supposed to do? We don't even have a doctor here, let alone any knowledge of Ollallan physiology and life cycle phases." The Norwegian Forest cat tried to pull her paws away from the hedgehog, but his little paws only clung on harder. "We'd better just take her back down. Surely, the Ollallans have their own doctors—"

"No, no, no!" Korvax exclaimed, the squeak in his voice rising to an ear-shattering pitch. "They know nothing about this! Nothing!"

Captain Carroway suspected that the distraught hedgehog would have continued his tirade, but a soft sound stopped him. Lys's cilia-like mouth parts were shriveled, wrinkled little things now, but they wriggled as she tried to speak. All of her green skin had taken on a deathly pallor—more the shade of mold growing on fruit than the bright, glowing shade of lime she'd been before. And there was a crack beginning to form at the top of her forehead; under the crack, something gleamed. The only person present who recognized what he was seeing under the crack at the top of her face was Korvax—he'd seen it once before, years ago, with Kynnis.

Under the crack, the crystalline face of her chrysalis was forming, smooth and expressionless.

CHAPTER 26
THE MANY BRANCHING FUTURES

Lys could hear the commotion around her. She heard the captain—the gruff cat with green eyes who she'd waited to meet for many years—get called away to consult on something in the engine room. She heard the kind squirrel man chittering to her about trees, branches, and roots. Something spiritual, something comforting. She could hear the sound and meaning, but the actual words had become muffled as her body tried to withdraw deeper inside itself, shedding the outer skin that was supposed to still be her, still be her for many more years. She could feel the filaments of the mushroom creature's hands extending out, infiltrating the space under her skin, between the old self that was trying to die and the new self—crystalline and unfinished—getting ready to begin.

She could also hear Korvax, squeaking and moaning, lamenting and bemoaning, as if this were happening to him and not her. But she also felt his paws moving up and down her body, the same gentle paws that had cared for her so many times before, touching her suddenly forming wrinkles, trying to smooth them away, trying to hold her together while her own body tried to tear her apart.

Korvax might sound like he was making her sudden affliction all about himself to the others, but Lys knew better. She knew he was there for her, as he'd always been and always would be. His feelings might be loud, but that was only because they were big. He loved with a heart too large to fit inside his small, quilled body.

Right now, Lys felt too large to fit inside her own body. She felt herself expanding, stretching, falling through layers of other dimensions. And then, beneath it all—or maybe above, maybe laced in and out, through and through—she heard a voice.

"Where do you want to go, little one?"

Lys didn't know what the voice could mean. What could it possibly mean?

"Open your eyes, little one," the voice said, filling her entire existence with its words. *"Not your old eyes, and not your new ones. Those aren't ready yet. Your other eyes. You know the ones. You can find them."*

Lys's old eyes were wrinkling and puckering, and they weren't something she opened or closed anyway. They were patches of photo-sensitive skin, always on, always looking. Her new eyes would be multi-faceted gemstones. Again, always open, always seeing in every direction, all around.

There. There, she found them. The *other* eyes, the ones that needed to open. They weren't really eyes, not in a physical sense. They were something quantum and hyperspatial, something neural and transcendent. A sense, more than an organ. And when she opened them, she saw so many paths, so many possible paths, branching and intertwining. They made her think of the branches and roots that the kind, gentle squirrel man kept chittering about.

Lys focused her inner eyes on a single thread and her understanding of it blossomed. She saw spaceships fighting, the Waykeeper being injured and limping away through space, leaving a trail of blood that the Zakonraptors would follow. It was a horrible future, and the longer she let her mind follow the thread, the more horrible it became. The Zakonraptors would invade the Waykeeper's forests; they would drill through the Waykeeper's shell, injuring the giant, gentle beast. The Ollallans would suffer, subjugated by the harsh lizard aliens, and none of the crew of The Wanderlust would ever get home.

Lys pulled her mind away from that thread and all the other similar threads tangled and twisted up with it. She didn't want to move that way through time and space. She picked through the other threads, looking for a better cluster, threads that led to better possible futures.

"You can't deliberate forever, little one, you must pick."

The voice was so large; it washed over her, crashing like a wave, trying to sweep her up with an undercurrent and tangle her inextricably with one of the cords leading to the future forever. But Lys's heart wasn't ready. She knew she could find a better option.

As the caterpillar lay on the floor, prone and quivering, her skin still dry and cracking, the mushroom officer continued to tend to her, their mycelial threads insinuating between shriveling skin and the organs underneath, holding her together, mending her caterpillar parts and keeping them from disintegrating entirely. The mushroom's ministrations kept Lys from fully entering metamorphosis, fending off her chrysalis state, and allowing her to stay in the strange in-between place where her mind could pick through the threads of possible futures, not yet committing to live in one, instead existing in a quantum fluctuation between them all.

As Ensign Mike tended to her, Commander Chestnut chittered prayers about branching trees to her, and Korvax cradled her head, gently stroking the side of her face with one paw and clutching her uppermost right hand with his other paw. The three of them kept her body safe as her mind explored the latent space that had opened up to her. She followed the threads and tangles, trying to untangle them, until she found the crisis point where so many of the threads diverged.

It was right here.

On this very ship.

Only moments from now.

The feline captain with the flowing fur and green eyes that Lys had been waiting for was in The Wanderlust's engine room right now, talking to a canine officer. There were millions of subtly different ways their conversation could go. The cat could be short-tempered and dismissive. The canine could be stubborn and snappish. There were countless ways for them to argue, for them to let their petty differences get in the way of working together.

But there was a path—Lys could see it—where the canine listened to the cat with green eyes, really listened to her, and the cat believed in the canine, encouraging her, pushing her to think harder, become more creative, and happen upon a discovery that would change everything. The whole future. Lys could alter the course of everyone's lives, just by picking the thread where the cat was patient, and the canine listened.

Lys selected that thread. She focused on it with her entire being, shoving all the other threads aside, and the Waykeeper's gigantic voice rolled over her like a wave that has already finished crashing and now just stretches peacefully along the shore, playing over the sand, pushing its foamy edge as high as it can up the beach: *"You will be lost to me, little one. The next time you enter this state, I will be too far away to help you. Be well my child. Our paths will not cross again."*

CHAPTER 27
METAMORPHOSIS DELAYED

Ensign Mike withdrew their mycelial filaments from the cracks in the prone caterpillar's wrinkled skin. The cracks healed and the wrinkles smoothed as the fungal strands pulled out of them, leaving Lys as young and healthy as she'd been before leaving the atmospheric bubble around the Waykeeper launched her into the throes of a premature metamorphosis.

The fungal officer had stopped her metamorphosis, staving off her chrysalis state.

"What happened?" Korvax squeaked, playing his delicate paws up and down Lys's worm-like body, checking every part of his surrogate daughter, as if she were but an infant and had fallen down, scraping a knee—or whatever was the closest stand-in for that on her body—for the first time. He could find nothing wrong with her, and so he burst into tears of relief and buried his pointy muzzle in the part of her tube-like body that most closely resembled a neck, just beneath her face, and sobbed disconsolately. He was sobbing with relief, but still, he was sobbing. Quite noisily.

"We fixed her," Ensign Mike said, their mushy voice beaming with pride. "She didn't want to transform yet, and so we located the hormone that was causing the changes, traced it back to its organ of origin, and palpitated the lymph gland in a soothing way until it calmed down and stopped overproducing unnecessary hormones."

"Good work, Ensign Mike!" Commander Chestnut chittered with genuine admiration.

"What?!?" Korvax blurted, all wet and noisy like a sneeze since he was still sobbing. "I don't understand."

Lys pressed several of her hands against the floor, rotating herself and pushing herself into a more upright position. Her tubelike body bent from a straight line to a jagged swerve. "You don't need to understand, Korvax," the caterpillar intoned prettily. "You only need to thank them for saving me."

"You're quite right, quite right," the hedgehog alien chittered. "Of course you are, my dear." Turning to the toadstool and choking back the last of his sobs—although, it sounded like he'd stored up a few for later—Korvax said, "Thank you most kindly, oh generous doctor, we owe you an endless debt of gratitude. What can I do for you to begin repaying it?" Korvax pulled a scrap of purple fabric off of the pointy end of one of his quills. "This is a particularly fine piece of silk. I'd like you to have it— not as a complete repayment, mind you. I plan to devote myself to repaying you! But as a token, yes, a token to show that I'm sincere and will do whatever I can to repay you for saving my dearest Lys from an early metamorphosis that would most likely have led to an early—" He was going to say 'death,' but instead, his voice choked off in a squeak and some of the sobs he'd been saving up started to leak out.

Ensign Mike took the scrap of purple fabric from Korvax's quivering paw and looked at it somewhat bemusedly. The toadstool didn't know what to do with a square of silk. They also weren't sure what to do with all of the words Korvax had said to them about repayments, and one word, in particular, stuck out at them: *doctor*. They weren't a doctor. Were they?

Or... if they weren't a doctor... yet... could they maybe become one? Perhaps that was what Ensign Mike wanted to do—not handle any of the stressful things that happened on the bridge of this chaotic ship, but instead, focus on healing people. Ideally, one at a time. That seemed much more like their natural speed. And The Wanderlust didn't have a doctor. More than that, a ship on a long-term mission like this was going to need one.

"You have repaid us enough," Ensign Mike said, their voice plopping like droplets of water on soggy leaves. "We think, maybe, you've helped us discover our purpose in life." Still unsure of what to do with the scrap of purple fabric, Ensign Mike tied the small square around one of their wrists. It looked quite decorative there. It wouldn't be regulation, but then, Ensign Mike had noticed that a number of the Anti-Ra crew members wore non-regulation ornamentation with their uniforms—such as Ensign Diaz's necklace of braided reeds or Commander Chestnut's rows of golden earrings. Ensign Mike liked the idea of wearing an ornament as well, especially one that would remind them of the moment when they realized their calling.

CHAPTER 28
THE SPARK OF INSPIRATION IGNITES

Meanwhile, in the engine room, Captain Carroway kept pressing Ensign Diaz, gently but firmly, to think harder. They needed a way to help the Waykeeper, while also escaping from the incoming fleet of Zakonraptors themselves.

The wolf-like officer kept insisting it couldn't be done. The fur on her hackles had raised, and a growl crept into her voice as she countered every one of Captain Carroway's proposals. The Norwegian Forest cat's suggestions barely deserved the word 'proposals.' It was more like she kept rattling off the basic specs of The Wanderlust—electron torpedoes, blazor canons, lumo-projectors. None of it was useful or inspiring, and Ensign Diaz felt increasingly wild and angry listening to the cat pressure her.

"No matter how well-armed we are," Ensign Diaz snapped, "we're one vessel, and there's a whole fleet coming! You've already had the whole crew brainstorm. *Why are you pestering me like this?* I'm not a miracle worker."

"I don't believe you," Captain Carroway meowed. "And based on how Commander Chestnut talks about you, I don't think he'd believe you either."

"You don't believe me that I'm not a miracle worker," Ensign

Diaz woofed in a stunned tone. This big fluffy cat was unbelievable. She seemed to think that if she just stood by her ideals, everything in the universe would fall into place for her.

The universe didn't work like that. At least, it never had for Ensign Diaz.

"What about the vacuum bomb idea?" Captain Carroway pressed. "The suggestion from last time—" The Norwegian Forest cat pedaled one of her forepaws in the air, like she was trying to pull a memory back to her.

"What? The thing about firing the vacuum bomb so that it dissipates across the Waykeeper's hyperspatial slipstream? That was always a crazy suggestion."

Captain Carroway's pointed ears flickered, wanting to flatten in irritation at this Xolo-Lupinian who didn't even seem to be *trying*. But instead, she held them upright, and she stared the wolf-like officer down.

It was a moment of patience, a moment that could so easily have not happened, so easily have gone in a different direction.

But it went this way.

And Ensign Diaz stared right back at Captain Carroway, wanting to chew her out and complain more to this rule-follower who had fired the exact same vacuum bomb they were still discussing at a sun only a few days ago, killing one of her best friends. The wolf-like officer wanted to give Captain Carroway a real piece of her mind, lecture her about the natural wonders of Lupinia and how it was cats and dogs like Carroway who were causing that lovely world to be destroyed by Reptassan colonizers who'd moved in and begun strip-mining beautiful forests.

But Captain Carroway wouldn't care.

Lupinia was galaxies away.

And suddenly, a spark flashed in Ensign Diaz's mind. A connection drew between the idea of firing the vacuum bomb into the Waykeeper's hyperspatial slipstream and the fact that, somehow, firing that same vacuum bomb only a few days ago had thrown two spaceships halfway across the cosmos.

But it was impossible.

Ensign Diaz didn't even know where to begin, trying to calculate how the power of a vacuum bomb, interacting with the Waykeeper's slipstream, could echo in a patch of space several galaxies away...

Except, that wasn't true. Mathematical equations started pouring through Ensign Diaz's head, and she could barely turn toward a computer console and begin typing numbers and variables with her paws fast enough.

Captain Carroway watched the Xolo-Lupinian work with the smugness that only a cat can express. Her whiskers rose with the Cheshire smile curling its way across her muzzle.

The moment had passed, and now, The Wanderlust and her crew were set on a course Lys had chosen for them.

Ensign Diaz finished her calculations and shook her head, disbelieving her own work, right in front of her, staring back at her. "It's not possible," she woofed softly to herself.

But of course Captain Carroway heard. The Norwegian Forest cat was standing right beside the Xolo-Lupinian, watching her work, failing to understand all the mathematical equations now written on the computer screen but still gamely continuing to try. "What's not possible?" she asked softly, barely a whisper.

Ensign Diaz continued to stare at the mathematical equations covering the computer screen as she spoke, almost as if she were talking directly to the work she'd been doing and not answering the captain at all: "If we fire the vacuum bomb directly into the path of the Waykeeper, it will... flinch? To change course and avoid the explosion. But since it travels by way of hyperspatial slipstream... it doesn't flinch or, uh, change course, rather, in the same way as any other vessel..."

Ensign Diaz's soft woofing tone was raising in volume, getting more excited and confident as she talked her way through the calculations she'd just done. Suddenly, the Xolo-Lupinian turned toward the Norwegian Forest cat beside her. Ensign Diaz narrowed her eyes and looked Captain Carroway directly in the face. *"I can get us home,"* she woofed, tail wagging behind her.

"Really?" Captain Carroway breathed, too surprised and emotional to put any real voice into the word.

"Yes," Ensign Diaz confirmed, but then a look of uncertainty flickered across her face, skewing her muzzle into a frown and causing her bat-like ears to flag. "I think so. Let me double-check."

Ensign Diaz's paws returned to the computer console and flew over it like they had a life and mind of their own, like she was playing a concert piano, or maybe like her paws were dancers and the equations she was writing were the steps of their dance.

Captain Carroway watched Ensign Diaz's paws fly with bated breath, almost afraid that if she breathed, it would make the Xolo-Lupinian's discovery disappear. The equations were so delicate, a single breath might melt them, like snowflakes in a beam of sun.

But Lys had chosen this reality.

The Wanderlust and Waykeeper were set on a course, and nothing Captain Carroway did at this point could change that.

Ensign Diaz shook her head again. "I can't believe it," she woofed. "I just can't believe it."

"What?" Captain Carroway asked. "What can't you believe?"

At this point, a small crowd had gathered at the entrance to the engine room, eagerly watching the captain and engineer. Ensign Melbourne was still on the bridge, piloting the ship, with Ensign Werik working a support console and Lt. Cmdr. Vossie manning the captain's chair. But Ensign Risqua and Lt. Lee, along with Commander Chestnut, were all crowded at the mouth of the engine room, watching what was happening between the Norwegian Forest cat and Xolo-Lupinian.

"We have a choice," Ensign Diaz said, turning firmly away from the equations she'd just written. "If we fire that vacuum bomb into the Waykeeper's path, we can cause this whole world turtle to flinch in one of several directions."

"What is the choice?" Captain Carroway asked, a gulf hollowing out inside her as she realized: whatever the choice was, it would fall on her shoulders.

"The Waykeeper's hyperspatial slipstream is extremely powerful," Ensign Diaz intoned, sounding like she was speaking down to a child, presumably for the captain's benefit. "And the explosion of a vacuum bomb is extremely powerful too."

"Yes, of course," Captain Carroway agreed impatiently. Fortunately, her patience was no longer necessary. The moment of realization had passed. All that was left was for the players on the board to play out their parts, exactly as Lys had seen they would, before they passed far enough into the future that the many threads she'd seen would become tangled again, indecipherable to her.

"Combining those two powers was strong enough to fling two vessels across the cosmos, bringing us here," Ensign Diaz. "I've calculated paths that would allow us to travel back home, while also flinging the Zakonraptors in the opposite direction—"

"Excellent!" Captain Carroway exclaimed, feeling a rush of joy that she hadn't expected. It was wonderful to be exploring the universe, and she probably wouldn't keep her captain's chair long once they got home.

But they would be home.

Except, then, Ensign Diaz explained the alternative.

"—or we could fire the vacuum bomb in a slightly different direction across the Waykeeper's path, and the force from the vacuum bomb and the flinching would be applied to.. well... a different object."

"What object?" Captain Carroway asked, her ears splaying in confusion. She couldn't imagine what object would be more worth moving than their own ship and the Zakonraptor fleet.

"Lupinia," Ensign Diaz answered.

And standing in the doorway to the engine room, Commander Chestnut gasped.

CHAPTER 29
A BETTER USE FOR A BLACK HOLE

"You can move Lupinia?" Commander Chestnut asked, scurrying his way into the engine room and pressing his way between the much larger cat and canine blocking his view of the indecipherable equations Ensign Diaz had been writing. His brushy reed of a tail flipped about wildly, expressing more excitement than seemed like should be able to fit into such a small mammal.

For the moment, Ensign Risqua and Lt. Lee, along with Lys and now Korvax stayed in the doorway, looking uncertain, raising the stakes of everything that happened, because it was all being watched.

"It's chaos theory," Ensign Diaz explained, not very helpfully. "Basic chaos theory."

"What do you mean?" Captain Carroway's ears flattened, irritated that she had no idea what the canine was talking about. She vaguely remembered an academy physics class, many years ago, that had brushed past chaos theory far too quickly for her to have really learned anything about it, and she didn't see how it was at all relevant here.

Ensign Diaz held out a paw, as if she were about to hold up an actual useful explanation. Instead, she barked, "A butterfly flaps its wing on Earth and two hundred years later there's a rebellion against the Reptassans on Avia." As if that made any sense.

"Or in this case, a butterfly flaps its wings on the outer edge of the Tetra Galaxy," Commander Chestnut chittered, getting excited, "and we fall through a black hole to the other side of the universe."

Captain Carroway wasn't sure if Commander Chestnut actually understood what Ensign Diaz was talking about, or if he was just really excited about the idea of moving Lupinia. To be fair, it was an interesting idea. If Lupinia weren't in contested, neutral territory between Tri-Galactic Union and Reptassan territories, then it could be properly defended, properly made a part of the Tri-Galactic Union.

But Captain Carroway didn't see how they could possibly move an entire planet. Especially from several galaxies away. She was about to say as much when Lys came inching her way into the engine room with her strange worm-like way of moving.

"Or a butterfly doesn't flap her wings," the caterpillar said in a singsong voice. "Because she hasn't grown them yet, thanks to your ship's lovely and brilliant doctor. Butterfly is the word your people use for my species' adult form, right?"

Instead of answering Lys, Captain Carroway asked a question of her own: "We have a doctor?" This day seemed to be just one surprise upon another. This whole week, actually. At least this might prove to be a good surprise. She wondered who among her crew had proven to have enough medical training to qualify for such a position...

She didn't have to wonder for long.

"That would be Ensign Mike," Commander Chestnut chittered proudly, as if the golden-mantled squirrel had helped the fungal officer realize their purpose himself rather than just watch it happen.

Captain Carroway's ears—which had perked up at the idea of a doctor—flagged again. She still didn't like Ensign Mike. But she supposed they did need a doctor pretty badly. Badly enough to count a computer program animated by mushy fungal tissue as a substitute for one, she supposed. Begrudgingly. Regardless, that was a problem for later. There were bigger problems to deal with now. Planet sized problems. "I still don't understand how any of this means you can move Lupinia," Captain Carroway meowed forcefully, trying to cut through all the nonsense to the heart of the issue.

Ensign Diaz drew in a deep breath through her muzzle and started to explain, "Think of it like this: when our ships were pulled across the universe, they... well... sort of carved a groove into subspace."

Intrigued in spite of herself, Captain Carroway asked, "Like wearing a path into a forest by walking through it the same way over and over again?"

"Yes, kind of like that," Ensign Diaz agreed. "Except since we were pulled through so forcefully, it was almost more like..."

"Carving a groove out with a plow?" Commander Chestnut suggested.

"Yeah, sure, why not?" Ensign Diaz rolled her eyes at how this metaphor was getting away from her. She was dealing with physics and hyperspace, not footpaths and farm equipment, but the Xolo-Lupinian didn't have a better way to explain her equations to officers who simply didn't know as much math and quantum physics as her. "The important thing is—we can essentially... uh... roll Lupinia along our path, jumping it from orbiting its own star to the star in the Dirt Cloud."

"That's huge," Captain Carroway breathed in awe. Her tail had begun swishing behind her, expressing her excitement and agitation. This was all a lot to deal with, and she was going to have some very big, very weighty decisions to make. Very soon.

"To the Dirt Cloud?" Commander Chestnut asked. His tail was whipped about even more frenetically than Captain Carroway's.

"Yes, that's the only place we can move it to," Ensign Diaz confirmed.

"That's neutral territory," Commander Chestnut chittered.

"Which is a whole hell of a lot better than Reptassan territory!" Ensign Diaz barked angrily.

Commander Chestnut's tail stopped moving. The golden-mantled squirrel froze, absolutely as still as a statue, as if the much larger canine's bark had triggered a deep self-defense reflex from the time before golden-mantled squirrels had been uplifted and could be a large canine's commanding officer.

Eventually, Commander Chestnut thawed out and said, "I didn't say it wasn't better."

"You implied it with your statement," Ensign Diaz growled.

"Hey now," Captain Carroway meowed, holding out her paws between the two Anti-Ra officers in a placating way. It was strange for her to be playing peacemaker between two colleagues who had both been her enemies a few days ago. "Commander Chestnut was just stating a fact. We don't shut people down for stating facts. Facts are good. Collecting them is the foundation of science."

"We're not talking about science," Ensign Diaz growled through gritted teeth. Very long, pointy gritted teeth. *We're talking about my homeworld.*"

At this point, Ensign Risqua stepped forward from where she'd been watching in the doorway to the engine room. Her red and blue feathers were puffed out, making her look larger, but also more nervous than usual. "We can't just go around moving planets," the reptile-bird squawked. It wasn't clear if she was trying to calm the Xolo-Lupinian down—if she was, Ensign Risqua had picked entirely the wrong strategy.

Ensign Diaz had very short dark brown fur, but it was clearly all standing on end, prickled out by her feelings and passion. She was literally gnashing her sharp teeth. This was not a subject that Ensign Diaz could be rational about...

And that was fair.

Captain Carroway had to acknowledge: the Xolo-Lupinian was right. They weren't talking about science or political boundaries anymore. They were talking about Ensign Diaz's home.

Wilder's home. Maple's home. Even though they would never go to go back to it. They'd been swallowed up by the complexities of physics and the brute force of a vacuum bomb.

Captain Carroway had begun this whole journey by doing the wrong thing—firing a vacuum bomb at a star, trying to cause destruction.

Was this a chance to do something right?

With the same vacuum bomb?

"Are you saying—" Captain Carroway placed her paws on Ensign Diaz's shoulders as she spoke, forcing the Xolo-Lupinian to look at her. "—that if we fire this vacuum bomb just right, we can safely move Lupinia from orbiting its current star to orbiting the star in the center of the Dirt Cloud?"

"*Yes*," Ensign Diaz woofed, almost choking on the single word, as if it encompassed an idea too large to fit through the narrow passage of her throat.

"Then we have to do it," Captain Carroway meowed. And it was that simple. She was going to save a world.

If Lupinia were moved to neutral territory, then the Reptassans would no longer have a claim over it. And inside the Dirt Cloud, the Anti-Ra forces would be able to easily protect it. This was what the Tri-Galactic Union should have been trying to do all along. Although, to be fair, it sounded like the wouldn't have been able to do it without a little help from a giant tortoise flying through the far side of the universe.

The universe is a strange place. Captain Carroway hoped it always stayed that way.

"But..." Lt. Lee was still standing in the entrance to the engine room. His butterfly-like ears were held as low as Captain Carroway had ever seen them. "...I thought... didn't you say... we could go home? But... only... if we didn't move Lupinia?" The pretty little dog's voice quavered. He wanted to go home.

And it broke Captain Carroway's heart to see him like this—so close to what he wanted so desperately, but also so very, very far away.

Because Captain Carroway wasn't going to make the choice he wanted her to make. She wasn't going to take this ship home. Not at the expense of an entire world.

"Lupinia needs our help," Captain Carroway meowed, as reasonably as she could. "That's what our whole mission here has always been about, and now, we have a chance to truly fulfill it."

Feelings flickered across the Papillon's face like sunlight flickering on a rainy day. But there was no rainbow to be found here. Lt. Lee was such a good officer, such a good dog, that he would do what he was told. But saving Lupinia from political unrest and turmoil would be cold comfort to him as he slept in the crowded barracks of a tiny ship on the wrong side of the Tetra Galaxy for months on end, worrying about his mother back home in the Milky Way, certain her only son had died in the line of duty.

"Wait... really?" Ensign Diaz's bat-like ears flicked up and down, and the expression on her long muzzle wavered nervously between anger and elation. There were a lot of uncertain feelings in The Wanderlust's engine room right now.

There were probably going to be a lot of uncertain feelings aboard The Wanderlust for a long time. The remainder of their journey home, however long that took, most likely.

Captain Carroway thought for a moment: perhaps what her crew was really missing, more than a doctor, was a therapist. Maybe the fungal officer would find a way to fulfill that role too. Though, the Norwegian Forest cat doubted it.

"Yes, really," Captain Carroway meowed. "If you have a way to move Lupinia into a safe orbit around the star at the center of the Dirt Cloud at the same time as protecting the Waykeeper from the oncoming Zakonraptor fleet, then by all means, we should do it. I'm giving the order: save two worlds with one vacuum bomb."

"Well, that's kind of overly simplistic—" Ensign Diaz began to bark, but Commander Chestnut could see that his star officer was about to undercut her own position by over-explaining the science involved to a captain who was clearly more swayed by metaphor than raw math.

So, the golden-mantled squirrel stepped up to her again, cutting the much larger canine off, and said, "You have an order, Ensign."

The Xolo-Lupinian bowed her head, leaving the science half-explained, at best. If she had her commander's faith and her captain's order, that was all she needed. It was time for Ensign Diaz to save her home world.

CHAPTER 30
THE VOYAGE BEGINS

Once again, the vacuum bomb sailed away from The Wanderlust, looking like nothing more than a thin streak of light on the viewscreen. A shooting star. But this time, Captain Carroway didn't try to wish on it. She wondered how many of the members of her crew did.

The bridge of The Wanderlust was much more crowded this time. Everyone aboard had gathered together to watch. And now, not only were there two crews melded together aboard The Wanderlust—Union and Anti-Ra—but also three newcomers, two guests from the Waykeeper's back and the strange amalgamation of circuitry and mycelia who now insisted they were a doctor.

Captain Carroway could never have imagined what a strange crew she would find herself in charge of, nor the sheer scope of the mission they would be on.

The Norwegian Forest cat might have preferred a crew composed entirely of loyal, tested, Tri-Galactic Union officers, and she would definitely have preferred the safety and security of a voyage closer to home. But her best friend, Lt. Cmdr. Vossie was still with her, and the first officer who fate had thrown her way had proven a perfect compliment to her own leadership style so far. Everything she'd seen of the rest of their crew—Lt. Lee and Ensigns Melbourne, Diaz, Risqua, and Werik—suggested they were all extremely competent officers. Korvax, Lys, and Ensign Mike were all complete wildcards, as far as Captain Carroway was concerned, but she was sure her crew could find a way to manage them, some kind of way to integrate them in.

If a crew of Tri-Galactic Union officers and a crew of Anti-Ra officers could find a way to work together, fusing into one combined crew, then certainly, they could figure out how to handle a hedgehog alien, caterpillar flirting with metamorphosis, and a mushroom convinced they were a doctor.

The streak of light on the viewscreen intersected with the invisible barrier of the edge of the Waykeeper's hyperspatial slipstream, and light spilled outward from its point of intersection. The slipstream lit up, glowing brightly, as the light from the vacuum bomb washed around the turtle, illuminating the oval shape of the hyperspace field. The brightness grew and grew, until the whole screen flashed with brilliant white light, causing every member of the crew to turn away.

Except for one.

Lys stared at the brightness with her eyespots, unflinching, knowing with complete certainty that this was the moment she'd always been meant to see. This was the brightness that kept the darkness at bay. Before Lys's egg had even been laid, her mother had seen that this moment could stop the Zakonraptors.

The flash of light ended, and the crew blinked with sun-spotted eyes at the screen.

The Waykeeper looked the same—verdant forests, marred only in a few places by the work of the forest fires, covered the dome of the giant turtle's back. Green and glowing. Profoundly alive.

"I'm glad you're bringing some cuttings from the Waykeeper's trees along on our journey," Korvax squeaked, disrupting the gravity of the moment and presumptuously coopting ownership of The Wanderlust's journey with the carelessly—or care-fully?—chosen word 'our'. "I'm going to miss those forests! Now what are you bringing the cuttings along for again?"

"Scientific study," Lt. Cmdr. Vossie said drily, sounding more like himself than he had since losing his implant. Perhaps he was starting to adjust. Captain Carroway certainly hoped so.

"Did it work?" Captain Carroway asked, turning to look at Ensign Diaz who was manning one of the engineer's consoles on the bridge. "Can you check?" The Norwegian Forest cat was too hyped up to sit in her captain's chair and instead, paced the length of the bridge while waiting on her answer.

"Lupinia is on the other side of several galaxies," Ensign Diaz woofed sarcastically. "I can check just as soon as you can get us within scanning range of it. But I guarantee you: my calculations were correct. I wouldn't play with the safety of my homeworld."

"So you're sure it worked?" the Norwegian Forest cat pressed, even though she logically understood that none of the officers on her ship could give her the reassurance she was looking for.

Lt. Lee announced from his post, "The Zakonraptor fleet is entirely gone."

"That's an exaggeration," Ensign Diaz woofed, looking annoyed. "It's not like we killed them or anything. They just fell through a space-time hole that dropped them far enough away from the Waykeeper, back in the direction of the Tetra Galaxy, that they'll never catch up to the world-turtle again."

"But *we* might run into them again," Captain Carroway concluded grimly.

"It's a possibility," Ensign Diaz admitted, seeming mostly untroubled by the idea. *"But Lupinia is safe."* There was a profound peace and contentment in the Xolo-Lupinian's words as she spoke them, like she was able to stop worrying for the first time about something that had been weighing her down for years, something she cared more about than her own personal circumstances.

"Assuming it worked," Captain Carroway grumbled, under her breath, not wanting to upset the canine's contentment but also unable to leave the loose thread alone.

But then Lys inched her way forward, farther onto the bridge, and said in a sing-song tone, "It worked. I know it did." And she did know. Because the Waykeeper knew. And although their connection was about to be severed forever, when Captain Carroway gave the order for The Wanderlust to fly away only moments from now, at this moment, the Ollallan's mind was still tied to the giant turtle's. And because of her mild telepathy, somehow, when Lys said that it had worked, Captain Carroway believed her. The caterpillar's mind reached out and soothed the feline mind, all jangled up with guilt and uncertainties, smoothing those feelings out until Captain Carroway could let go of the fear that she'd wasted their only way home for nothing.

It hadn't been for nothing. Lupinia was safely circling a different sun, away from Reptassan space, and easily defended. The Waykeeper was on its way, deeper into the space between galaxies.

There would be a lot of anger and hurt feelings aboard The Wanderlust in days to come from officers who would have chosen to take the quicker path home, leaving Lupinia in its untenable state, fought over by Reptassans and Anti-Ra. Officers who wouldn't have cared if the Waykeeper were left to fend for itself. But Ensign Diaz was happy, and so was Lys. And Captain Carroway thought that the large canine's contentment probably mattered more for the stability of her crew than any other individual. The Norwegian Forest cat felt confident that she could handle the rest of them.

It might take a long time, but she would get them home. And she would hold them together until they got there.

"Commander Chestnut," Captain Carroway meowed to her first officer, "could you clear the bridge of off-duty officers?" It was time to clear the crowd. It was time to begin their journey in earnest.

The golden-mantled squirrel nodded smartly and then shep-herded everyone off the bridge except for Ensign Diaz, Ensign Melbourne, and the captain herself.

The Norwegian Forest cat settled comfortably into her captain's chair, letting herself relish the way that it sat at the center of the bridge, giving her an optimal view of the screen that still showed the beautiful world turtle, flying away from them already.

Speaking to the white tom cat at the pilot's console Captain Carroway meowed, "It's time to start covering some distance. Ensign Melbourne, please set a course for home."

ABOUT THE AUTHOR

Mary E. Lowd is a prolific science-fiction and furry writer in Oregon. She's had more than 200 short stories and a dozen novels published, always with more on the way. Her work has won four Ursa Major Awards, ten Leo Literary Awards, and four Cóyotl Awards. She edited FurPlanet's ROAR anthology series for five years, and she is now the editor and founder of the furry e-zine *Zooscape*. She lives in a crashed spaceship, disguised as a house and hidden behind a rose garden, with an extensive menagerie of animals, some real and some imaginary.

For more information:
marylowd.com

To read Mary's short stories:
deepskyanchor.com

For news, updates, discounts, and deals:
marylowd.com/newsletter

ALSO BY MARY E. LOWD

Otters In Space

Otters In Space

Otters In Space 2: Jupiter, Deadly

Otters In Space 3: Octopus Ascending

Otters In Space 4: First Moustronaut

Otters In Space Spinoffs

In a Dog's World

When A Cat Loves A Dog

Jove Deadly's Lunar Detective Agency (with Garrett Marco)

The Entangled Universe

Entanglement Bound

The Entropy Fountain

Starwhal in Flight

Entangled Universe Spinoffs

You're Cordially Invited to Crossroads Station

Welcome to Wespirtech

Beyond Wespirtech

Brunch at the All Alien Cafe

Xeno-Spectre

Hell Moon

The Ancient Egg

The Celestial Fragments (A Labyrinth of Souls Trilogy)

The Snake's Song

The Bee's Waltz

The Otter's Wings

Tri-Galactic Trek

Tri-Galactic Trek

Nexus Nine: A Tri-Galactic Trek Novel

Voyage of the Wanderlust: A Tri-Galactic Trek Novel

Commander Annie and Other Adventures

The Necromouser and Other Magical Cats

The Opposite of Memory

Queen Hazel and Beloved Beverly

Some Words Burn Brightly: An Illuminated Collection of Poetry

Furry Fiction Is Everywhere (with Ian Madison Keller)